Cruel SAINT

VICIOUS EMPIRE: ONE

LUNA KAYNE

Cruel Saint by Luna Kayne

Book cover design: Pretty Little Design Co.

Cover model photographer: Wander Aguiar

Cover model: Kyle Kriesel

Editor: Caroline Knecht

First Printing, 2022

ISBN (eBook) 978-1-989366-30-1

ISBN (paperback) 978-1-989366-31-8

Luna Kayne, Kayne Publishing

For my girls, E and Q.
Be brave, be kind, be fierce.
Above all, be you.
I love you.

She took pride in how guarded she was, building her charming house with so many beautiful windows to see out, but no doors to let anyone in.

— LUNA KAYNE

PROLOGUE: RYDER

FOUR YEARS AGO

"I'm asking you to let her go." Grayson leans back in his seat with his feet propped against the edge of my bed. He pushes his chair onto its hind legs while repeatedly tossing a baseball toward the ceiling and catching it.

I don't tell him to elaborate. I know who he's talking about.

Amara.

His little sister and my dark obsession.

It's no secret Amara is mine. Our parents decreed as much when they made the decision to arrange our future marriage.

What no one knows is, with or without their ridiculous blessings, Amara belongs to me.

"What do you know?" I hold my attention on the note I'm writing at my desk, keeping my back turned to him.

Information is power in my world, and Grayson is the best at gathering it for me. At twenty-two years old, we are both often overlooked as children among my father's associates, and Grayson uses this to his advantage.

"They're downstairs right now. My mom is speaking to your father. It's about my dad—and Amara." The wooden legs of his chair knock against the floor as he shifts in his seat, and I remain in place, staring at the piece of paper that started as a thought and devolved into a series of scribbles as soon as Grayson started talking about his sister.

"What about them?" *Her*—I want to say "her," but that would give my intentions away.

Grayson and Amara's father passed away suddenly a few weeks ago of a heart attack. They took the news as well as can be expected, but that is a testament to their father being a neglectful dick to his kids. You can't mourn the loss of someone who never made an impact on your life when they were alive. It's an opinion I've never shared with my best friend, but they lost the parent lottery on both counts.

I'm not saying I won. My old man isn't much different. But my place in life more than makes up for having a hard-as-nails father who works late and cares conditionally—his attention always comes with a price. Unfortunately for Amara and Grayson, their parents never quite landed as high in society, and they lived within lesser means.

"My mom is asking that the arrangement between you and Amara be dissolved without *consequence or malice*." I know Grayson's tone; without turning around, I can tell he's throwing up air quotes. "That's what I heard her say on the phone earlier, when she was setting up the meeting. Do you know what it means?"

My attention creeps to the mirror in front of me as I check Grayson's reflection in the space over my shoulder. Tossing the ball onto my bed, he rises out of the chair to his full six-foot height and walks to the window to watch the rain fall.

The weather has been an accurate reflection of my mood. I almost expect a bolt of lightning to strike us all into oblivion any second now. It still wouldn't compare to the tempest of emotions brewing inside of my soul at this upsetting turn of events.

"No idea," I lie.

I do know.

Amara's mother is downstairs in my father's office asking that her daughter be released from a marriage both sets of parents agreed to. What Grayson doesn't know is that the promise of Amara's hand was bought, not given. It was done without my knowledge at the time. I didn't find out about it until recently, when my older brother Dagen stumbled on information he shouldn't have.

Amara's parents offered her to us for a price, and it was a deal my father jumped at in order to keep me in line and test my loyalty to the family. It was a test I gladly passed. They didn't know how I already felt about her.

My father thought tying me into an arranged marriage would ensure my obedience. It would give me something I would come to want, something he could hold over my head as a way of keeping me on a short leash. When I accepted the eventual marriage, it was a sign of fealty in his eyes.

No one knew I was already entirely invested in her.

Amara is my sin eater.

She consumes my darkness like it's her lifeline. What I once thought were my worst parts are made beautiful around her.

No one knows about the things we've done, the things I've done to her. I've pushed her, corrupted her, and molded her into my missing piece. Don't get me wrong, I didn't drag her down my wicked path on my own—she willingly followed. Little by little, she sought me out, and I didn't turn her away.

There's a monster inside of her no one sees.

No one but me.

The sharp look of disgust on my face snaps me out of my

rage as I catch my own reflection in the mirror. My lip is curled up in a sneer that rattles me. I look primed to kill. I school my features before Grayson turns his attention back to me, because my anger isn't meant for him. It's for his parents, who betrayed Amara when they sold her like cattle.

Lifting my hand to my mouth, I slip my tongue through my lips while keeping my eyes trained on Grayson's back through the mirror. If he knew what I did to his little sister behind the pool house not even an hour earlier, he would be furious. I still taste her on the salty tips of my fingers. The memory of her contorted face and her feeble whimpers as she wildly bucked her hips against my fingers as I fucked her with them makes me want to find her and punish her for making me feel weak.

But no one can know.

Grayson is as protective of Amara as I am, and it pains me knowing I can't show it. My secrecy is my way of keeping her safe. While I'm sure that not loving her at all would be the best way to shield her, I can't do it. I'm a selfish son of a bitch, and I won't deny myself the pleasure of the one thing in this world that grounds me.

But now, her mother is in my home, asking to take Amara away from me. She wants to keep the money my father gave her, and she wants to be released from the promise both she and her dead husband made.

I can't tell Grayson any of this.

Knowing would destroy him.

Since becoming an adult, Grayson has distanced himself from his parents in inconspicuous ways. On some level, I think he knows his parents are opportunists. If this came to light, Grayson would be pulled down into his mother's fall from grace, and I won't allow anyone to hurt my closest friend.

No. Grayson and his sister both belong to me, and I will always protect what is mine.

I've been quiet for too long, and Grayson turns his attention away from the rain tapping against the window. Before his eyes settle on me, I lean over, scribble nothing on my little piece of paper, then slide it into my drawer as though none of this information concerns me.

"The marriage was arranged, and now neither of you needs to go through with it. Maybe this is good news." Grayson's tone has changed, and his statement sounds a lot like a question. My silence has fueled his suspicion.

I steady myself with a breath, then stand and turn to face him.

"Maybe it is." Another lie.

"You know me, man. I am in this with you for the long haul. But a piece of me wonders if Amara is better off away from... you know. What we do."

What we do.

It's as though if we don't label our actions, they can't be held against us. Once you give something a name, it is classified: good, bad, acceptable, depraved.

At first glance, my family lives up to the sanctity of our surname, but its shiny veneer washes away when you stare a little too long. When the gloves come off, the Saints are not a family to mess with because we mess back ten times as hard.

A knock at the door breaks our silence, and I roll my eyes. If it were one of my three brothers, they would have opened the door and waltzed right in. My father never comes to us— we are always summoned to him—and my mother has taken to texting me ever since I showed her how to use a smartphone.

That leaves those on my father's payroll, which means I've been summoned.

"Yeah."

The door opens, and a maid pops her head in, first seeing

Grayson, then scanning around until she meets my apathetic glare.

"Mr. Saint wishes to see you in his office."

"You good?" I nod to Grayson.

"Yeah. I'm meeting up with Sloane in a while. Dinner with her folks."

I don't respond. Instead, I turn to follow the woman out of my room as the muscles in my neck tense with envy.

I'm not jealous of Grayson's relationship with Sloane. I'm envious because I don't have the luxury of publicly declaring my intentions with Amara.

I follow quietly behind the small woman, my mind drifting to my sinful little flower as it always does.

The door to my father's office is ajar. Pushing it the rest of the way open, I step in and acknowledge the man who beckoned me: my father, Sebastian Saint. He lifts his chin in my direction, a silent order to close the door behind me, and I comply.

As I take my seat across from him, my eyes fall on a glass half full of amber liquid. My father's drink of choice, and he's poured me one as well.

He begins by telling me information I already know. Ms. Scott dropped by to discuss some business, and I shift in my seat, pushing down my restlessness.

"As you know, Harry's death has been a shock to us all, but more so his wife and kids." He breaks long enough to take a sip, and I use his pause to ask for the point.

"What does this have to do with me?"

"I've asked if there is anything we can do to help, and Amara's mother has made a request."

I already know this part, and I clench my teeth, hoping to stop my impatience from manifesting across my face.

"She has asked that you and Amara be released from your future obligations to each other—and I have agreed to allow it."

"Why would you do that?" My voice cracks, and I recover. "Going back on an agreement is seen as a weakness, and we are not weak men." I hope my tone is taken as a challenge rather than the plea it is.

"Are you questioning my decision, boy?"

"I'm merely voicing what our adversaries will whisper behind our backs."

He takes a long pause to scrutinize my reaction before responding. "This was a widow's wish, and it has been granted."

His answer is final.

Any further push to hold on to our union will damn me and Amara both.

"I have one condition."

His eyebrows shoot up at my audacity. "You? You have a condition for me?" His laughter holds no humor.

"You forget, I was a part of this arranged marriage without my own wishes being heard. I stepped forward and took the place you wanted me to. And it is I who is also losing face in the termination of this agreement. One that was decided without my own reservations being heard."

The next minute ticks by in uncomfortable silence as I watch him assess my words before one corner of his mouth curves just enough to expose one of his tells.

He's impressed.

My father wants nothing more than four versions of him taking over the family business: my three brothers and myself. I know, if he were in my situation, he would use this as an opportunity to take something for himself.

"Spit it out. What do you want?"

Leaning forward, I lift the glass off the desk before taking it back into the chair with me as I make myself comfortable.

"I'm off the table."

"How so?"

"I can no longer be used as a bargaining chip in any type of arranged union. You want someone to offer up? You have three other sons. My choice is my own, when and if I ever decide, and it is no one else's business. I've done my time." My words are cold, harsh. There is no hint of the fire raging inside of my soul.

If I can't have Amara, I want no one.

I down the drink in one go before setting it back on the desk while he considers my demand. When he's drained the contents of his own glass, he slams it down.

"Very well, son." My lips twitch at the term. We are only his sons when he is proud of us.

Losing Amara now is a setback in my plans. I've earned my freedom, and, as far as my father is concerned, I've chosen my family yet again.

Amara isn't going anywhere. She's still mine, and I will have her back with me soon enough.

"Is there anything else?" I brush a nonexistent piece of fluff off my pants and wait for him to dismiss me.

"We'll just go and wish them a safe trip."

I don't dare look up.

This is information I wasn't aware of, and I can't ask for clarification. Amara is supposed to be of no concern to me.

"Sure."

I stand and wait for my father to walk past me before I allow the uncertainty to appear on my face as I follow him out the door.

Where are they going that I would need to wish them a safe trip? And why didn't Grayson mention this to me earlier?

The walk down the hall to the sitting area is shorter than I remember, and I catch the look of surprise on Grayson's face as I watch him release Amara from an embrace. Tears are running down her face.

Grayson didn't know.

His own mother didn't tell him she was leaving. He's old enough, and she's cutting him loose. But Amara is just shy of her twentieth birthday. While she's an adult and can do what she wants, she's as much a prisoner to her family as I am to my own. She's still in school, living at home and under her mother's thumb.

Amara follows Grayson's stare to me, and she takes an instinctive step in my direction, only stopping when she remembers we are not alone.

"She's moving me away." Her words crack on a sob as she takes a half step toward me and lowers her voice to a whisper. "Don't let me go."

She fights to hold back her sobs as I see a glimmer of hope fill her golden-brown eyes. I want to brush my fingers into her chestnut waves, cup the back of her head, and pull her into me. I shove my hands into the front pockets of my pants to stop myself.

She's too good for this place.

She's too good for me.

I'm not strong enough to protect her yet, and claiming her now will damn her. Even if I spoke up and fought for her, my father would most likely send her away to punish me for keeping something like this from him.

At this moment, at my very core, I understand what sacrifice means. There is only one option left to me, and I need to let her go.

"There's nothing for you here, Amara." My words slice my own heart open.

I promised I would never hurt her. Her parents used her for their own gain. Only Grayson wanted what was best for her. It was going to be me who gave her everything she deserved. But instead, it's me who is setting her hopes ablaze as she watches, helpless to fix the hell I've cast her into.

"But you promised me—" Tears fall freely down her round face, which is now patchy with heartache. My father crosses his arms, catching her attention, and she doesn't finish her thought. When her eyes return to my own, I know.

This is breaking her.

Her lips pinch together, and her open palm swings back before it happens. I remain unmoved. I don't block the slap. I welcome it.

As my head snaps to the side, I allow her to replace our love with hate. She'll need it to carry her away from here until I am strong enough to protect her properly.

My father clears his throat, a sign we are done.

As I step back to allow them to leave, I realize this, too, was a test—and I passed.

But I also failed.

I don't deserve Amara; I'm not sure I ever have. But one day I will, and when I do, no one will stop me from taking what's mine.

1

AMARA

There are two things I hate most in this world.

The second is surprises, and specifically surprise *appointments*, which my secretary Penny springs on me with a calm voice that contradicts how I feel when I hear the words, "Your one o'clock is in the Platinum Room."

She tips her head to the side and back, pointing me in the direction as if I haven't been working here for the past three years.

"I don't have a one o'clock." I hold up my phone to indicate the calendar I carry around with me.

My phone has been permanently attached to my hand since I accepted my promotion ten months ago, and my entire workday is always just a click away. I glanced at it as I was coming back from lunch only five minutes ago, and I was clear for another hour.

"It was last minute. They arrived just after you left for lunch." The clicking of her nails on her keyboard grates in my eardrums.

"You know our procedures. Why didn't you schedule them

for another day so I could find out what they want and look into them?"

That's my job, after all.

I'm the gatekeeper for the CEO of the company. I manage his schedule, find opportunities, vet potential contacts, handle mundane tasks, and, most important, act as his proxy in handling people who wish to hold meetings.

"Mr.—um—Smith"—realization dawns on her features, and she winces as she says the generic name—"said he was only in town today, and he wished to speak to you about an important business opportunity." Another cringe.

I roll my eyes.

Everyone's business opportunity is "important."

"I'm sorry, Ms. Scott. I should have rescheduled. It's just that...well, he was very convincing—and handsome." She has the sense to mutter the last part to herself.

My gaze wanders down the hall toward the closed door. I lower my voice to a conspiratorial whisper. "Why are they in the Platinum Room?" The Platinum Room is our most exclusive meeting room on the executive floor, and it's rarely used.

"The other good rooms are all taken, and I didn't want to send him down to the staff conference rooms. He doesn't look like the type of person who meets in regular rooms."

My phone lights up with an alarm, reminding me my lunch is over. I've kept my unexpected guest waiting long enough.

"Have an intern prepare some refreshments and join me in five minutes."

I remove my notepad and pen from my bag, which I drop along with my winter jacket behind Penny's desk before making my way toward the meeting room. I slide my phone in my pocket as I go.

This meeting better be worth my time. I have a pile of

important business opportunities on my desk, screaming for my attention.

"I apologize for the delay, Mr.—"

A chill runs down my spine when a familiar scent hits me. Memories crush my heart, forcing the air out of my lungs.

Ryder Saint.

"Hello, Amara." The seductively low timbre in his voice grates through me like nails on a chalkboard.

My body mutinies, refusing to move as Ryder leisurely lifts himself out of his chair, buttoning his suit jacket over what I remember are washboard abs. My mouth waters at the thought, and I swallow to prevent myself from drooling stupidly, because this is not how today is going to go.

He still has a visceral effect on me, and I'm disappointed in my knee-jerk reaction to him after all this time.

When my father died of a heart attack four years ago, my mother decided she was moving away and taking me with her. I was sure Ryder would speak up for me and keep me with him. But no. He cast me out when I begged him not to abandon me.

The world I've pieced together over the last four years snaps me out of memory lane and into reality—my reality, in which I loved a boy who promised never to hurt me just before he publicly broke my heart and sent me away.

So, while I hate surprises second most in this world, the man standing across from me, wrapped up in his expensively tailored suit and staring me down, takes the top honor.

"Mr. Saint. My apologies. My receptionist *mistakenly* wrote down Smith."

His lips twitch into a loose grin.

I've amused him.

I will my feet to take the painful steps to the table. The gentleman standing behind him joins us, drawing my attention. A second, more devastating memory swells in my heart.

That used to be Grayson's job. My brother was Ryder's best friend and right-hand man until he was murdered almost three years ago, a year and a half after I moved away. They never caught his killer, which leads me to think it was someone close to him. Someone in the Saint family. The Saints are never punished for the crimes they commit. With deep pockets and connections to organized crime, they are close to untouchable.

Pressure builds behind my eyes, and I can't afford to succumb to my heartache. Not here in front of him. Sucking my lips between my teeth, I bite hard enough to ease the pressure, and my tears subside.

I reach across the table. As Ryder leans in to meet me, extending his arm in a handshake from the other side, I feel a rebellious fire spark to life inside my soul. A moment before our hands connect, I drop my fingers to the console in the middle of the table. I narrow my eyes on him as I push the intercom button, leaving Ryder standing with his hand outstretched.

"Penny, hold the refreshments. They aren't staying long. Please, join us."

Ryder's smile doesn't falter. Instead, he motions for his new right-hand man to take a seat at the table, and the sweet taste of my little victory drowns in my sour stomach.

I thought Ryder took everything I treasured away from me before he tossed me out like trash, but I was wrong.

When Grayson died, the last bright light in my world left with him.

"Is this your new BFF?" I motion to the man standing quietly beside him. "At least until someone puts a bullet in his head too, am I right?"

Ryder's smile falters, and I know my emotional punch has landed. The guy beside him only glances at the table in awkward silence.

The door opens, and Penny enters. I take the break to pull

out my chair and sit down. Ryder doesn't dignify my outburst with an answer as both men settle into their seats.

My anger festers inside of me, and I focus my emotions onto the items in my hand. I place my notebook down and line it up so its pages are aligned with the edge of the table, then I lay my pen in a straight line, one inch away from the notebook. The orderly sight fuels me to get this over with.

"Mr. Saint." I roll my eyes. "You told Penny you had an *important business opportunity*." I say the words with as much mocking derision as I would behind their backs, and a look of shock rushes to my receptionist's face.

"Yes." His dark eyes glance in Penny's direction. "And it is something I would like to speak to you about in private."

Penny closes her notebook and places it in her lap as though she expects me to dismiss her.

"This is as private as it will ever get for you, Mr. Saint. I'm busy, and I don't appreciate having my time wasted."

Penny rolls her chair half a foot away from the table, no doubt distancing herself from the growing tension.

Ryder shifts his attention to Penny, and she shrinks back a few more inches before he returns his focus to me, dragging his teeth over his bottom lip.

"Very well." His smile morphs into something sinister. "Before we begin, tell me, how is my ex-fiancée doing?"

Penny's gasp makes me regret telling her to stay.

How could I forget that one of Ryder's favorite things was calling me on my shit and putting me in my place? Unfortunately for him, my place is no longer under his thumb.

"Funny. You never called me your fiancée in public when we were actually promised to each other. You never acknowledged anything about me."

"You know why." His expression turns serious, and the boy I used to know makes a fleeting appearance.

I used to love that boy.

The thought hits me with a wave of nausea, and everyone around me suddenly looks small. Their heads tilt up. Wide eyes stare at me in silence, and I realize that at some point in the last few seconds I must have stood up. I reach for the table as my head swirls.

"Amara." His tone sounds a little like a warning.

I lift my hand, telling him not to speak.

He lost the right to have any concern for me a long time ago.

I can't release any of my control to him. I won't allow him to find a foothold back into my life in any capacity.

Clearing my throat, I push my chair back and suck in a deep breath to steady myself for a graceful exit. "I—um. I'll be a moment. I need to use the restroom. Gentlemen."

I don't wait for anyone to excuse me.

I'm one position under the damn CEO.

No one excuses me.

I count each measured step to the hall. Once the door to the Platinum Room closes behind me, I sprint into the women's bathroom.

"Shit," I mutter under my breath as I close the distance to the sink and run the cold water. While the *shh* of the flow usually calms me, the shock of seeing Ryder after all this time is too much to process. I want to leave this bathroom, run out of the building, and leave Penny to deal with them.

"If you run away, he'll know, and he'll use it against you." I act as my own voice of reason as I stare myself down in the mirror. "You can do this," I tell my reflection. "Just get rid of him. Don't let him know. Don't—"

My stomach knots as the flush of a toilet draws my attention over my shoulder to the two closed stalls behind me. I turn my back as the lock clicks open and shove my hands under the frigid water.

The woman approaches the sink beside me, and we exchange a hesitant smile in the mirror. She looks vaguely familiar. In a company of over three hundred people, it's easy to forget a face, and I relax once again as I dry my hands and make my way back to the room.

The men half stand, then return to sitting as I walk into the room with more determination than I had when I left.

"This meeting has gone on long enough, Mr. Saint. You said you had a business opportunity to discuss." I grab my pen and tap it against my notebook. I'm two seconds from ending everything and getting on with my life...I mean, my day.

Ryder keeps his gaze on me but holds his hand out to the silent man sitting beside him. A folder is handed over, and he places it on the table in front of him, then slides it across to me.

"I represent a party who is extremely interested in purchasing this company."

Penny is quiet beside me. These types of deals are rarely good for the employees who work hard and rely on the company to live.

"Well, that's an easy one. Our CEO is not interested in selling, but I will take your offer and run it by him at my own convenience. Someone from our office will get back to you. Now." I slap my notebook on top of the file. "If that's everything?"

Before he can answer, the door opens behind me. So much for my opportunity to run out of the room and hide in my office for the rest of the day.

The woman from the bathroom enters, and I exchange a look of confusion with Penny, who only shrugs. I'm hopeful we double-booked this meeting room and I can make my exit even quicker than originally planned.

My hope turns to internal panic when she smiles at Ryder and his buddy before circling the table toward them, and her eyes turn solemn as she looks my way.

I do know her from somewhere—but it isn't here.

How could I have forgotten her?

Sloane, my brother's old girlfriend, stops at Ryder's side and bends over to whisper into his ear.

Ryder's eyes don't leave mine as my heart thuds heavy into my chest, my words of encouragement I spoke to myself in the bathroom replaying in my mind.

His demeanor changes the longer she talks, a wolfish grin spreading across his face. When Sloane is done talking, she stands and steps behind Ryder without making eye contact with me. We both know she just ratted me out. Ryder reaches his hand to his suit and unbuttons his jacket as though he's making himself comfortable.

"Don't let me know what, Amara?"

All eyes turn to me.

Well, shit.

Anything I say now will be used against me. If I lie, he'll know, but I won't sit here and tell him the truth.

So I say nothing.

Like the grown-ass woman I have become, I cross my arms and sit in utter silence, staring him down. My jaw is clenched so tightly, my teeth will shatter before I reveal my secrets.

A painful minute passes before Ryder places his palms on the table and slides his chair back. Standing, he towers over all of us, his eyes burning into my own.

"Everyone, get out!" His tone is firm, commanding, and I can't blame any of them for obeying, which they all do.

Penny is the first to leave, followed by Sloane. I wasn't close with Sloane, since my brother was a few years older than me, but I feel betrayed. Before she leaves, she attempts a smile, but it doesn't light up her eyes. It looks a lot like pity.

As Ryder's new right-hand man leaves as well, sealing the door behind him and cutting off my escape route, I realize I never even got his name.

The door is closed, not locked, I remind myself.

Taking a deep breath, I stand, pushing my own chair back before turning to leave.

"You're not going anywhere, Amara. Not until I'm done with you."

I stand still, my back turned to him. I would like to think I'm in charge of this entire situation, but we both know it isn't true.

I'm not in control of anything. Not when he's around.

From the moment I entered this room, I've been slowly sinking into a trap. It was one of the things I craved about Ryder Saint when I belonged to him. I loved it when he stalked me like I was his prey, always drawing me closer to my eventual demise. He was methodical, precise, a master at fueling my need to be hunted and taken by him.

That's why I won't turn to face him. I can't afford to lose any more ground today.

"What do you want?" I pull my shoulders back, preparing for his answer.

"It's time to come home, Amara."

Home.

The word is foreign.

My home abandoned me four years ago.

My home was murdered two and a half years ago.

I have no home.

I jump and spin around when I feel something brush against my hair, coming face-to-face and inches away from the lips I used to kiss and suck on for hours on end.

"I've missed your smell." His gravelly tone sends a shiver through me that I hope he doesn't notice.

He used to tell me he could smell my arousal. My body betrays me as heat flushes my cheeks at his insinuation. But he had his chance, and he threw it away when he cast me out. He has no right to miss anything about me.

A little voice in the back of my head screams warning after warning, and I take a step back to place some distance between us. As quickly as the space is created, it is recovered as he steps into me until my back hits a wall and his fingers graze my throat.

He leans in, lowering his voice, his words hot against my cheek. "Do you remember that time in the pool house? Because I do, my little flower. I remember your eyes rolling back into your head as you sucked in as much air as I allowed while I pressed you up against the wall. I remember my hand covered in your spit as I clamped it over your mouth to quiet your moans as you rode my palm into oblivion, your panties stretched tight around your knees. Do you remember that, Blossom?"

I whimper involuntarily at his old nickname for me, and I immediately hate myself for allowing my emotions to show.

Unable to look him in the eyes any longer, I lower my gaze.

His low chuckle hums into my ears as he lifts his hand to his mouth, slipping his tongue through his lips to his fingers. I watch, mesmerized, as he licks the pads while keeping his eyes trained on me.

"I swear I still taste you on the tips of my fingers."

My body stiffens as he removes his hand from his mouth before tracing his wet fingers over my lower lip. My heart hammers in my chest. Of course I remember that time. It was the last time he ever touched me, and an hour later, he let me go.

Unable to bear my close proximity to him any longer, I slide my body along the wall. My grace long gone, I bumble out of his hold.

"Nope." I say the first thing that comes to my mind, and Ryder's eyebrows pinch together. Straightening my shirt, I lift my chin and correct myself. "I'm not going anywhere with you. You can't just show up here and make demands. I have my own life now, and I make my own choices. You need to leave."

With deliberate attention, he adjusts the cuffs of his sleeves before he addresses me again.

"Remember this moment, Amara. Remember that, just now, I gave you a chance to make this easy for yourself. You can make all the choices you want, but every decision comes with the heavy responsibility of being accountable for the outcomes that follow."

Stepping back from me, he turns to the table and lifts the file and my notebook before offering them to me with a smile that hides his intentions.

I reach out to take them. He combs a loose strand of my hair off my shoulder before walking to the door. As it clicks open, he turns to face me.

"This isn't over, Amara. I'll see you again. Soon."

2

RYDER

*N*ash's text lights up my phone on the table in front of me: **She's on her way in**.

Five days. That's all it took for me to go above Amara's head, speak to the CEO myself, and buy the company. Everyone has their price, and her boss isn't as committed to his employees as she would like to think. He took the money and ran. I can't blame him; my offer was well above a fair price.

While I waited for everything to transfer over, I asked my brother Cole to gather more information on my little flower. It's been a while, and I'm not making assumptions or taking any chances with her.

Letting Amara go four years ago paled in comparison to living without her. The first few months blurred into each other. I incessantly looked for her on social media, but she had closed her accounts and hid herself away from me.

I couldn't ask about her, as she was supposed to be inconsequential to me. Back then, my father was a couple of years away from loosening his tight grip on the family business and allowing his four sons to step up. I had no choice but to let her go until I had a better grasp on my family's company.

I told myself it was a small amount of time to wait, and I would talk to Grayson and get his blessing before taking Amara back—but I never had the chance.

A year and a half after I lost Amara, Grayson was murdered. He was found, shot in the head, in one of our own warehouses. In a flash, the two people who meant the world to me were gone.

I push the memory of my best friend down as the click of the handle catches my attention.

"Good afternoon, Mr.—oh!" The rest of her sentence dies on her lips, but her mouth forms the word "no" and my cheeks tighten, stretching a smile across my face.

"Ah, Ms. Scott. There you are. I was just—"

Her eyes narrow on me. "I'm not here for you. I was told I have a meeting with Mr. Traeger."

"No," I correct her as I lean back in my chair, crossing an ankle over my knee. "You were told you have a meeting with your CEO, and as of"—I stretch my arm out, sliding the cuff of my sleeve off my watch, and check the time for dramatic effect —"one hour ago, that is exactly what I am."

As she stares daggers at me in silence, I replay Cole's initial assessment of Amara in my mind.

My brother wasn't able to dig up much on her.

In the few days he had, he found no close friends, no boyfriend, and, other than yoga on Wednesdays, no social life.

The most shocking piece of news he had was about her mother, who doesn't call or visit. Phone records show it is always Amara calling her, which was odd to me because her mother was so adamant about moving her daughter away with her when she left four years ago.

Amara did, however, stick to a predictable schedule that

Cole was able to piece together after only a couple of days of watching her.

The wild, carefree girl I knew is now guarded, precise —*controlled*. The thought makes me jealous. There was a time when she surrendered her control to me.

"You didn't." Her shaky voice breaks me of my thoughts.

"Shut the door and sit down, Amara. We need to talk." Uncrossing my leg, I shift in my seat. The curious fear in her voice catches me off guard and triggers a craving I haven't entertained in a long time.

Her lips pinch together in defiance. Up until five days ago, she has never denied me anything.

Her fingers tighten around the items she's carrying. As she tentatively walks toward me, her skirt hugs her curves with each step. She pauses at the chair before pulling it back and taking her place at the table, and I smile at her.

It isn't returned.

She drops her gaze to the space in front of her and doesn't look up to speak to me. "There's nothing to talk about." Instead, she places the folder on the table, straightening it before setting her notebook on top. She adjusts it as well before setting two pens on the table, and I notice a small tremor in her fingers as she fumbles with one. It rolls a couple of times before coming to a stop.

"I disagree."

I begin by telling her about the buyout. As I talk, I watch her zero in on the pen; the one that rolled away. She picks it up and sets it neatly in line with the first pen, and her fingers fidget on it until it is perfectly parallel to the first.

"You can't do this." She's lost the confident tone she had when she first spoke to me, and it's just as well. The sooner she accepts her fate, the easier it will be for her.

"It's already done, Amara. It's time to live with the weight of the choices you've made."

Her lips curl into a snarl at my attempt to claim my authority. Straightening her back, she places her palms on the table and pushes herself up, just as I did when we were first in this office.

I know she's going for intimidating, but watching her attempt to assert control ignites something dark inside of me. Thoughts of what I would do to her in order to break her spirit, if we weren't expecting company shortly, make my pulse race.

"If you think for one second—" She freezes mid-sentence as the doors behind her open and a line of employees file into the room.

These must be the managers and executive team I've asked to meet with, and I rise, quickly circling the table to Amara before she notices.

Disoriented, she hasn't realized I've moved until she turns back and startles before going for her notebook.

I'm quicker, and I cover her items with my hand before leaning in to whisper in her ear, "Sit down, Blossom."

Maybe it's just my own need playing tricks with me, but I'm sure I hear her whimper before she clears her throat at the name I used to call her and takes her seat.

Nash, my first in command, enters the room at the end, closing the door behind him. I see the familiarity dawn in Amara's eyes. Nash was with me during my first visit.

Once everyone is settled, I begin by announcing the takeover and notice the exchange of glances between employees.

After I finish telling everyone that I have no intention of changing anything about the company, I notice sighs of relief being exhaled around the table.

"There is one personnel change, and it is effective

immediately." I extend my hand down and to the right. "Amara Scott will oversee the smooth transition and will be working directly under me from now on."

My announcement had the effect I intended.

Amara's body goes rigid. I can't see her face from my standing position, but I expect she's plastered on a tense smile as everyone around the table looks at her.

I know from Cole's digging that she isn't particularly close to any of the employees, with the exception of a few, and she's earned an interesting nickname for herself from those who work below her.

"I'm sure many of you have questions, and we will be meeting with all departments over the next week to address all of them, but for now—" My sentence is cut short when the *Ice Princess* stands beside me with a calm, determined expression. "Excuse us for a moment." I hook my hand around Amara's upper arm. "My associate, Nash, will fill you in on any information you need before we leave for the weekend." I casually slide my chair out of my way and lead Amara toward the window. She reluctantly moves with me.

I was right to ask that notifying the staff of the change be left to me. I've caught Amara off guard, and the uncertainty of a situation that is slowly growing out of her control has made her compliant. But she won't remain this way for long.

Amara recovers quickly.

I turn her to face me, leaving her back to the room, and keep a relaxed smile on my face as I speak. "What do you think you're doing?"

She looks up at me with animosity in her eyes, and my stomach flutters at her ferocious glare.

No one provokes me like she does.

"I am not part of the deal you made, Ryder. I owe this company nothing. And I sure as *hell*"—she grits the word through her teeth in a hushed tone—"don't owe you a damn thing. So you lose, Ryder. I'll just resign." Her anger morphs into a triumphant smile.

I love the determination in her tone. It almost makes me regret what I'm about to do.

My lips pull back, exposing my teeth in a hungry grin, and the poise on her face falls for a moment. She remembers me well enough to know when I am about to strike.

As I lean in to her, she draws in a breath of air, holding it in anticipation of my retaliation. My smile hides the dark promise in the words I'm about to speak.

"I'm telling you now, Amara, you aren't going anywhere. If you announce you are anything but eager to work with me when we return to the table, I will gut this company and everyone in it. Now sit down and smile like my good girl." My threat tastes delicious on my tongue.

I ache to show her her place.

I'm gambling that my sweet Amara is still inside this controlled and cold woman standing in front of me. The woman who, although she appears distant and reserved, still cares a great deal about the people she's worked with for the last few years.

A war rages across her face. The lips I want to claim once again pinch together, no doubt holding back everything she desperately wants to say to me.

I have my answer when Penny coughs, catching Amara's attention and draining her of her resolve. She breaks our stare but doesn't turn to look at everyone behind her. Instead, her gaze travels out the window and over the city. The golden flecks in her eyes glimmer in the sun, and the urge to reach out to her chips away at my own restraint.

I flex and fist my fingers to hold myself back from touching her.

After a minute of silence, Nash raises his voice to catch my attention as he wraps up his spiel and nods at me.

Amara notices the exchange and lifts her chin, pulling her shoulders back and composing herself before she turns and rejoins the table with a forced smile.

She knows what I expect of her.

Everyone watches Amara closely as she pulls her seat out and sits down. I return to my own chair beside her, yet no one is looking at me.

They are waiting for her to lead them. Even though they refer to her as the Ice Princess, they respect her leadership. The thought fills me with a surge of pride.

Amara adjusts the pen beside her notepad until it is straight before speaking.

"This news is as much of a surprise to me as it is to you, so we all have a lot to consider over the weekend. That being said, the company's new owners have just finished telling us they don't expect any changes, so we continue with the work we've always been doing."

As Amara addresses the managers and department heads around the table, her arms tremble in her lap. Her hands are fisted, and she is squeezing so tightly that the effort is making her forearms shake. Above the table, she looks calm and professional. But below the surface, I watch her struggle to maintain her guarded exterior.

She suggests we all break for the weekend to spend time with our families. She looks around the table at each person as she tells them we'll reconnect on Monday morning for further information, and everyone nods like sheep before I stand.

"Thank you, Ms. Scott, for your welcoming words. Ladies and gentlemen, I look forward to discussing this in more detail next week." My words are meant to excuse everyone at the table, but all glances defer to Amara.

Interesting.

She nods, and everyone gathers their things and files out of the room. Nash holds the door, nodding to everyone as they pass.

Amara stands, and I extend my arm to take the handshake she denied me on Monday. She hesitates. Her hands are still clenched at her sides, but I won't let it go this time.

This time, she will acknowledge her new circumstances.

Lifting her palm into my own, I shake her hand with a tight smile on my lips, and she follows my lead. Before breaking away, I pull her in and lean close to her bowed head, my lips so close I could lick the spot on her ear that used to tickle her. "You will do well to remember I always get what I want, Amara."

Her insincere smile falters.

I don't give her the chance to recover into the spitfire she is this time. Stepping around her, I join Nash at the door before turning to dismiss Amara from my company's conference room.

If I give her the opportunity to defy me, she'll walk out of here with her head held high. She'll feel emboldened, and that's the last thing I want. Right now, I want to live in her head all weekend. I want her thinking about the things I've said to her and anxiously wondering about what next week will bring. I want her to kick herself over and over again, thinking about all of the witty little comebacks she would have come up with if only I'd given her the time.

I want her to think about me because, since Monday, I haven't been able to get her out of my head.

Amara reaches the entryway, and I see her fight already returning to her. Before she has the chance to say her piece, I cut her off and hold my hand out, gesturing for her to leave. "Thank you for your time today, Ms. Scott. I will schedule our next meeting at my own convenience. Enjoy your weekend."

She glares between Nash and I before spinning on her heels and leaving without a word.

We both stand in silence, watching her walk down the hall toward her office.

Nash clears his throat. "Your father texted. Says he's been trying to reach you."

I roll my eyes. "Of course he has." My definition of "retired" is very different from his. "I'll deal with him later."

Nash reaches out, catching my attention, and my gaze drops to the tissue in his hand. I silently stare at him, and he offers more information. "For your hand. You're bleeding."

Confusion sets in, and I turn my palm up to examine the smears of crimson on my skin. I trace my fingers along the blood. "It isn't mine," I mumble to myself.

Since entering the room, I've only touched one thing.

Amara.

I shook her hand. The same hand she clenched under the table. She must have dug her nails into her palm, breaking the skin in order to hide her emotions from me. Knowing she would rather bleed than face the feelings she fears is all I need to know.

I once took my mother to have her palm read as a birthday gift, and I remember the fortune-teller pointing out the various points on my hand. It's fitting; the blood Amara marked me with is creased into my love line.

I will have all of her: blood, sweat, and tears. Her heart, her body, and her mind will bend to my will. The thought is as powerful as the urge to have her as close to me as I can.

As my fragile flower turns the corner to her office, I lift my fingers to my mouth. The metallic taste of her fury is sweet on my tongue.

She's still mine.

She knows this, and it terrifies her.

3

AMARA

I've spent the last two weeks waiting for the other shoe to drop.

After Ryder announced his takeover to our executive members, I was flooded with meeting requests. I trained Penny to temporarily fill my position while I oversaw the transition. It meant a higher rate of pay for her, and I know she needs the additional income.

I kept waiting for my meeting with Ryder, but he never scheduled it, and there was no way I was going to seek him out for something I never wanted to be a part of in the first place.

Nash acted as his liaison for the first week and only told those who were curious that Mr. Saint had been called back to Seattle on business and would return as soon as possible. Which was fine by me—until he returned at the beginning of this week.

By then, Penny was up to speed. Still, I made sure to pad all of our meetings with additional staff. I provided detailed updates so there would be nothing further to discuss, and when Penny and I were tasked with setting up an executive cocktail party to say goodbye to Timothy Traeger and welcome our new boss, I threw myself into the task, keeping myself busy and off of Ryder's radar.

Now, four days later, I'm in the ballroom of the Courtyard in my black cocktail dress, clutching a glass of white wine for show and standing as close as possible to a large ficus in hopes of going unnoticed by all of the attendees—one in particular.

Networking is like a dance. Men and women move around the room from conversation to conversation. Managers flow from Timothy to Ryder, covering their bases and their asses while they wish one well and welcome the other while a sinfonietta plays a delicate yet upbeat song.

I get the odd smile and the lifting of a glass as people notice me trying to hide, and I smile in return.

I know what they call me.

The tune changes.

As soon as the first chord is played, I know what song it is: Canon in D Major. I know because I played it over and over again the night I found out Grayson had died. I mourned by myself and drank until I passed out, but not before sobbing on my bathroom floor. It was the single worst night of my life, and I was alone for it. It was also the last time I allowed myself to lose control.

The day Ryder sent me away, Grayson told me I deserved the world. He said things looked bad but they would get better. He told me he'd never be far away from me, and he'd still be there to share every wonderful moment. He said he'd even walk me down the aisle to that *cliché wedding song I liked*, and he told me our lives were just starting.

I believed him.

My throat tightens, and the room in front of me becomes fluid as my sadness threatens to spill down my cheeks. I use the cocktail napkin to take the tears away before they fall, and I bite my lips between my teeth to push back the urge to succumb to my pain.

Maybe this is my sign. Ryder showing up here and buying the company isn't random, and I will use this as my opportunity to get justice for Grayson's murder.

The song ends prematurely, pulling me out of my thoughts, and I glance to the musicians when his piercing stare hits me.

Ryder stands just to the side of the band, speaking to the group's lead. His expression is serious; his eyes are on me.

The band immediately picks up with another song, this one more lively, and Ryder turns his attention to someone at his side: Fiona from HR, who seems to be falling out of her dress and trying to get her time in with him.

"Thank you, Amara. This is beautiful—and appreciated." The man attached to the deep voice joins me in my hiding spot.

I straighten when I realize who it is. "Mr. Traeger. You're welcome. Are you enjoying yourself? Can I get you anything?"

"Please, call me Tim. I'm having a great time, and no. You're off the clock. I just wanted to tell you personally how much I value you. I know it wasn't an easy job, but you sure made it look like it was."

"Thank you, Mr.—Tim."

"Mr. Traeger." Penny joins us with a glass of champagne in hand. "A bunch of managers were asking if they could steal you away for a moment."

He turns to me with a smile, and I shrug knowingly. Everyone always wants a piece of the boss.

He takes a step to follow Penny away, then stops and faces me once more.

"You know what I valued most about you—and Penny?"

I tilt my head, waiting for his response.

"You never concerned yourself with kissing my ass. You just did your job. You were my greatest asset, Amara."

I blush at his comment.

"Now she's my greatest asset." Shivers crawl up my spine, and my arms prickle with goosebumps as Ryder takes Tim's vacant place by my side.

Like a predator, he waited for the perfect time to strike.

Ryder's double entendre is lost on my old boss, who nods in agreement and excuses himself, leaving me standing alone in my hiding place with the very person I was hiding from.

"You're trying to avoid me, Ms. Scott." His small talk is anything but.

A stray manager catches sight of us and takes a few steps in our direction, no doubt wanting time with the new boss. My temporary feeling of relief is shattered when Ryder simply takes a sip of his drink, lifts one finger off the glass, and shakes his head, warning him off with a charismatic smile.

"I don't know what you're talking about, Mr. Saint."

I feel like a child saying those words. I know I'm feigning ignorance.

His sardonic chuckle tells me he knows it too.

"You look stunning tonight." His shift in conversation unnerves me. "Both powerful and delicate." He takes another sip. Speaking casually, he surveys the room as everyone mingles around us. "Do you know why they call you the Ice Princess?"

I take my first gulp of wine.

Of course Ryder knows about my nickname. He always gathered as much information as he could on all of his enemies and assets, and right now I'm both.

I am standing in between him and the one thing he wants to own, which also happens to be me. I still don't know why.

He takes my silence as an invitation to continue.

"You are an impressive woman. Powerful." A long pause has me waiting for his next words. "Dominant." He catches my attention with that word, and I turn to look at him, but his gaze remains forward. "None of them will ever own you. They can't wrap you in a pretty package and put you in their pocket. You will never belong to them, so they've given you a label. The label is theirs, and it is all they will ever have of you"—another casual sip of his amber liquid—"and you let them have it because you are so far out of their league, they can't touch you."

I drop my gaze to the floor in front of me. This is the deepest conversation I've had with anyone in years. My heart thuds painfully against my chest.

When I lift my attention back to Ryder, his stare bores deep into me.

"But I can touch you, Blossom. I can peel back your petals and you'll give me anything I want—eventually. You know this, and this is why you are trying to avoid me, and it worked for you this week, but your time is up." His fingers graze my bare arm, and I hug myself against the shudder stirring inside of me.

"What do you mean?"

I realize too late I shouldn't have asked the question. I'm not prepared for his answer. I should have walked away when I had the chance.

"Your replacement is trained, and your time in Portland is done. I require Nash for other matters. You'll be returning to Seattle with me next week, and you'll continue working as my liaison from there. I've arranged to have your apartment packed up this weekend. It's time to come home, Amara."

I break from his scrutiny, blinking rapidly to quell my emotions and organize my thoughts, but the room feels like it's swaying.

Stepping away, I place my glass on an empty table, and some managers take advantage of the space I created to get in their time with the company's new owner.

I exploit the break and move steadily away from the group

that's growing around Ryder. Then I find my way out the doors and into the hall.

My dress feels a size too tight. I need a quiet room to gather myself in. Luckily, this hall is lined with doors, and I try each handle as I make my way down the hall away from the party. On the fourth try, the door opens, and the room is dark and perfect.

Before the door shuts behind me, I hear my name from down the hall. I spin around, backing into the dim room, and hoping I wasn't seen.

The handle jiggles, then the door opens, and my stomach knots as Ryder follows me into the room, shutting us in without a word.

I open my mouth in the darkness, but nothing comes out. A small part of me hopes he doesn't know I'm here, but we met each other's eyes when the light from the hall illuminated the room.

A small lamp by the door is turned on, and I panic.

I hold up my hand. "Give me a minute." There is no point in asking him to let me stay here, in Portland and away from him. The best I can hope for now is a moment to gather my feelings and accept my fate.

Ryder stands in front of the only exit, filling the area in front of the closed door and adjusting the cuff on his jacket while he watches me. He doesn't respond.

"Please. I need you to go." I'm rattled. The desperation in my voice sounds pathetic.

"No, Amara. I won't allow you to hide yourself away from me. I'm not going anywhere."

He abandoned me four years ago when I was at my most vulnerable. Without time to push my hurt down, my anger builds at an unstoppable pace.

My voice rises. "That's a big change from when you told

me to leave, Ryder. You have no right to come back into my life. And that's just what this is." I wave my arms around me. "I'm living just fine without you. You have no right."

His composure cracks as he takes a step toward me. "I have every right!" His words are sharp with disdain. I take a step away, but he takes another toward me. "You're surviving, Amara. That is all you're doing. You sure as hell aren't living. And I won't allow this to continue."

The cruel accuracy in his words cuts me open.

After all this time, how does he see me so easily?

"That's not fair. You don't know me."

I don't realize I've been stepping back until I'm stopped by heavy velvet curtains, and Ryder takes his last step into my space.

He lowers his voice to account for our close proximity. "I know you better than you know yourself, Blossom." Hooking his finger under the strap of my dress, he tickles a line across my shoulder to my collarbone as he levels himself directly in my line of sight. "Tell me, how many men have there been since me?" His lips twitch into a harsh grin, and I realize he doesn't know *everything* about me. Not yet.

I find my fight.

"It's none of your business, but there have been many." I bite the words of my confession at him. He studies my expression for signs I'm lying before blinking to snap himself out of his certainty. As his confidence wavers, my strength grows.

I've got this.

"Did you think I would spend my time pining for the boy who threw me away? You did me a favor, Ryder Saint. You don't know me." I repeat myself. My tone isn't as sure as I would like it to be, but it's steadier than it was.

As I wait for his response, I reach my hand around behind

me and fist the soft fabric of the curtain to avoid digging my nails into my palm like the last time.

Ryder mutters, "It doesn't matter." I don't know if he is speaking to me or himself, but his clenched jaw tells me my answer matters a great deal, and I feel a stab of regret even though hurting him pales in comparison to how he hurt me.

I didn't lie to him; there have been many men since Ryder. But he asked me the wrong question, and I'm thankful some of my secrets are still safe with me.

The silence between us stretches on, and our nearness becomes more apparent as we stare at each other. The scent of whiskey on his breath makes my mouth water, and his lips are only inches away from my own.

I've missed his smell. I've missed being his and feeling him all around me. I've been broken ever since, and I still want him. I'll hate myself for admitting this later, but my traitorous heart still wants him.

His gaze flits fervently between my eyes and my lips, and I swallow hard. Clearing my throat, I lick my lips and hope my next words get me out of the hole I'm sinking into. I open my mouth, unsure of what is about to come out, when he surges forward.

Soft, demanding lips crash into my own before taking me over and pulling me under.

He tastes like home.

The warning in my head shuts off, and I let go of the curtain and wrap myself around his muscular body. I feel him tense as I lean in to him, returning his desire with my own.

I haven't felt whole since him. His chaos welcomes me in. He's right. I was only surviving. I haven't been living; I've been dying. My heart has been slowly wasting away.

The desperate will to live once again pulses through my veins, and my needy heart eats this connection up.

Strong arms swing me around and walk me toward the back of a couch. I try to turn my face away from him, but he stops me.

"You'll look at me." He growls hungry words as his hands search for purchase, one sliding along my jaw and wrapping around the back of my head, the other on my hip, guiding me to my place in front of him.

A reckless urgency consumes my sanity, driving me crazy with need. I don't recognize myself, and I don't hear the door open.

"Oh, I'm sorry. Thought this was the washroom." I can't place the male voice.

I pull my shaking hands to my face in shame at the horror of what I've done. I've let myself lose control, and at a work function no less. I crumbled for Ryder in a matter of minutes.

"GET OUT!" There is no mistaking the assertiveness in Ryder's tone, and the door immediately shuts.

Dropping my hands from my face, I find myself in darkness. Ryder wrapped his jacket around me to cover my identity.

As he lowers his arm, his eyes meet mine.

I could easily lose myself in him once again, and I can't allow that to happen. I will return to his home, find my brother's killer, and cut the ties that bind my heart to Ryder.

Placing my palms on his hard chest, I gently push, and he steps back. I shift myself away and straighten my dress. "Um, I'm going to go."

Ryder draws his thumb along his lower lip. "You should stay."

It's a challenge.

Ryder has always been big on consent. So, while he took control and dragged me down to the depraved depths of my debauchery, I was always the one who took the first step toward my dark demise.

I don't allow myself to say another word. Dropping my gaze, I shake my head and turn to leave the room, burrowing my nails into my palm to keep me from giving in.

His melancholic tone makes me pause at the door, one hand on the handle. "I know you try to control everything around you so that nothing can control you."

The sincerity in his tone crushes me more than the painful truth itself. I've been on my own for four years, but it wasn't until this very moment that I allowed it to hurt.

No one has ever challenged me like Ryder has, but the difference between then and now is that I felt safe with him then. No matter what I faced, I wasn't alone, and nothing could hurt me. He challenged me to push myself, and I became addicted to the rush of flying high knowing he was there—until he wasn't.

I don't respond. Instead, I open the door and run away.

I needed this to make me stronger, I tell myself as I leave the party behind. I need time to focus on what I want, and what I want is to find out who killed my brother.

4

RYDER

As soon as the elevator doors open onto her floor, Amara's frustration carries all the way down the hall when she yells from inside her apartment, "JUST GIVE IT TO ME. I'LL DO IT MYSELF."

Her door is ajar, and I push it the rest of the way open, letting myself into her home.

She's faced away from me as one of the movers hands her a potted plant, and she reaches out to grab a second planter from the table beside her. Clutching them to her chest, she turns to walk away, but freezes as her gaze locks on mine.

Her cheeks flush; I've witnessed a vulnerable moment for her.

It was the same look she had when she realized I caught her looking distraught at the cocktail party. I had a feeling it was the classical song the band was playing. She'd seemed fine during the previous forty-five minutes I was secretly watching her hide behind that artificial tree.

She shuts herself away, and she considers it a strength.

Her fingers tighten around the succulents in her hand.

She looks like she hasn't slept much. "I'm not ready to leave." Her timid tone tells me her words carry more than one meaning.

"I know," I answer, pulling out my phone to check for a text message.

My brother said he'd be here by now.

Cole always got along with Amara, so having him here as a buffer made sense.

The loose ponytail on Amara's head is a sharp contrast to the formal woman I've seen in the office, and her yoga pants are doing damage to my restraint.

Visions of her sobbing put me on edge. The memory of her lips on mine on Friday night, her fingers digging into my skin through my suit, make me want to pick up from where we were so rudely interrupted—but this is not the time.

Amara is distressed. It's written all over her face. She's an emotional wreck, and she has no control over the dismantling of the life she felt secure and safe in. This is not the type of vulnerable I want her to be when I have her.

And I will have her.

The sound of glass shattering in another room causes Amara to jump. She is wound so tight she looks like she's going to snap, but instead of rushing out she does something that surprises me.

She looks at me. It's a brief exchange. I'm sure she doesn't notice, but she just deferred to me to excuse her.

I nod and turn away.

I don't want her to realize what she's done. It won't strengthen her, and it will only encourage her to remain closed off from me.

Instead, I look around the room where she lived away from me. I want to think she was happy, that all of her treasured possessions and photos of her loved ones are packed away, but something tells me these three boxes on the floor hold most of her memories, and two of them aren't full.

I check my phone for a message from Cole once more, and an incoming call lights up my screen, but it isn't a number I recognize. I step onto the balcony, slide the door shut behind me, and answer it.

"Ryder, is that you? It's Mrs. Scott." The haughty, entitled tone makes me roll my eyes.

I pinch the bridge of my nose and drop my head with a sigh. I knew I'd be hearing from this one. I just didn't expect her to come crawling out of the woodwork so soon.

"Alicia. What can I do for you?" I refuse to address anyone with a title they don't deserve, and Amara's mother is the bottom of the barrel as far as authenticity goes.

"It's been brought to my attention that you are interested in my daughter. I thought we resolved that business years ago." Her tone carries a confidence it really shouldn't. I'm not the boy she remembers.

Alicia and her husband sold Amara to my family in some secret transaction they all believe I know nothing about. My father thought tying me down would reign me in, so he jumped at the chance without knowing the secret Amara and I kept between us.

She was already mine.

When Amara's father passed away from a heart attack, Alicia asked to be let out of the deal without having to repay the money, and my father granted her that one wish.

I sensed Alicia was jealous of the close connection Amara and Grayson shared. Cole tells me that any calls between Amara and Alicia are always initiated by Amara, so her interest in her daughter's well-being is suspicious.

"My business with Amara is none of your concern." I will never owe this woman an explanation.

"It's every bit my concern. She's my—"

"She's nothing but a payday to you, Alicia, and that stops now."

A part of me hoped her mother took her away to help her heal from losing her deadbeat father, but Cole's digging confirmed that shortly after her mother moved her here, she pretty much dumped her on her own.

She took Amara away from the only home she knew and the only family she had left. She took her away from me, then left her to fend for herself without any support. This is unforgivable.

Alicia doesn't respond right away. They always thought I knew nothing about Amara's arrangement. It served my goals just fine, so I kept those cards close to my chest. But now, I have no further use for her wretched mother.

"I know you sold Amara to my father, and I know you never call the daughter you claim to care about. So drop the act, because I have no patience for you. I'll ask once more, and if you waste my time, we are done. What can I do for you?"

"I—" The line slips into silence for a few seconds. "I just think we can come to some kind of arrangement, like I had with your father."

I feel sick to my stomach. Grayson was the only family Amara deserved to have in her life.

Before I can tell Alicia all of the ways I am planning on crushing her out of existence, she speaks again. "Or I could call and deal with your father directly."

There's her play.

I always brushed our arranged marriage off as something I did for the family. I used my sacrifice to earn myself rank among my brothers. If my father knew how invested in Amara I was, I could be used as a puppet, and if he knew I lied to him all of this time, there is no telling how he would use the information to punish me.

Amara would end up collateral damage.

"Alicia, I will offer this one time, and there is no room for negotiation. Amara is working for the company I just purchased, and I require her professional expertise only. This is an important business deal for me, and I would rather not have my father involved. And trust me when I tell you, you do not want that either. I will offer you a one-time payment, but let me be clear: I am not buying Amara. I am paying you to crawl back under the rock you just crawled out of and allow me to do as I please. I'm also paying you to be the mother Amara deserves. You will call her on holidays and on her birthday, and you will ask her questions and be a fucking mother to her or, so help me, I will use all of the money at my disposal to put you in the ground. I'll text you my offer shortly."

I disconnect without waiting for a response.

Movement in the living room catches my attention, and I slide the door open and join Amara, shaking the chill from my bones. Her hands tremble, and tears run down her blotchy cheeks.

I'm ready to tear someone a new one when the item in her hand stops me cold.

Glass remnants are nestled in her palm, and she cradles her hands close to her heart.

I know what it is instantly.

Grayson beamed with pride when she unwrapped this glass butterfly on her seventeenth birthday.

It's broken because of me.

Lots of things are broken because of me.

The unbridled little girl I once knew peeks through her cracked exterior, and I stand in stupid silence as I watch her fight with everything she has to push her vulnerability back down.

I've done business with criminal organizations. I've been threatened by my father's enemies, and I grew up with three headstrong brothers. None of that fazes me as fast as seeing Amara in a helpless state.

As she looks down at the jagged pieces of glass, I scan the room. The movers haven't joined us. I'm sure they are holed up in one of the other rooms questioning their life choices, and movement at her front door catches my attention before the soft knock catches hers.

"Hey. There's my girl."

Cole's charismatic grin is deceiving.

I've seen my brother at work. The guy is brutal when he is after something he wants, yet women flock to him like they don't know there's a demon lurking just below the surface.

Amara looks like she's about to have an identity crisis. "C-Cole? What are you doing here?" She straddles the fine line between the kind, warm person she was when he knew her and the cool person she's become as her expression swings between a friendly smile and reserved indifference.

Cole is the second youngest of the four of us. Since we were the closest in age, he often hung out with my friends, and he was usually home when Amara's family came to visit. I knew inviting him here today would help ease the strain, and he doesn't disappoint.

"In Portland? I live here, Sunshine. I'm on the west side." His smile is warm. It's just what Amara needs right now.

"And what's this?" Amara lifts her hands with the broken glass and points to her jawline, dragging her finger down to her chin.

I shift my focus to my brother. It's been four years since she's seen him. We've changed, but we haven't.

A flash of confusion crosses Cole's features before he lifts his hand to his face.

Understanding dawns when he runs his fingers through his beard. "Right. It's been awhile."

Amara's features soften into sadness, and Cole's smile fades as his gaze drops to Amara's hands. "Move not going well?"

Amara looks between both of us with a solemn pout. She's not sure how much to share with Cole. Back then, no one knew about us. It was a secret I kept to protect us both.

After Grayson died, I had a momentary slip when I wrapped my car around a tree after a night of drinking and fighting. Cole was close with one of the nurses who bandaged me up, and she called him. He covered for me with our father, and we grew closer as a result. I ended up telling him everything about Amara up until the day she left. He agreed the timing to keep her was wrong and said I was right to let her go.

Growing up, the four of us were always pitted against each other. It made all of us great competitors, but sometimes I feel like I lost out on knowing my brothers better. We were always trying to find weaknesses to exploit in order to gain the approval of our father.

Cole left town and moved to Portland a couple of years ago. He said it was so he could have more anonymity to handle our shadier dealings, but I know it was to get away from my father's control. He prefers to handle business by his own rules.

Cole breaks the silence. "Tell you what; I'm going to take care of all of this for you." He holds out cupped hands, and Amara looks from his palms to the glass she's still holding before stretching her arms out and giving the pieces to him.

"It's not garbage. I'm keeping it." Her little threat makes Cole smile even wider.

"There's a good girl. This is safe with me." He pulls his

palms into his chest, mimicking how she held it so dear, and Amara's shoulders relax. "I'm going to help you out. You don't need to be here to see this. I'll organize everything, and nothing else will break, or I'll start breaking legs."

The ghost of a smile tugs at my cheeks, but I force it away. Cole is almost brotherly with her, and it is softening her in ways only Grayson used to be able to.

"You'd do that for me?" Her round eyes are filled with surprise.

"I'll even pack some of it myself. I'll start with your panty drawer. No one will touch your unmentionables but me." Cole's wink earns him a blush from Amara, and, while the comment has me feeling possessive, I can't deny the genuine smile he pulled out of my little flower. "Now, go and pack a couple of bags, enough for a week, and get out of here."

Amara steals a glance at the broken glass butterfly in Cole's grasp then bows her head and leaves us.

He waits until she is out of sight before speaking again.

"So things are going well then." Cole lowers his voice, but not enough that I can't hear the sarcasm.

I ignore him and change the subject. "How are you doing on our little side project?"

Amara walks into her bathroom with a bag, and we both keep our eyes on her while Cole answers.

"My guy is still working on it."

The saying "No news is good news" is bullshit. No news is no news, and I'm becoming impatient.

One of the largest criminal organizations we do business with is about to go through some things. Elia Lucciano, the head of the Lucciano crime family, has been ill for a while, but his months left have been given a limit. After that, his entire syndicate falls to his heir. But there's a problem: no one knows where his only son is.

I'm in the business of knowing things, and Cole has someone in their group who is keeping us informed of any changes so we can prepare to protect our business if their organization breaks down and the infighting to find a new leader begins.

A couple of the movers are packing up plates in the kitchen, and Amara is still in her bathroom while we both settle into silence.

Pulling my phone out, I pull up Alicia's number, then type a text with nothing more than a dollar amount before hitting send and sliding my phone into my pocket.

When I look up, I'm met with my brother's shit-eating grin.

"Spit it out." I won't give him another chance, and I already know he's about to enjoy whatever this is.

"When are you going to tell Amara you're engaged to someone else?"

5

AMARA

The Saint family home is an imposing place. There was a time I never wanted to leave. Then there was a time I was sure I would never return.

On the drive to Seattle, Ryder told me we would be staying in his parents' old home. His mother and father moved out when they downsized, leaving the home to Ryder and his brothers.

I now know Cole moved to Portland. Ryder told me Dagen, the second oldest, is a bit transient. He wasn't clear on what he contributes to the family business, and I didn't push it. Lennox, the oldest brother, was always distant from the rest of the guys. Apparently, the distance has only grown. Ryder told me that they all have access and a room at the home, but he is the only one currently living in it full time.

Ryder was uncharacteristically forthcoming with information in the car. I expect it's because of my meltdown in my apartment. He doesn't want to add to an already volatile situation, and I'm embarrassed I couldn't be stronger.

This house holds a lifetime of memories for me. Many

moments in time that I cast out of my heart, just as Ryder cast me out of his life.

I'm thankful for the spare room I now call my own, as it isn't one I have ever been in. Once I closed the door, I was able to mentally pretend I was in another house. This room is the farthest down the hall from Ryder's bedroom. Another small mercy.

I finished unpacking my bags in twenty minutes, and I spent the next twenty minutes moving things around to the point where I felt more comfortable.

The Saints threw many parties when I was younger, and my parents would always drag me along. Grayson would take off as soon as he got here. He'd tear up the stairs and head straight for Ryder's room, leaving his awkward little sister behind. I couldn't blame him, I was in grade school, and he was heading out of middle school when we first started coming here.

I was often left to explore on my own with the only rule being "If it's locked, it's off-limits." I would walk the halls pretending I was a princess locked away in a castle.

And this is exactly what I've become. I chuckle sourly before finding my backbone.

I chose to be here. I chose to do this for the people at my company, and I am choosing to be here for Grayson. I will not cower like a helpless prisoner. It's early afternoon, and I must have a couple of hours before dinner.

Opening the door to my room, I glance down the wing of the second floor. The occasional sound travels upstairs from the main floor, but this area seems quiet, and I start walking down the hall, looking in the rooms that are open.

Ryder was my first crush. I used to spy on my brother and the Saint boys when they would hang out. I would hide and listen to them talk about dumb things that didn't make sense to me. The first time Ryder noticed me spying, he did nothing. He only smirked and left me in my hiding spot to listen in awkward silence as he stole glances in my direction, making me feel immature and inexperienced. At the time, the difference in the few years between us felt like a lifetime.

I'm relieved to see that the door to the room beside Ryder's is shut. I'm not ready to look in there yet. I'm not sure I'll ever be prepared enough for that.

Stopping in front of Ryder's open door feels like déjà vu. When our parents had parties, they left us to our own devices. One of those nights, I wandered up to the very spot I'm standing in now, and the memory rushes in.

Muffled voices through the door catch my attention, and it sounds like a girl is crying. I step closer to get a better look, and that's when I see them. Two people in Ryder's bed. They are under the covers, and she isn't crying.

Morbid curiosity won't let me walk away. At the same time, I am crushed that Ryder is with another girl. I have no right to be jealous, but the stray tear falling down my face doesn't get the memo, and I stand there like a pathetic groupie watching Ryder fuck another girl in his bed.

Only it isn't him.

While I watch like a voyeur from a distance, Ryder sneaks up behind me, clamps his hand over my mouth, and whispers in my ear—

"See something you like?" My memory collides with my present at Ryder's seductive baritone, and my heart hammers into my chest, jolting me out of my thoughts and causing me to spin around as he says the same words he did on that night.

"I—what? No. I was just looking around." I prop my hand on my hip, but the action doesn't feel natural so I cross my arms in front of me.

Ryder tilts his head to the side before a grin tugs at one corner of his lips.

Lifting his hand to my throat, he wraps his open palm around my neck, and I soften into his grip. Pressure under my jaw from his middle and forefinger catches my attention too late.

He's checking my pulse.

I can lie all I want, but my heart will always tell him the truth.

"Oh, Amara." My name slips through his lips like silk.

His thumb guides my jaw to the left, and my body follows as Ryder turns me around to face his room, just like that night.

His free hand cups my hip as he pulls my back into his chest, and I move with the rise and fall of his breath.

I shiver as his lips tickle my cheek, his voice inviting. "I remember finding you that night. Such a curious little thing you were. Do you remember?"

"Yes," I whisper. There is no point in lying; his fingers are still monitoring my hammering heart rate.

"I know you do." Soft lips run along my ear, pulling a whine from me then a growl from him. "Do you want to know a secret?" I don't trust my voice not to sound desperate, so I nod, and he continues, "I was wandering around the house looking for you that night. And there you were— looking for me. Look at my bed, Blossom." His head tilts to his door.

My skin heats under his touch as he pulls me down memory lane.

His room is empty, but I see everything as though no time has passed.

"You thought it was me in the bed. I felt your tears when I covered your mouth with my hand. Do you know what you did to me?" He punctuates his question by pulling me closer. His length is hard against my backside. "Do you remember what I said to you?"

I nod again.

"No. This time you'll say it. What did I tell you?"

I clear my throat. "You said if I wasn't ready, I could leave, and you'd let me go." I ball my shirt in my fists at my stomach to steady myself.

"And what did you say to me?"

"I told you I was ready."

He tsks me. "What else?" His fingers knead into my hip.

"I told you I was a big girl." My cheeks warm in embarrassment.

"And are you still a big girl, Amara? Or are you going to run away?"

He's taunting me.

His tongue glides the length of my neck, and I tilt my head to give him complete access to my throat.

I take too long to answer, and he fills the silence. "Or are you going to let me stick my hand down your pants to feel how wet you really are?"

I whimper and adjust my stance. Releasing my shirt, I drop my palm on top of his hand and guide him to the waist of my yoga pants.

The vibrations from his growl against my neck make my stomach clench, and he takes control of his movements.

His fingers slide beneath the waistband and find my panties, easily pushing under the fabric. He wastes no time gliding over my mound and into my slick folds, where he moves around as he always had.

Ryder knows every inch of my body; he knows where to touch, how hard or soft, and how to work me into a frenzy.

My eyes roll up as my head falls back, resting on his shoulder, and I glide myself on his palm, waiting for his fingers to claim me.

He pulls me into a gentle sway as he whispers into my ear, "You were my little flower growing among the weeds of this place. You smelled sinfully sweet. So sweet you made my cock ache." Ryder grinds his erection into my ass as his fingers find my entrance, and I lose myself in waves of euphoria. "You made me want to ruin you. And I did. I made you watch as they fucked, and I fingered you until you came, whimpering into the palm of my hand. It was the first time someone else made you come. I was your first for everything, Blossom, and I will be your last."

Ryder walks me into the room, dropping his hand from my throat and closing the door behind us. The intense rubbing ceases as he pulls his hand from my waistband and lifts his fingers to his mouth, lazily licking my taste off of them before dropping his other hand into my pants to take their place.

My scent fills my nostrils when he covers his palm over my mouth as he continues fucking me with his fingers, and I groan into his hand, brazenly humping my hips and taking what I need.

Ryder tells me how good I'm being for him, and his praise tosses me over the edge. The crest of my orgasm hits me without warning, and I scream into his palm. He angles his body back, pulling my weight into him to hold me up while he pulls every last bit of tension from me.

Fragmented moments pass as my body settles and I lift my

head from his shoulder. His arms loosen, letting me go, and I take a step away.

The silence in the room is more prominent now. There are so many words left unspoken between us.

As I turn to meet Ryder's gaze, he takes a step toward me, his arms lifting for an embrace, and I raise my palm and place it on his chest. He stills, confusion replacing the softness in his features.

"I'm not that girl anymore." I mean for my words to sound like a warning, but I hear the sadness in my voice.

This is the part of me I can't give him.

This is the part of me I won't give anyone ever again.

A sound from the hall catches my attention, and I step to the door before Ryder's hands reach for me. "Wait. There's something you need to know."

The concern on his face is disconcerting, and I hear the noise again. I read Ryder as easily as he reads me. He's trying to buy time.

Tugging my arm out of his hold, I walk to his door, open it, and the light from the hall floods into the room.

A startled Sloane jumps and spins to face me.

"Oh—hi—Amara." She's speaking to me, but her eyes jump up and down the hall, and I wonder if she's looking for Ryder.

"Sloane? What are you doing here?" Ryder's unmistakable presence joins me as I ask the question.

Grayson and Sloane used to hang out here all the time, but now it seems odd to see her in this house. And so late in the evening.

She glares over my shoulder at Ryder as he joins us. They exchange a glance before she returns my gaze. Her mouth opens and closes on a series of nonstarters, and Ryder answers for her.

"Sloane is my fiancée." His words are cold, detached. There is no further explanation, and I feel sick to my stomach.

At once, I've been reduced to a dirty secret, just like I used to be.

I let my guard down, and I should have known nothing would change. This is still a game, and we are all mere playing pieces for Ryder to move around as it suits him.

Pulling my shoulders back, I straighten myself and fist my hands at my sides. The pinch of my nails biting into the tender skin on my palms quiets the voices and eases the pressure building in my heart.

"I see." I force the muscles in my cheeks to pull my mouth into a smile while my heart crumbles all over again.

I have no idea why I'm here. After all this time, why drag me back into a life I had completely disconnected myself from, only to show me how happy he is with my dead brother's ex-girlfriend?

I open my mouth to excuse myself when the giggle of a child freezes me in place.

Sloane's hesitant demeanor instantly changes into a playful smile, and she steps to the side, exposing a little boy. He can't be any older than two.

"There you are, you little rascal! It's time for bed." She tugs him into her, hugging and fussing over him just like a—

A clammy wave washes over me as the blood drains from my head.

She lifts him up, settling him on her hip as he rubs his eyes. "This is Henry. Henry is—"

"Your son." I answer for her, and she smiles.

I won't turn to look at Ryder. I suddenly need to distance myself, and I remember I have a room full of things that are out of place.

"It's been a long day. Um, I need to—" I finish my thought with a shake of my head. There really isn't anything to say.

"It is nice to see you again, Amara." Sloane reaches her free hand out to me, and I pull my fists closer to my body and return her smile with my lips pinched together.

Once again, my nails have cut into the skin on my hands. I'm keeping my palms closed to stop my blood from trickling onto the floor.

I leave them standing in the hall without another word. That little boy is too young to notice my awkward exit, but I'm sure both Ryder and Sloane feel it. I can't bring myself to care.

Ryder says something funny to Henry, and he giggles again. Their voices grow faint the farther away I get.

Ryder hurt me once.

I won't give him the chance to do it again.

6

RYDER

This isn't how I thought tonight would end.

I half thought I'd be lying in Amara's bed, wrapped around her naked body and reconnecting with every inch of her. Instead I'm sitting in my office with a hard-on that hasn't gotten the message that this isn't the kind of fucked we are right now.

I can't be entirely mad. Not at Henry or Sloane.

I was supposed to tell Amara about them before we returned.

This is all on me.

Twirling a USB stick between my fingers, I contemplate what it holds. Information is power, and I got this a couple of years too late. Now I'm forced to play catch up, and I'm making mistake after mistake.

I was supposed to tell Amara I was engaged to Sloane. Instead, she defied me on day one, and I made it my mission to put her back in her place.

Every time she challenges me, I accept.

Every time she surrenders to my touch, I claim.

She acts, I react.

Together, we are the perfect storm.

The more Amara tells me I don't know who she is, the more determined I am to strip her bare and show her how wrong she is—about everything.

Trailing my fingers along my lower lip, the vision of her riding my hand torments me.

She's exactly who I think she is, and she's trying to hide it from me.

Sloane doesn't bother knocking.

"What the hell, Ryder?" Closing the door behind her, she joins me, hovering over my desk and crossing her arms. "You told me you'd tell her before she got here. I love you, but you're a piece of shit sometimes."

I ignore her question with one of my own. "Did Henry get to sleep okay?" I set the USB stick on the desk beside the laptop and pick up the second glass of whiskey I've poured since coming down here after the incident with Amara.

Her anger dissipates only a fraction before she shakes her head. "Don't change the subject. You were supposed to prepare her. We agreed."

"Things changed." My voice hitches, and I clear my throat, shaking my head at Sloane, silently telling her to drop it. "Why do you care anyway?"

She looks at me like I have two heads.

"You know why. She's Grayson's sister. She doesn't deserve to pay the price we both agreed to pay. I know I was never close with her, but I always liked her. I see pieces of me in her." Shaking her arms out, she adjusts her tune. "It doesn't matter. What matters is you fix this, Ryder. You can't have it both ways."

All my life, I've been told what I can't have. It got old a long time ago.

"I'll remind you of the part you played in Amara's return," I tell her. "You are not blameless. Besides, it's too late to stop moving ahead with our plans. I can't undo what's been done."

My eyes drop to the USB stick once again.

When I return my attention to Sloane, her expression is solemn. She knows what file it holds.

Alicia Scott recently sent over a box full of Grayson's belongings, and this was among his things. A video file, only a few minutes long, filmed on the same day he was murdered. I imagine he left it on his computer for me to find, but his mother packed up his items before I got to his place, and it was never turned over to the police.

Grayson expected me to have it over two years ago. Instead, it arrived a couple of months ago, and it sent me into a tailspin.

All I know is, the night Grayson was murdered, he found out some disturbing information, but he didn't have enough to give me an update. He was still checking it out.

Grayson asked me to take care of Sloane if anything went wrong. It was something I would have done anyway.

I often wonder if he knew he was in trouble since the second part of his message was odd.

I attempt to set us back on track. "We need to stay focused. It's the only way I can protect you and Henry. We still don't know who killed Grayson or why, and until we do, neither of you are safe. It could be someone who has access to this house."

Sloane is already shaking her head as I accuse my oldest brother without saying his name. She's always fought me on this. Sloane and Lennox have a history, and it clouds her judgment.

"I'm going to find out what happened to him, Sloane. I'm going to keep you and Henry safe, and I will take back everything I gave up for this so-called family business—no matter who it is. They will pay."

Sloane and I both know I'm listed among the suspects in Grayson's murder. I will clear myself and crucify whoever is responsible. Nothing and no one will get in my way.

"You need to make this right." She points to the ceiling, and I know she means what happened with Amara upstairs earlier.

"I'll deal with Amara in a bit."

Sloane looks like she wants to argue, but I shake my head before downing my drink. Amara is right; it has been a long day, and my patience for any opposition is gone.

"I'd like to get to know her better. Amara needs someone to talk to who isn't you. She needs a friend. Grayson would have wanted that." Sloane plays the only card she knows will tug at my cold heart—my dead best friend.

"I'll think about it."

Sloane opens her mouth to object as my phone lights up with an incoming call.

I've put this conversation off long enough. Pointing at the door, I excuse Sloane and answer.

"I was beginning to think you didn't want to talk to your old man."

"Just wrapping up some loose ends. I asked Nash to update you on business. Has he not been filling you in?" I already know the answer.

Nash has been meeting with my father every few days, and there is nothing new to report on the companies our family owns. My brothers and I have been running everything without incident since we took over for him a couple of years ago.

"He's been doing a fine job. That's not why I'm calling. I understand you bought a company in Portland recently."

I roll my eyes but keep my audible sigh to myself. "That's my business. Bought with my own funds, but it may be beneficial for our combined ventures in the future."

"Everything is my business, son. Tell me about the Scott girl. Is there a problem there?"

Amara has only ever been a pawn to him, and now he's calling me to gauge her worth.

"The girl happened to work for the company I took over. I used that to my advantage. Nothing more. I'll remind you, I'm engaged." I attempt to knock Amara off of my father's radar.

I wait for the pause in conversation to pass. If I talk first, it's a sign I'm keeping something from him.

After a minute, he fills the silence. "And how is your lovely fiancée? Your mom has been asking about her." The tone of his voice tells me he doesn't care to know my answer.

If it doesn't make him money, he has little time for it.

"You can ask her yourself. You're coming for dinner this week?"

"Yes. Your mom has been chatting with your brothers. I believe we'll all be there." His answer surprises me, but I won't show it.

It's been a while since all four of us were in the same room together.

I see Cole and Dagen regularly, but Lennox keeps his distance from us. Being the oldest, he got the first pick of which piece of the family empire he wanted to run. He chose my father's heart of the company, Eros, a group of sex clubs and associated businesses.

I took almost everything else. Cole manages a nightclub and a couple of restaurants in Portland. He's a hands-off kind of guy, unless you cross the family. Then he takes great joy in exacting payback and taking what is owed to us.

Dagen is the only one of us who went out on his own, making a name for himself as a freelancer for hire of sorts.

My earliest memories of Lennox conflict with the man he is

today. I used to look up to him. He was more of a dad than my own father, but things changed as we grew up.

Then we grew apart.

"I look forward to it." I answer to another long pause, except this time I fill the void. "How's Mum?"

"She's doing better since the doctor switched her medication." I hear my father's stress in his answer.

My mother started showing the first signs of Alzheimer's a year ago. It was a bumpy start when she had a negative reaction to the first prescription her doctor gave her.

I use the reset in our conversation as my cue to end the call. I palm the memory stick before shutting the laptop and pouring half a glass to take with me.

Walking through the quiet house, I reach the top of the stairs and look down the corridor toward my room. The room I just pulled an orgasm out of Amara in.

She opened up to me easily. Her body writhed under my touch. She's still as passionate as I remember, but there is one stark contrast to the woman I knew.

It isn't lost on me that she came out of her euphoria quickly. She was ready to run away from me at the flip of a switch. She went from being mine to taking everything back without warning, and it's left me feeling confused.

I can't put my finger on it, but there is something off-putting about it.

As I ponder what happened, I turn away from my bedroom toward the room at the end of the hall. I chose this room for Amara because it was the farthest from mine. I knew she wouldn't want the one right next door, and I wasn't so sure I could stay away from her if she were any closer.

I guess, in the end, it doesn't matter. I can't stay away from her no matter how far down the hall she is.

The light from her room shines through the crack under

her door. The occasional shadow gliding along the threshold tells me she's still up and moving around.

Amara can tell me all she wants that I don't know her, but I've become great at reading people. It's what has made me good in business. It's Amara who doesn't know who she is anymore. She's hidden herself away so well that she no longer connects with the woman I know.

A quick walk through her office in Portland spoke volumes. Her workspace was made to look sterile; it was a place without feeling, and her home had no heart.

Sure, there were some pictures on the table behind her desk. They were mostly photos of landscapes with no one in them. It makes me wonder if she took trips by herself.

Those were the photos she faced out to the people who entered her office. There were no pictures on her desk, facing her. Seeing that made me curious, so I opened her desk drawers. There was one picture in a bottom drawer that held nothing else. The photo was a family portrait. It must have been taken about ten years ago. This told me she tries to keep the memory of her family close, but she hides her past away, and, judging by the thin layer of dust I saw on the glass frame, she hadn't looked at it in a while.

Amara's room goes dark, and I'm left wondering what her last thought before she goes to sleep will be.

I want it to be of me.

I turn as quietly as I can and make my way back to my own bedroom. If I can stay focused a while longer, we'll all get what we want.

I used to have a long list of things I wanted.

Now that Amara is back, it's getting shorter by the day.

7

AMARA

Every little thing was removed from my bags and placed in a spot before I climbed into bed last night. An hour later, I was up and reorganizing my room. I unfolded and refolded every piece of clothing I brought with me. I matched up my work outfits hanging in my closet. Then I sat in the dark with only the light of the full moon shining in, examining my broken butterfly to make sure all of its jagged pieces were there before carefully setting it on the nightstand.

Around three in the morning, I opened the doors to the balcony and stepped out to take in the night sky. The cold seeped into my bones, my breath floating from my lips in bright swirls and gusts in the moonlight. Everything looks bigger out here. This place is a stage, my insignificance on full display under the vast canopy.

The Saint family home is near the edge of the city on a large acreage, and it's removed enough from the compacted lights of downtown that I found four constellations right away. I wonder if anyone else hears a sad song in their head when they look up at the stars. I used to imagine they watched over us, documenting eternity, and I wondered if they were pleased with how life was unfolding.

The lights from downtown Portland drowned out those stars after Ryder sent me away. They abandoned me at the same time he did.

My parents would often stay late into the evening when they came over to the Saints for a party. I'd wander on my own until I got tired, then I'd find a couch or rug and curl up and go to sleep. The next morning, I'd wake up at home, in my own bed.

One night when we went over, Mrs. Saint had a surprise waiting for me. She had made one of the spare rooms into a bedroom, a place I could go when I got tired. She placed me beside Ryder's room, telling me I would be close if I needed Grayson for anything since he was always hanging out in there.

Having four boys, I imagine decorating the room was a lot of fun for her, and she beamed when she showed it to me. She spent most of the night sitting with me in there, going through the dolls and books she'd brought in.

It was nicer than my room back home, and that made me sad, but I didn't show it.

The sun broke across the horizon before I closed my eyes early this morning for the six hours of sleep I was able to claim.

I missed breakfast, and no one tried to wake me up. I found out it was because no one was home when I finally got up, showered, and had a quiet lunch by myself.

Guilt settles into my bones as last night's revelation hits me.

Ryder is engaged—to Sloane, and they have a son.

My stomach rolls, and I leave over half of my food on the plate to return to my room in search of a distraction until Ryder tells me what he requires of me. I text Penny to ask how the office is doing, and we go over what the big issues are this week before she asks me about my email and phone number to forward some things.

Nothing is set up yet, and I tell her I won't know for a few days as I settle in. I hope it won't take longer than that. I function better knowing I have a schedule both in and out of work.

Over an hour passes before commotion in the house tells me someone has arrived. I wander to the top of the stairs and peek around the corner to see that Sloane and her son have returned.

Henry runs in through the front door, dropping his winter jacket on the floor, and makes a straight line toward the dining room. I assume he's heading to the kitchen for a snack. His laughter floats through the large house, and although he sounds happy, I feel anything but.

I meet Sloane's gaze as I return my attention to her, and she smiles up at me, waving.

I don't deserve her kindness.

I force a smile and return to my room to hide. While I answer a couple of emails, I notice a message from an address I haven't seen in a long time.

How is it that my first thought at seeing an email from my mother is that her account must have been hacked? I'm still not convinced after opening it to find a simple message to check in and see if I need anything.

After I read it three times, my stare travels up from my computer to see the reflection of my face contorted in confusion in the mirror across the room.

Closing my laptop, I stretch and look around for something to do. My clean and organized room glares back, mocking me. There isn't anything to do here. I'm hiding, and I know it.

I move my laptop to its spot on the dresser before straightening out the sheets on the bed where I just sat before gathering the courage to go downstairs toward a set of voices coming from the front room.

Henry bounces between the man and woman standing at the door while Sloane tries to settle him enough to get his winter jacket on him. Ryder is standing behind her, and his eyes follow me down the stairs as the woman with them says something about her double shift at the hospital.

No one else notices me until I'm halfway down.

"Hello, Amara. I'm not sure if you remember my parents." Sloane stands, blowing a strand of hair off her face with another smile I feel guilty accepting.

I've never really spoken at length with either of them, but I do remember them. I smile, but something nags in my mind. They both look surprised to see me, but I feel like there is something else, and I wonder if it's my conscience beginning to gnaw away at me.

At first, I tell myself I'm imagining things, but as Sloane talks about how Henry is going with them for a sleepover, I realize there is something going on here. Neither one of her parents looks me directly in the eyes.

An awkward chill crawls up my spine as I wonder which one of the many things it could be that would force both of them to avoid my gaze. It could be that Sloane used to date Grayson, my brother. It could be because she is now engaged to Ryder, my ex. Or it could be because they know what I all but begged Ryder to do to me last night in his bedroom.

My shame returns, and I deserve to feel this awful. I hate Ryder for bringing me back here. I hate him because I never stopped loving him, and now my heart is being used against me. I hate him for showing me how weak I am.

When Henry tugs at his grandpa's sleeve and asks to go, I wave and step away. I'm wrapped in a cloak of humiliation no one sees but Ryder. His dark gaze follows me while he stands there playing the loving fiancé, wrapping an arm around Sloane and waving their goodbyes to her parents.

My bravado is fading quickly. As soon as the door shuts, I wrap my arms around my midsection and turn to retreat back up to my room. But Ryder catches my attention.

"I asked the staff to prepare an early dinner. I'm told you missed breakfast and didn't eat much of your lunch."

He extends his hand as I turn to look at him, stretching it out toward the dining room, and Sloane leads the way. My feet stay put for a moment as I watch her leave. Then, I crumble under his austere expression and follow her to the table.

My stomach growls at the sight of roast chicken, vegetables, and potatoes on the plate in front of me.

The sound of utensils scratching across porcelain fills the void for a few minutes as we all choose to hastily start our meal in silence, and I keep my eyes lowered to my food.

Sloane is the first to speak, saying something about how excited Henry was all day to see his grandparents.

I don't belong.

I am not part of this conversation, and I'm not part of this world.

Isolation sets in, and I finally look up, taking in my surroundings.

I mutter my thoughts to myself: "It feels like he was never here."

Sloane looks at me in confusion, but Ryder knows exactly who I'm referring to. He stops chewing his food and places his knife and fork on either side of his plate before taking a sip of water to swallow his bite down. His eyes are fixed on me, his jaw clenched.

Sloane attempts to comfort me. "Henry will be back tomorrow."

"How could you forget about him? He loved you." My guilt

morphs into anger. I'm not here to make friends. I'm here to stand up for my brother, and no one seems to care that he's gone and they'll never see him again.

Sloane's face falls.

"That's enough." Ryder's raised voice startles me, and I drop my fork on the plate as a single tear escapes down my cheek. "You are out of line, Amara. Apologize."

Chastised.

I've been forced out of my old life and dragged back to the place that never wanted me so I could be scolded like a child and made to watch the life I used to want being lived without me.

"No." I defy Ryder, earning myself his full attention. "Why did you bring me here?" My last word is delivered on a half sob.

Ryder opens his mouth to respond, but it's Sloane's voice I hear.

"He didn't bring you here, Amara. It was my idea. I just wanted you to know." She stands, removing the napkin from her lap and placing it on her plate. I stare at her in confusion as I watch her make her way to the door before speaking to Ryder. "I'm going to join Henry at my parents' for the evening." She hesitates between us before continuing, "I think you—"

"That's fine, Sloane." Ryder nods once, excusing her from the room, his judgmental stare weighing heavily on me.

I stare hard at the plate in front of me, unable to bring myself to look at him. The hairs at the back of my neck tickle under his attention. After a few minutes, I lift my fork and pick at my food, willing myself to swallow everything down along with the hard lumps that are forming in my throat.

Footsteps finally descend the stairs before the front door opens without any further goodbyes.

An anxious tension seeps through my limbs as I fork a

broccoli floret and continue eating as though nothing happened.

"Apologize, Amara." With a detached tone, his words call me out, and I look up to see he hasn't moved. He hasn't taken a bite. He's been sitting and watching me since Sloane left the room.

"She's not here." My food becomes tasteless in my mouth, and I lower my fork to the table beside me, making sure it sits perfectly parallel to my knife.

I know Sloane loved Grayson as much as he loved her. I don't understand any of this.

My outburst is a reflection of my pain. Why can't he understand this?

My gaze follows the movement of my hands as I straighten the knife and fork.

"To me. Apologize. To. Me." At first I don't think I heard him correctly.

I pinch my brows together at the suggestion he is blameless in all of this.

If I didn't know better, I would say he was genuinely wounded. But Ryder will never be a victim.

Pulling my own napkin off my lap, I take care to fold it before setting it on my unfinished meal. Then I push my chair back and rise. Ryder's stare follows me up.

"I don't think I will." I attempt to make my stand. My voice is meek, and I divert my eyes. "I'm also excusing myself for the night."

"You are under my roof, and you are excused when I say you are excused."

Ryder isn't challenging me. He's drawing a line. A line I used to crave. It anchored me.

Now it terrifies me because I have no business responding to it. I shouldn't feel a surge of need; I shouldn't want him to sink himself into my life, consuming my fears and setting me free from this control that shackles me with guilt and shame.

There is only one way I'm leaving this room.

I clear my throat and adjust my stance.

"May I be excused?" I ask, my gaze focused on the fingers brushing along his lower lip as he measures my request before answering.

"No."

He returns to his meal, leaving me to continue standing in front of him as he cuts off a slice of meat and chews it while he watches me.

The room feels warm. I know he expects an apology as part of my rejoining him at the table, and I can't bring myself to sit down.

"P-please." His eyebrows shoot up in surprise at my second attempt, and I humble myself, trying again. "May I be excused?" I hate how weak I sound.

I watch in painful silence as he considers my plea. He reaches for his glass of water, draining the contents before rendering his decision.

"I said *no*."

I flatten my hands against my thighs to stop myself from opening the wounds on my palms, and I push the chair back, taking a step away from the table.

Disappointment rages through me. I humiliated myself in front of him yet again.

I excuse myself. No one excuses me. The thought makes me take a step away with my chin held high, and I turn to walk toward the door.

The scraping of his chair along the floor behind me grates into my ears, and I freeze.

He's standing up.

"Amara." The low growl in his voice is a final warning.

There's no turning back now. Fear sinks its tendrils into me. My spirit crumbles, and I cower. I run out of the room and up the stairs, hoping the sanctity of my small bedroom will hide me from the repercussions of how badly I've just damned myself.

8

RYDER

I wait until her footsteps thump all the way up the stairs before allowing myself a grin wicked enough to match my mood.

My body vibrates with the desire to run after her and have it out, but my emotions are unpredictable, so I cross the room to pour myself a stiffer drink.

I'll deal with her when my fire is burning hot, but my raw anger at her outburst about Grayson needs to come down a couple of notches or I'll lose control of the situation.

She has no idea what I've done or what I would do for the ones I care about, and I remind myself she's hurting too.

I was selfish. I will always be selfish where Amara is concerned.

I brought her back without regard for her heart because I wanted to take her back and make everything okay for her like it used to be. I didn't think about the painful road we both still need to walk to get to that point.

The first time I noticed Amara watching me was in this

room. I knew she used to hide out and listen in on our conversations long before I let her know I knew she was there.

Her innocent curiosity drew me to her at first. I'd often steer the conversation in certain directions when I knew she was listening in. Topics I knew she shouldn't know much about yet since she was a few years younger than me. I wanted to plant seeds to see what would grow, and Amara impressed me as she blossomed.

I leave my glass at the table and make my way out of the dining room.

I take my time.

There's no one else here tonight.

Memories of Amara keep me company as I stroll through the house, turning off the lights in the rooms I no longer need tonight.

The library was one of Amara's favorite rooms. She would usually surface there at some point in the evenings of my parents' parties.

I always lost track of her. I had no idea where she'd wandered off to until I found her in the library one night. I startled her while she was lost in whatever she was reading. She jumped up, knocking the magazine from her lap to the floor. That same look morphed into terror when I lowered myself to pick up the item she dropped, only to see she had found a stash of my father's erotic magazines.

At the time, I chuckled to myself, and she blurted out how she had just found it and wasn't looking at the pictures before she ran out of the room.

I realized a while later it wasn't horror on her face, but shame, which gnawed at something dark inside of me.

I had always thought of Amara as a fun distraction.

It wasn't until a year after that incident when a couple of visiting boys went missing from our group at one of our parties.

Cole and I found them in the library. They had cornered Amara against some bookshelves and were asking her questions about sex. Her flushed cheeks spurred them to continue picking on her.

Cole asked what they were talking about, and one of the kids said they were asking her if she was a virgin.

I saw red.

I wanted to push him down, climb on top of him, and beat him until he stopped talking. I didn't understand my reaction until a minute later, when the other kid broke my rage-filled haze by asking her who she wanted to lose her virginity to.

I wanted it to be me.

Her eyes remained lowered; she didn't respond. Cole moved the guys away to give her some space when it happened. When no one else was looking, she lifted her gaze and met my own, and I saw her answer written all over her face.

From that moment on, Amara Scott was mine.

The memory is bittersweet. It's a reminder of all the time I lost, of what I could still lose if I don't stay focused.

I stop in front of the door, unsure of how I got all the way up here without noticing it.

I raise my hand, fingers fisted and ready to knock, before I stop myself.

I more than lost Amara four years ago.

She lost herself.

And I want her back.

I drop my hand to the handle and open the door to find her hugging herself as she looks out the window at the winter-ravaged land around us. Her head turns to the side before returning to the view.

We never talked about the day I sent her away, and she hasn't asked.

I contemplate tiptoeing around her, but Amara never

thrived when handled with kid gloves. She flourished when I challenged her to face the tough truths. "I know you're afraid."

Rounding on me, she adjusts her arms from a comforting self-hug to a defensive stance. "I am not afraid of you."

I'm glad I took my time before coming up here. This comment would have set me off. Instead, I'm ready with a controlled reply.

"No. You're not afraid of me, Amara. You're afraid of yourself. I know you aren't the person everyone else sees, and no matter how hard you try to hide it—no matter how deep you dig your nails into the palm of your hand—you never will be." She flinches when I mention the weakness she thought she was hiding from me.

"Who am I then?" I know she means to challenge me, but her question comes off sounding like a plea for help—an answer.

"You're mine." My answer is flat and without hesitation.

Her eyes soften into sadness as her arms return to grip her body tighter. "I can't...be *that*."

I shrug. Her response is inconsequential. Whether she thinks she can or can't, she just is.

"Now, I gave you the chance to apologize." I step further into her room, and she takes a step to the side since the doors to the balcony are directly behind her.

She drops her hands to her sides and fists her palms, and I drop my gaze, waiting for her to prove me right and cut open her own skin. Again.

Her hands flex open in response. "I'm so—"

I hold my hand up to silence her, and she heeds my warning. "I said I *gave* you the chance. That's off the table now."

Her gaze jumps from me to the exit I am currently blocking

before she looks to her feet. "I can't have sex with you. I can't—do that to—" It isn't lost on me she says *can't* instead of *won't*.

I know she wants to. She can't because of Sloane and Henry, and, oddly enough, her moral compass is one of the many things I love about her.

"First, if you'll recall, sex with me is never a punishment." I smirk, eliciting an eye roll from her before laying down my ground rules. "But you must be made to understand: my house has rules you will follow, and I'll take your apology out of you in another way."

"You won't hit me." She doesn't say it as an accusation. She's trying to figure out what I *will* do to her, and I'm sure she's running through the various methods I've used to punish her in the past.

She knows how creative I can be.

I scoff. "There's a difference between being an abuser and—"

She cuts me off. "And what? Being an asshole? Don't worry, Ryder. I have no doubt which one you are."

Touché. A little glimmer of the woman I remember returns.

"Remember why you came back," I chide, and she tilts her head, willing to hear more. "You can take your punishment or you can leave, but I know you agreed to come back for a reason, and that all goes away if you walk out the door." My stomach turns at the thought she might actually leave, but I'm betting she won't.

She has a heart bigger than anyone I know, and, whether she agrees or not, it is a strength of hers.

My confidence falters when she takes a moment too long to think about her answer, so I challenge her.

"You're a fighter, Amara. Fight."

She glares at me, and I recognize little pieces of the woman staring me down, the glint of something wild in her beautiful eyes.

I used to take great pleasure in dominating the little hellion standing in front of me.

I drop my gaze to check her hands when the broken glass butterfly on the nightstand beside her catches my eye. It's not the same as it was when it was whole. It's different now, and it has the ability to be something new, maybe something stronger than it once was, and I draw the parallel.

"I'd like to think about it."

"You are wise to consider your choices carefully," I reassure her. She should be thinking hard about her options. She knows what type of man I am and what I will demand of her if she chooses to stay. "I'll be waiting in the same room you just ran out of. You can join me by ten o'clock, or you can pack your things and leave."

I don't say it in anger. She knows me better than that. I hear the sadness in my tone, and it matches the expression on her face.

Bowing my head, I give her time. I leave her to her thoughts, and I return to the dining room with some thoughts of my own.

Amara is my glass butterfly. She's my treasure. Perfection is where she started, but she's so much more now. She's fractured, but her broken pieces fit flawlessly into my own, and it's those cracks that make her who she is. It's in those devastatingly stunning breaks that I find myself.

She's perfect because of her imperfections. No one will ever be her, and that is what makes her precious.

I enter the dining room feeling more relaxed. The top drawer to the hutch creaks as I slide it open and pull out an old set of dominoes.

My phone vibrates as I slide my chair to the table and open the box, the wooden pieces clattering on the hard surface.

Cole normally doesn't call this late, and I ask if he's found more information on Amara.

"I'll get to that in a minute. We got a fucking lead!" Cole announces incredulously.

My blood runs cold, and I will myself not to get my hopes up. He could be talking about any number of things.

It's been over two years.

"Gray?" The vulnerability is evident in my low tone, and he confirms my assumption. "How?"

"I was…balancing some books"—this is Cole's way of saying he was settling a score or collecting a debt—"and the guy offered information in exchange for a month's extension on his loan. I asked him what he had, and he said he overheard some regulars talking in one of our bars in your neck of the woods a while back. Something about missing security footage of a murder in a warehouse on Saint's Wharf from a couple of years ago."

A garbled string of unintelligible profanity fills my head. I have a hundred questions, a thousand thoughts all rushing in at once.

Grayson's murder was never solved because the warehouse security video was removed. We assumed the killer must have taken it.

The fact that the footage was gone when the police came asking for it did us no favors. It only put the entire Saint family at the top of their list of suspects.

The most telling piece of information is that the area is only called "Saint's Wharf" within our organization because we own all of the surrounding buildings.

"What happens now?"

"Well, now me and Lucky are looking into some things." This is the closest Cole has ever sounded to giddy.

"Who's Lucky?"

"This asshole right here." I imagine Cole is still standing next to his new informant. "Aren't you?"

I hear the faint weasel of a voice actually respond to him on the other end. "It's Ted."

"Go stand by the car, Lucky." Cole's back to business with his low don't-fuck-with-me tone.

There's no sound on the line for a few moments, and I check the face of my phone to confirm we're still connected before Cole returns sounding more like my brother.

"So yeah, give me some time on that. I might actually hand this one off to Dagen to deal with since finding lost items is kind of his thing. Also, I don't like Lucky." There's a rustle on the line. "For that other thing; Mr. Lucciano has been given a date. Doctors say he has six months to a year. There's no word on his heir, but I'm working on some stuff with upper management. I know where the divide is in their group, and we definitely want to be on a certain side of it. I'll set up a casual meeting."

"And what about Amara?" I check the clock on the wall.

Nine forty-five.

She has fifteen minutes.

"Alicia Scott accepted the payment." Cole's scornful distaste for Amara's mother is evident even through the phone. "I don't have much else yet. I'll get everything to you soon. I'll call if there's anything urgent. Anyway, I should get back to business. Lucky looks pale. Fucker better not yack on my car."

"You coming for dinner tomorrow?"

"Are you kidding me?" Cole barks. "The chance to watch you and Lennox aggressively stare each other down while your ex-fiancée and your current fiancée hang out? I cannot fucking wait. I'm bringing pie."

I disconnect the call to the sound of my brother chortling like a chucklehead.

I am not looking forward to dinner.

9

AMARA

I don't need the time to think about Ryder's ultimatum. I need the time to prepare myself for what it means to stay.

I have no doubt Ryder would gut the company just like he threatened should I leave, but I'm not sure I can hide behind that as the reason I'm going to remain.

I will use this as an opportunity to find out what happened to my brother. In order to do so, I need access to the Saint family and their associates.

But staying is proving to be harder than I thought. Not because I can't stand Ryder—it's just the opposite.

Ryder is a force.

Distance didn't make me stronger, it gave me a false sense of power that crumbled the moment he walked back into my life.

Seeing him again affects me in ways I thought I had under control. Just the thought of being punished by him again after all this time makes my traitorous body react. My mouth is dry, my panties are wet, and I'm constantly half a second away from begging him to take me back to the way we were before. My disappointment in myself is immense, but I want what I want, and I worry I won't be able to stay focused around him.

This is why I asked for some time to think. To remind myself I create the power I have. There is one thing I will continue to hold on to, one thing I won't give Ryder because, the last time he had it, he threw it away.

There are four minutes left until Ryder's deadline.

The house is quiet as I leave my room and walk down the hall I used to do cartwheels up and down as a child. I left that little girl around here somewhere. Her schoolgirl crush on Ryder was so pure at first, and what I feel now is the furthest thing from that innocent moment in time.

Lying to myself will only hurt me in the end.

I know what I'm walking toward. I'm walking toward the man who hurt me the most. Out of everyone I trusted, Ryder's betrayal devastated me.

I accept how I feel when he's around, how painful it is to merely look at him, let alone listen to his voice, smell his scent, and feel his touch. Every piece of my soul wants the lie I thought I once had, if only for a moment more.

But there is one thing I won't allow myself to have again.

The wooden door slides open on its rail, and it isn't until I reach the edge of the table that I realize what Ryder is doing.

His eyes glance up to meet my own before returning to his task of setting up dominoes. His expression is emotionless.

"Did Sloane come back?" I ask, hoping to earn some points by offering to apologize to her.

He doesn't look up this time. "No. She's gone for the night."

I get his message loud and clear: we won't be disturbed.

"I don't understand what's going on with her, with everything."

Ryder has always been fiercely loyal. Marrying his best

friend's girlfriend and bringing me back here when he has a son and a fiancée is out of character for him.

He shifts his gaze to demand my attention, and his glare holds me in place. "My arrangement with Sloane is none of your concern. It has no bearing on the arrangement I have with you."

Of everything Ryder has said to me since waltzing back into my life, this is the moment I realize he is no longer the man I once knew.

"But you have a son."

Ryder's father was never hands-on unless it was about the family business. He was never faithful to his wife, and Ryder grew up in that environment. I know he never wanted that for his own child. He always said he was going to be better.

"I see you've made your decision." The topic has been changed.

"I have." The corner of his lip twitches into the ghost of a smile as I continue, "You said you won't fuck me."

His smirk fades just as quickly as it came. "No. You haven't earned that."

My stomach does a flip at the hint of a promise, and I hate myself a little more.

"You've told me yourself, you can't count the number of men you've been with since me, and how easy it is for you to spread your legs, and how little you think of the act itself."

I break our stare and drop my attention to the dominoes he's holding.

His words hurt. They shouldn't, but they do, and it's because I've given him some power.

My attention snaps back to him, and he remains sure and unmoving.

He knows what he's doing to me.

"I won't fuck you, Blossom. By the time I'm done, I'll

fucking own you." I've never seen Ryder look more sure of anything in his life, and the threat scares me. Not because of what he'll do to me, but what I am afraid I will allow. "You know I'm a patient man."

Ryder slowly, methodically places a domino on the table, taking care to make sure it stands on its edge without tipping over.

I'm frozen in a trance, watching him as he continues to speak.

"I'll wear you down." He speaks as though my future is a foregone conclusion, placing another domino on the table. "I'll fracture your defenses."

I watch with rapt attention as he sets another domino on the table in front of him. A line is forming.

"I'll make you feel everything you once felt for me." His admission makes my stomach knot as another domino is set in place. "I'll make you crave the connection I know only we have."

My heart hammers in my chest as the bite of tears stings my eyes.

I zero in on his strong hand as another domino is carefully set on the table. Those fingers that used to know every inch of my body. His actions are gentle, but what he is promising will tear me apart, and I don't know what pieces of me will rise in his wake.

Worry sets in.

"I'll make you desperate for my touch"—domino—"my praise"—domino—"my love."

Another domino.

My mouth waters, and I don't know if it is in fear or desire.

Or do I fear my desire?

How easy would it be to surrender to him, to allow him to lead me to my ruin all over again?

The comfort in his tone doesn't match the words he speaks. "You should know I will break you down. Piece by piece, you are no match for me, Amara." He sets the last domino in its spot. "None of this will be easy for you."

Ryder takes a moment to appreciate the line of dominoes before lifting his hand ever so slowly. His attention drops to the first domino as his finger lazily draws a line on the table beside the wooden piece.

With a tap, the first one topples, knocking it into the next and so on until the last domino falls. It skitters across the table and drops off the edge. I watch it fall, my gaze following it to the floor.

I startle as Ryder juts his palm out and catches it before it lands.

The metaphor isn't lost on me.

The only difference is, Ryder isn't the one who set up my dominoes. I've created new pieces of me. I've made a life without him. I'm sure he doesn't even know the worst of my sins yet.

He's telling me, if I accept and stay, he's coming for me.

He doesn't just want one thing.

He wants everything.

The thought both terrifies and excites me, and I'm not confident I will be able to trust myself.

His thumb casually rubs over the face of the domino he caught, his eyes boring into my own.

I can't afford to be that last domino. I can't fall with only the hope he'll catch me.

I blink rapidly, snapping out of the trance I fell into as I take a deep breath. Losing myself to Ryder will only end in disappointment.

The pain from the last time I fell hasn't dulled. Those wounds haven't healed.

The chair scrapes along the hardwood as Ryder stands to his full height, setting the domino back on the table in a standing position.

Another metaphor.

"Do you accept your punishment?"

My words won't come out. Somewhere between the time I first walked in this room and now, he managed to get into my head. If he can do it so easily, while we are simply talking, I know it will be much, much worse for me once I give him permission to let loose.

Can I take this step? He's asking me to leave the person I worked so hard to become at the door and step back into his world, and this is the threshold.

"Consent is everything, Amara. You will understand the role you play in your surrender to me."

I'm swept back to four years ago, when I was his. The way he would look at me like I was his beautiful secret. How his eyes raked over my body as though he could taste me from where he was standing. I ached to be lost in him. My body craved his chaos, my mind desperate to surrender. The intoxicating pull of free-falling for him, granting him permission to ruin me because those were the moments I felt like I was alive, and nothing has ever felt like that since.

Walking around the table, he stops a step away from me. I breathe in his crisp, ginger scent with the hint of tobacco even though he doesn't smoke.

His strong hands cover my own. Twisting gently at the wrist, he turns my palms up. His firm fingers pry open my own, showing me the thin red lines forming half-moons on the tender skin of my palms. I didn't break the skin this time.

Releasing my hands, his fingers brush along my forehead, taking my hair out of my face.

"You've been holding on for so long." Ryder's pensive tone makes my heart sad. "Just let go."

His fingers continue to brush through my hair as his free hand wraps around my upper arm, his thumb caressing my skin in the same way he rubbed the domino.

Ryder drops the strands of my hair. Hooking his finger under my chin, he tilts my head until he is looking into my soul before brushing his fingers along my jawline.

With a whisper, he pushes.

"Say yes, Blossom."

10

RYDER

Amara drags her teeth over her lower lip before releasing it exeruciatingly slowly. And damn me if I don't feel the gesture viscerally, as my cock strains against my pants to get to her.

I told her I wouldn't fuck her. As much as I want to, I'll refrain.

Her round eyes blink in a daze a few times, and the need to bury myself deep inside her body and rail us both into oblivion becomes unbearable.

I pull my hand back from her heated skin, fisting my fingers to keep myself from reaching out for her again.

I understand her need as though it's my own, because it is.

But there's something else I need out of tonight.

Understanding.

I want Amara to know what I expect from her and what the price is for disobedience. My plans work better for everyone if she accepts she is not in control here.

"Yes." The bow in her posture is barely noticeable. Her fire from earlier is subdued, replaced instead with humble deference.

We'll see how long that lasts.

Amara is a passionate woman. I'm asking a lot of her, and I'm nowhere near finished with her tonight.

Stepping away from her, I stand beside the table, my fingers tapping the surface while she waits for my next move.

With purpose, I reach my arm out and knock over the one domino I left standing on the table. The clattering echoes in the quiet room.

I will break her if I have to in order to protect her.

Amara watches me, apprehension written all over her face.

Message received. Good.

This isn't going to be an easy lesson for her to learn.

"Take off your clothes."

"I—I—" Her objections come fast as she shakes her head. Her focus shifts around the room as though someone else is with us. She looks over her shoulder at the door behind her. "What if—"

"I won't ask again."

Her shoulders drop in resignation. She knows what I expect of her.

To her credit, she takes a few steps into the room while her hands lift to her top. In one smooth motion, the fabric slides out of her jeans and over her head. Her expression falters, granting me a glimpse of the curious and eager woman I remember.

I know she's still in there.

Her fingers fumble with the button on her pants as she takes another glance over her shoulder toward the door, nervously biting her lower lip.

She's worried we'll be disturbed.

I already know Sloane is staying away for the evening, and my security at the gate will inform me if anyone comes through.

"None of this is sexual, Amara," I half lie. It's mostly sexual, but I won't act on it right now. "This is about you knowing your place. We won't be disturbed tonight." I offer her a sliver of assurance in reward for her good behavior.

She bends over, taking off her jeans and stepping her bare feet out of them before standing up. Her hands move to her panties, and my lungs swell with a held breath.

"Leave those on. Over the table." I point at the spot where the fallen pieces lie.

If I see what is under that thin layer of fabric, my promise not to have her would be broken.

She joins me then turns to face the table; her upper thighs press against the edge.

Placing one hand on her lower back, I make a point of clearing the dominoes out of the way, and she bends over, taking their place.

My fingers feel cold against her flushed skin, and I splay my palm wide, feeling the soft flesh just above her underwear.

The muscles in her arms are defined, and her ass is tight. She is in better shape than when she lived here. Cole mentioned she frequently attended yoga classes.

The desire to knead and feel just how strong she is overwhelms me, and I step back to compose myself out of her line of sight before rejoining her. I rest one palm on the small of her back and hold her firmly to the table.

"Ask me to punish you, Amara." It's been too long since I've entertained this side of me. I choose not to call her by my pet name for her right now in an effort to retain control over my own needs.

I'm too close to the edge.

Lifting her head from the table, her cheeks pull against the surface made sticky with the heat of her body.

Her gaze meets mine.

"Please punish me, Ryder." Her doe eyes plead with me as she says the words.

Motherfucker.

I wasn't prepared for the punch her request delivered, and, in a moment of weakness, I clear my throat to steady my nerves.

"Why should I punish you?" I tickle my finger along the seam of her panties, waiting for her answer.

"I was rude to Sloane, and I wouldn't apologize."

I draw my finger along. "And?"

"And I ran away from you when you told me I wasn't excused."

Lifting the seam, I idly run my finger under the elastic, enjoying her pliant flesh.

"Whose house is this?"

"Yours."

"And whose rules have you agreed to follow?"

"Yours."

"Yet here we are." I raise my hand and land my palm in a smack across the fleshiest spot on her cheek.

Her breath hitches, and her feet shuffle for a better position.

I spank her again. She takes another steadying breath, and her hands fist on either side of her head.

"Palms flat on the table." I won't allow her to administer her own pain to negate the punishment I'm delivering.

The moment her fingers open and her hands flatten, I take another strike. A little lower, where her cheeks meet her upper thighs.

I continue, building rhythm and intensity until her back rises and falls prominently as she pants, desperate to maintain control.

It's a control I'm ready to strip away from her.

"Spread your legs." I watch her step out, but it isn't good enough. "Wider."

She's wound tight with tension, and her hips buck in surprise as I reach down to tap the inside of her thighs. One by one, she steps her feet out until her legs are spread so wide only her big toes touch the floor.

I strike again.

This time, she has no choice but to take each strike as it comes. There is no bracing herself against the floor; there is no digging her nails into her palms.

She is focused only on her punishment.

Warmth floods my face as I punish Amara, setting her firmly into the place meant for her.

This is the place meant for me.

I know Amara feels it too. With each smack, her body relaxes into the table, accepting me, but it isn't enough, and this isn't meant to be pleasurable.

Without warning, I angle my hand from her ass and deliver a swat between her legs, covering the length of her pussy with my palm.

Amara reacts, jumping up to standing. A look of shock and shame fills her cheeks with a rosy glow.

I don't have her complete surrender yet. For that, I need trust. My actions and the years apart have washed it all away.

I narrow my focus on her wide eyes.

"Get back on the table. Or have you decided to run away again?" I taunt, staring her down without emotion.

"I never ran away the first time," she mumbles before resuming the position.

There's her spark. She's right. She never ran away the first time. Four years ago, I sent her away. It was the only way I could protect her. Now, the only way I can keep her safe is to keep her under control.

I spank her in the same spot she fought against, and her legs go tight, trying to hold herself in place. I wonder how this is affecting her as I spank again.

I used to make her come in almost this exact way. Just a little softer and combined with rubbing, and I wonder if it's pulling the memory out of her.

On the next strike, I feel the heavy warmth soaking through her panties, and I clench my teeth so tight a pain shoots into my temple.

I return to spanking her ass to keep myself from exploring her desire further. I build up and spank her the hardest I ever have, and she stays still for me.

The flesh outside of her underwear turns pink, then red, and I desperately want to see what my marks look like all over her, but I don't. Those damn panties need to stay on.

I continue to spank her through her gasps and jolts until she whimpers.

She takes a deep breath and releases it in a shaky stream as she tries to steady her breathing. I lean over the table, making eye contact as I draw my finger gently over her punished bottom.

I see you—all of you. My delicate flower.

Her chin trembles at our connection, and I stay silent, holding an apathetic expression on my face and waiting for her to give me what I want—and she does.

First her chin trembles, then she attempts to pinch her lips together to hold herself in. Her breathing slows as her eyes threaten to release her pain.

Then she breaks and cries for me.

Her silky strands are soft against my fingers as I comb her hair away from her face.

I take the time to commit her to memory. Her eyelashes

stick together with her tears as she sniffles then sucks her lips into her mouth before gently biting down.

I shift her hip, allowing her to pull her legs closed and stand her weight onto her feet. Then I guide her upright with my hands on her upper arms.

"I'm sorry." She whispers her apology. Her eyes meet mine.

I know she's sorry, but there is something else. A combination of anguish and regret hits me, reminding me of another time.

Her punishment is done, and I worry for a moment I've pushed her a little too far into something she wasn't ready to face as she hugs her arms around her chest.

Stepping into her, I tug her docile body into mine to comfort her, and the air between us shifts.

She goes stiff in my embrace.

I try again, tilting her chin up to look at her, and her neck moves in rigid awkwardness. She pulls herself away from me before I realize what she's doing, and I release my hold on her.

"May I go to my room?" The request is out of place for her, and it's one I wasn't prepared for.

I gather myself and nod. The cold realization of what we've become settles painfully into my bones as she gathers her clothes and leaves, stealing herself away from me.

I let her go.

The memory of the night Amara's father died hits me as the door to the dining room slides closed. Grayson brought Amara by to spend the night at our place. He brought her to us and asked my mother to care for her while they made arrangements.

I found her lying in the spare room my mother made up, clutching onto a pillow and sobbing herself to sleep. It was the first time I couldn't fix her pain—I could only be there for her while she fell apart in my arms, trusting me to hold her while she cried herself to sleep—and I did.

She never wanted to go in that room after that night.

Less than a month later, I sent her away.

The one thing Amara's never denied me was the chance to care for her—until now.

By the time I make my way upstairs, her door is slightly open, and her light is off.

The need to comfort her hasn't eased up, and I want to crawl in bed beside her just like that night. I want to pull her into me, wrapping my body around hers and granting her a safe space to free herself.

But I know that is something I haven't earned.

Self-preservation.

The epiphany hits me as I crack her door open further and look in at her sleeping form tucked under the covers.

Amara has become fearful of trusting anyone, and she's gotten used to relying on herself. This way, she can't be disappointed or hurt ever again.

Bringing her back here, at this time, was a rash decision, and I wonder if it was a mistake. I'm not in the position where I can earn her trust and give her the peace I want her to have.

I'm not able to make any of this better for her right now. In fact, it will most likely get worse. Starting with my family dinner tomorrow night.

11

AMARA

I woke up feeling both better and worse than I have in a long time.

Sleep came surprisingly fast after my time in the dining room with Ryder. My release from my punishment relieved my anxiety and provided an outlet for the building tension between us, but I woke up feeling the weight of my guilt.

I went in meaning to suffer my punishment, not enjoy it. The pooling dampness between my legs as Ryder spanked me exposed my shame.

I stop in front of the wooden doors to the dining room to clear my head. The sound of utensils clanging on a plate tells me I won't be eating alone this morning.

I'm determined to approach today differently. I will stay focused, and I will avoid any situation that places me under Ryder's control.

The door slides open, and Nash looks up from his plate of bacon and eggs as he sits back and reaches for his coffee.

He's alone.

The smell of sugar and cinnamon hits me, and I glance to

the hutch, where an assortment of muffins and fruits awaits.

Unsure of my rules regarding speaking to Ryder's men, I step to the side of the breakfast spread and grab a coffee while I take the time to decide how much of a breakfast I really want.

My tummy grumbles at the sight of all of the food, but eating means sitting at the table, and I'm not up for company right now.

"Good morning, Ms. Scott," Nash says from behind me, and I turn to see him smile.

"Oh, um, good morning."

"Why don't you join me?" His hand reaches out, pointing to the chair across from him.

I smile, then lift my empty cup. "I was just going to take this to go." I turn my back to pour the coffee.

"Ryder said you might skip breakfast. He asked me to make sure you eat something since you didn't finish your dinner last night, and I'd hate to tell him you refused one of his requests." I swear I hear the grin in his tone.

Groaning inwardly, I roll my eyes at the wall. While last night came with the release I needed, I'm not ready for another round so quickly, and defying Ryder's wishes will get me there fast.

I take my time adding the cream and sugar before covering my grimace with a smile and turning to face him.

"Of course." I scoop some fruit onto a plate then join him. "And where is everyone?"

Nash resumes picking at his breakfast. "Sloane is still visiting her parents with Henry. She should be back later this afternoon, in time for dinner." He watches me while he speaks, and I wonder how much Ryder has told him about me. "Ryder is at the office for the day. He's asked me to tell you, you have one more day here to get settled. Your office space is almost ready. He's asked you to be ready for dinner at seven. The whole family is coming over." My fork clatters to my plate with a piece of apple in its prongs. I recover it without missing a beat, jamming the fruit into my mouth as he continues on about needing to leave shortly, and I couldn't be happier with my impending seclusion.

Excusing himself, he walks out with his coffee, and I wait until I am fully alone.

As soon as the front door closes, I release the breath I was holding in. Dinner with the whole family, except this time I'm alone. My brother and father are dead, and my mother is nowhere to be found.

Shaking the worry from my head, I finish my coffee and take a cinnamon bun with me to nibble on while I explore the Saint home further. The sugar rush reminds me of all the treats and desserts I used to have when I'd visit as a little girl. At the time, I thought Mrs. Saint baked them all herself. I didn't know they had staff to do it for them.

My family cooked for ourselves. Our dinners usually came out of a box or a can. I used to stuff my pockets with cookies when we came over. They were so soft and chewy, and they tasted fresh and sweet. I don't think my mother has ever baked a thing from scratch in her life.

A moan leaves my mouth at the sweet, buttery taste of the bun as I step into the office on the main floor. This door always used to be locked. It was off-limits.

That must have changed when Mr. Saint moved out, taking all of his secrets with him. Now it looks like a common area. There is an open laptop on the desk. Licking the last of the icing off my fingers, I reach down to tap a key, and it comes to life, no password required.

I press a few more keys, and I see why there is no security on it.

There is nothing on it to secure. This must be for the

brothers to use to look things up if they need. There are no downloads or files to be found.

I abandon the office in search of another room. As I step into the main area, my feet instinctively turn to the left, leading me deeper into the house, toward my favorite room—the library.

A stab of anger hits me as I enter the old room, which smells of paper and leather. When my parents first started coming here, I remember my mother asking if it was okay for me to be on my own. When Mrs. Saint said it was fine, my mother leaned down and whispered to me that we were going to play a game of hide-and-seek. She started counting, and I took off running to find the perfect spot.

They never found me.

As I grew up, I realized they never looked.

They just wanted me to disappear.

Rounding one of the bookshelves near the back, my breath hitches in my throat.

Of course the leather chair is still here, looking just as worn as ever.

After a while, when my mother told me to go hide, I would take off for the library. I knew I wouldn't be disturbed. I'd grab one of Mrs. Saint's old romance novels or Mr. Saint's erotic magazines off the shelf at the very back, and I'd curl up on the fluffy carpet, wedging myself in between the chair and the wall to hide away and read all of the dirty stories I wasn't supposed to know existed.

I did that until the time Ryder found me entranced by one of her dirty books, and I was trapped in my little hiding place with no way out. It wasn't the first time he caught me reading something I shouldn't have in there.

"*Show me what you're reading,*" he demands, standing over me, and I feel the deep shade of red across my face as I try to look around him. He lowers his voice. "*We're alone.*"

Closing the cover, I turn the book over and let him look. I am terrified he's going to laugh at me like he has once before. Instead, he takes it from me and opens it, flipping a few pages until he finds something. Then, placing it back in my hands, he crouches down so his eyes are level with my own.

He points halfway down the page. "*Read it to me. Starting —here.*"

I stutter through the book, my voice dropping to a whisper at the most vulgar words. Ryder stays still, listening to every syllable and nodding for me to continue every time I look up, hoping I'm done.

Finally, he takes the book from my feeble grasp and closes it before telling me these aren't stories for little girls. Shame fills me, and I want to tell him I am not a little girl, that I am almost a woman, but I just look away until the distant sounds of boys' voices enters the library. Fear washes over me at the thought that everyone will soon know what I am doing here, but Ryder steps away from me, catching their attention and leading them away from my hiding spot without another word.

I still remember the strange tingle I felt being so close to him while he made me say those things. I remember wanting him to do those things to me without knowing exactly what they were.

I'm already onto my next destination, climbing the staircase before the memory of him leaves my mind.

His door is open, and I remind myself of the Saint rule: *if it's locked, it's off-limits.* I justify that that must make the opposite true as well, and I take a step into his bedroom.

His room looks different in the daylight. It's more grown-up than I remember, but it still smells like Ryder, like the scent I caught off him the first time I saw him again in my conference room after all that time.

I tell myself I won't snoop.

I won't go through drawers or dig through closets, but the thought leaves me when I spot a box of items in a corner.

I tell myself I won't dig, but that changes when I spot a white envelope on top with Grayson's name on it. It's written in my mother's handwriting.

My fingers glide over the paper, and I feel something inside. I pull my fingers into a fist, determined to walk away, when I see a hat just below the envelope. Grayson's hat.

A nagging voice in the back of my head pushes me to look, and I do. I owe it to Grayson, even if it's nothing.

The envelope is already open, and in it are a few photos of Grayson and Ryder together, along with a USB stick. Twirling the little drive in my fingers, I decide to take a look at it. This box may not be here tomorrow, and I can't let this go if it gives me any information about my brother's death.

I leave the photos in the envelope and make my way down the hall to my room. My laptop fires up, and I plug the stick into a port and wait for the drive to pop up on the screen.

There's only one file on it, a video file, and I open it.

I try to smile through my sadness as Grayson's face comes on the screen, and I fumble to turn the volume on when he starts speaking. Seeing him again makes me realize how much I miss him.

He addresses Ryder in the video, and I feel an anxious knot form in my stomach as Grayson talks about looking into something going on in the Saint organization. I pause the video to check the timestamp, and my blood runs cold when I realize this was filmed the night he was murdered.

I hit play again and sink myself into his recording, oblivious to everything around me.

When Grayson is done telling the camera his plans to gather more information, he changes his tone, saying he was wrong to ask Ryder to release me, that he didn't realize how he felt until he saw a change in him after I was gone.

He finishes his video by saying he's lifting his request to let me go. He's offering his blessings, and none of his words make any sense.

It doesn't matter now because years have passed, and Ryder never came for me. What matters now is that Grayson was looking into something, and it is probably the thing that got him killed.

If he made this video, then at least Ryder knew he was up to something.

Someone in the Saint family knows something about my brother's murder.

I eject the stick and check my computer to make sure the file was removed completely before closing the laptop and making my way back to Ryder's room to set the file back as I found it.

The front door opens as I clear the top of the stairs, and I don't stop to see who's come in.

Barricaded behind my own door, I replay the video in my head.

Someone at dinner tonight will know something. Maybe the whole family is corrupt. I never wanted to consider Ryder capable of something so awful. He was Grayson's best friend.

I won't stop until I know what happened, and that starts now.

The only way to get rats out of a building is to start a fire and watch them scurry away. A nice dinner with the whole family present is the perfect time to strike the first match.

RYDER

Nash informed me he told Amara to be ready for dinner at seven o'clock, which is why I'm not surprised when the grandfather clock in the foyer starts chiming and she is nowhere in sight.

Her unpredictability is infuriatingly predictable.

Almost everyone has been here for at least twenty minutes already. Only Cole is running late because of an accident on the highway, and he had the courtesy to text to let us know.

Even though this is no longer his house, our family tradition dictates the head of the family sit at the head of the table, so my father takes the seat he's always had. He's been catching up with Dagen about some recent freelance work he's been doing.

My mother sits across from my father at the other end, and she and Sloane have been going on about wedding details and Henry since they sat down.

True to Cole's prediction, Lennox—who is sitting on the other side of my mother—and I have been shooting each other uncomfortable stares—that is, when he's not stealing glances at Sloane, who seems to be handling herself well.

Since I'm sitting beside Sloane, in the middle of the table, that leaves the seats beside me and across from me empty. The servers are busy filling glasses as everyone makes small talk.

The front door opens, and a few people glance toward the dining room doorway before returning to their conversation. A part of me is happy Cole has arrived first. He'll take the seat across from me, forcing Amara to my left, where she'll be easy to keep an eye on.

Cole is two steps away from the dining room when a body slips in front of him to greet him, and my features harden as Amara meets my eyes.

Keeping my gaze on her, I stand to pull out the chair beside me, silently showing her where to sit. She blocks Cole's entrance as she looks around the table, her eyes stopping at the seat across from me.

Her lips stretch into a confident smirk as she turns away from my side of the table and takes the seat across from me, defiantly maintaining eye contact.

A warning goes off in my head. Something feels off about her tonight.

My brothers and father rise as she takes her spot, and Cole makes his way to my side and sits at the last available seat.

The servers rush in to serve them, and I listen to Amara ask for a white wine. I don't hear Cole's order as I see a tray of food being rolled in, and more staff follow to hand out our plates.

My mother instantly catches Amara's attention and asks her to tell her everything that is going on with her. Sloane takes interest in their conversation, and I listen quietly as Amara only offers vague answers until my mother offers her condolences for Grayson and asks how Alicia is doing.

Amara reaches for her newly poured wine and takes a large sip before thanking her and attempting to change the subject.

She unconsciously adjusts the utensils beside her plate until they are in line.

It isn't lost on me that everyone around the table is listening to her answer, whether they are being obvious about it or not.

Forks start scraping against plates as we dig into our salads, and Dad asks Cole how everything is going in Portland. Cole gives him the PG-rated version, covering only our legitimate businesses. I have no doubt they will catch up on the rest later.

Out of the corner of my eye, I catch Lennox stealing more glances at Sloane, but she doesn't seem to notice. Or, if she does, she's hiding it well.

Our plates are cleared, and a creamy angel-hair pasta dish is brought in. My brothers dig in, and I watch my mom smile at Sloane and Amara as they eat with a boatload more elegance than the men do.

"And what brings you by for a visit? Are you staying long?" my mother asks Amara innocently.

I know how much she cared for Amara when she was younger. My mother always wanted a daughter, and Amara was the closest thing she had. It's why she made up that bedroom beside mine. She never had the chance to shop for dresses and dolls, and she lost out on hairstyles and makeup. Instead, she got four boys who competed against each other at every turn, all of us stubborn alpha males who can eat a plate of pasta in under two minutes.

I lean back, casually taking a sip of my drink as Amara answers.

"Oh, Ryder bought the company I work for and forced me back here to work for him as part of the purchase conditions." She offers her answer so matter-of-factly that my mother simply smiles as if to say, *That's nice, dear,* but everyone else around the table picks up what she's laying down, and my drink burns in my throat as I force a swallow and Cole chuckles beside me.

Lennox levels his glare on me. "You did what?"

So my oldest brother can still speak.

"I bought a business that Amara here happens to work for," I clarify. "I offered her the chance to oversee the transition, and she accepted." I level my stare at her. This is her first warning, and she takes a sip of her wine before nodding to confirm my side of the story.

"Did you consult anyone here before you just went out and bought a company?" Lennox looks to our father, Dagen, and Cole. Two of them shake their heads no. Cole stays out of it.

"The purchase was made with my own funds. I need no approval." As I answer, Amara waves down the server and points to her glass, asking for a refill. That's her second glass, and she's barely touched her food.

Lennox holds his thought. Instead, he shakes his head and takes a gulp of his own drink before returning to his meal.

Out of the corner of my eye, I catch Amara's fingers tapping nervously beside her plate.

Another warning goes off. She looks nervous, and I watch her take a deep breath before she opens her mouth to speak.

"Anyway. I figured I would use my time back here to find out who killed Grayson." Her voice is loud enough for everyone to hear. Her eyes stay glued to the middle of the table. She's not brave enough to level any one of us directly, but it's clear: she's calling out whoever it is she feels is responsible.

No one says a word.

Her eyes shift around quickly without landing on anyone in particular, and if I didn't know her better I would think she's trying to make herself sound stronger than she is.

I shift in my seat, unsure of what to say to get her to stop talking, when Cole moves beside me.

Leaning forward, he asks, "Do you have any leads?"

He says it with the hint of a smile, and he makes it sound as though he's curious, but I know Cole. He's challenging her to back up her unspoken accusations.

Now Amara looks up, provoked.

Her gaze moves from man to man before deciding on her approach, and I'm mesmerized by her fortitude.

When her eyes land on me, her intentions hit me like a sucker punch. She's sizing up me and my brothers.

"I'm still gathering information. I haven't started questioning anyone yet." Her eyes continue to roam, and I slowly shake my head when she meets my stare. I'm telling her to back off, and when she looks away I know it is a warning she has no intention of listening to. She leans in, levelling her attention on Cole. She's chosen her target. "But, now that I have you here, did you kill my brother?"

Cole's smile leaves his face.

Sloane starts choking on the morsel she was trying to chew, and she reaches for her water while everyone else pauses in shock at Amara's audacity. My father sits in silence, glaring daggers at me. I'm meant to deal with her outburst.

Since stepping down, he has given us a short leash to take care of business before he steps in, and I definitely don't want him dealing with this.

A small sliver of me, one that I will never admit to aloud, is impressed. No one would dare walk in here and accuse a Saint of anything in their own home—even if they had proof.

Yet here she is.

"Amara." This is my second warning.

She's dangerously close to becoming a target.

I take a glimpse around the table at my family. The truth is it could be one of us. My father's face is turning red at the blatant disrespect shown to our family. Lennox's glare is calculated, but he isn't giving anything away. Dagen is stuffing his face with a second helping of pasta, oblivious to the standoff going on around him.

A soft laugh from the end of the table catches my attention, and my mother brushes Amara's response off as though she was joking around. This seems to snap my father out of his anger, but Cole and Amara continue to glare at each other, and Cole looks ready to pounce.

Tilting his head, Cole tries a different approach. "You'd make a horrible detective, Sunshine." He's giving Amara an out.

Her features soften, and she releases a steady breath. She looks relieved at the olive branch he's offered her.

Shrugging her shoulders, she lifts her wineglass. "A girl's gotta try." Then she drains her second glass. Cole raises his glass in cheers, and she continues, "I know he was looking into something, and that *something* got him killed."

Where is this coming from?

I look to my right, catching Cole's attention as he's taking a sip, and he raises his eyebrows at me over the rim of his glass.

Something has definitely changed with Amara since we last spoke, and I feel like I'm starting all over again with her.

A server steps to Amara's side with a bottle of wine, and I catch her attention, shaking my head and warning her off. Amara doesn't need any more wine tonight.

"Sloane and I are going to pass on dessert this time." I speak for both of us and, thankfully, Sloane takes my lead and places her napkin on the table, indicating she is done.

Everyone follows suit and says good night. Amara won't look me in the eyes as we wrap everything up.

She knows she's in trouble.

Sloane walks my mother to the door, and my brothers follow close behind with my father. I turn to walk out, and I feel Amara's presence behind me.

Cole looks back, and I push my chin up, hoping he gets my hint.

When everyone has passed the threshold, Cole turns and slides the door to the dining room shut behind him, closing Amara in the room with me and the servers who are clearing our plates.

Stopping abruptly, Amara grunts as she runs into my back, and I turn on her, pushing her back against the wall.

The servers shuffle behind me, clearing out quickly. They've been here long enough that they know when to make themselves invisible, and right now is one of those times.

I dip my head, searching for her eyes and demanding her attention, but she refuses to give it to me.

"What did you do, Blossom?" I challenge her, the low growl in my tone daring her to answer me. Her lower lip trembles before she bites it, and I swear it is sending all the wrong messages straight to my cock.

I decide to intimidate her.

I lean in close, my face flush against the side of her head. I nuzzle my nose in her hair and take a deep, cleansing breath. The scent of her fear feeds my demons.

"You can be a brave little girl and tell me what you did, or I can pull up the house video feed from today and watch how you misbehaved."

I pull back to watch her reaction, and she gives herself away.

Her eyes flutter to the corners of the room, searching for the cameras she didn't know were there. Her guilt is written all over her face, and I go in for the kill.

"I'm warning you now, Amara. If I have to find out on my own, it will be worse for you."

13

AMARA

Of course someone as controlling as Ryder would have eyes everywhere, I think as the first little camera comes into view.

I would never have seen it if I wasn't looking for it. I almost don't see it now.

Ryder threatens me with a promise to make my punishment worse if I don't come clean and just tell him what he wants to know.

His jaw ticks as he hovers in my space, his eyes staring into my guilty soul, his scent filling my nostrils and reminding me of how horribly I handled my last punishment.

"Were the cameras...always there?" We stole so many secret moments in this house before I left, and the thought of someone watching us makes me sick with worry.

"No one else has ever seen what you've given me." He doesn't answer my question. In his eyes, I'm sure I don't deserve a full response.

Now it's my turn.

Ryder has told me he is a patient man, but I wonder if his

patience comes from the knowledge that if I don't tell him something soon, my punishment will be something more his style.

His threat rings in my ears, and I answer. "I saw Grayson's video."

His expression drops into surprise, and he pulls back to process what I've just told him.

"You were snooping in my room?" It sounds like a question, and he stares at me, searching for confirmation, and my guilt weighs my gaze down to the ground. I'm sure my averted eyes have given him the answer he was looking for.

I'm not the only one who should feel this shame, so I say my piece while speaking into his chest. "The video where Grayson gave you *permission* to *take me back,* like I'm some kind of toy that gets passed around. I'm not a thing. I'm a person." I can't help the tears filling my eyes.

Grayson made me sound like a commodity to be handed over. A thing without her own thoughts and needs. It wasn't up to him. Sniffling, I gather myself, then I realize Ryder hasn't moved or answered me.

When my eyes meet his, his wicked grin tells me I said the exact wrong thing. My heart thuds into my chest as he looks at me, his teeth bared into a grin like he wants to devour me.

He bulldozes over my attempt to deflect blame and keeps his focus on my sins.

"You walked into my room, Amara. You took something that belongs to me, and you looked at it without"—he pushes his face as close to my own as he can without touching me, his voice lowered into a whisper—"my permission."

This isn't good.

Now that he's saying it this way—I screwed up.

I overstepped his boundaries, and, in doing so, I invited him to overstep mine.

And he knows this.

"What else did you do in my room?" His fingers wrap firmly around my upper arms, and he holds me against the wall, removing one hand to run his fingers along the length of my neck.

"Nothing—nothing else."

His eyes lower to my lips, and he licks his own as I feel his breath blow hot against my face.

"No? Tell me, Amara, did you like it in my room? Did you feel close to me?" He places a pause between each question, searching my face for answers. The soft caress of his fingers dissipates when he splays his hand, wraps it firmly around my throat, and draws my eyes up to his own. "Could you imagine yourself tied to my bed, Blossom? Writhing under me while I fuck you?" Now his pause is longer. He wants an answer to that one, and I'm too chicken to give it to him.

He considers my lack of response for a long minute before speaking again. "I see you have no sense of boundaries, and that's okay because I don't want there to be any between us. No boundaries—no limits. You've touched my things without asking permission. Now it's my turn to invade something of yours."

I open my mouth to answer, but I'm too slow.

Ryder peels me off the wall, his hand pulling me by my upper arm like a child to the door of the dining room.

When he slides the door open, only Cole and Sloane are in the main area. It looks like everyone else has left, and I expect Ryder to drop his hold on me, but he doesn't.

And no one looks surprised.

Only Cole looks directly at me, the hint of a smirk on his face.

"I'll talk to you in the morning," Ryder says gruffly, and I'm grateful I am being dismissed.

Nodding, I take a step away from him, pulling my arm back, but he doesn't let go. Instead, he tightens his grip, tugging me back to his side, and I trip over myself. When I look at him, he's looking at me like I've lost my mind.

I think I have.

Sloane and Cole turn and head down the hall.

He was dismissing them, not me.

Without another word, he leads me up the stairs.

Once we reach the top, he turns away from my room and heads down the hall toward his own. My mind spins as I wonder how Sloane and Cole think this is normal behavior, then I realize Ryder has started speaking.

"...put you in the furthest room from me to give you space, but you've shown me you don't want that." My anxiety builds with each step closer to his bedroom. "You made the choice to enter my private space. You took something that belonged to me. You invaded something that was mine alone."

We stop walking ten steps away from his door, and I look from his room to him. He's standing still beside me, his eyes forward. After a moment, he drops his head, and he looks lost in thought before he looks up with determination on his face and turns us sharply to the room on our right.

The door is closed, and a flash of relief hits me. I don't know if I could handle being in Ryder's bedroom tonight. Not now, and not with Cole and Sloane just downstairs.

Ryder reaches for the handle and opens the door beside his, guiding me through the doorway. For once, I'm content to follow—until I take in the room around me.

It's a room that has been stuck in time, frozen with the last memory it held for me, and I stop in my tracks.

When Ryder's mother first showed me this room, I thought it looked like a castle. Three of the walls were painted a charcoal gray, with a feature wall painted in swirls of four different shades of pink. The little bed had a sheer canopy that hung down from the ceiling and the fuzziest pillows I've ever touched in my life.

Dolls and books lined the shelves, and a vanity held beautiful barrettes and hair ties. Mrs. Saint went all out decorating it, like only someone with an obscene amount of money and no daughter of her own could.

The last time I was in this room was when my father passed away. My mother handed me off to the Saints for a couple of days while she grieved and made arrangements. I remember I felt guilty because I wanted her to come and get me so I could mourn with her, so I could be there for her, but what I really wanted was her to be there for me.

I was alone.

My dad died, and I was pushed aside and abandoned.

She never checked on me.

I'm not sure she would have ever come to get me.

It was Grayson who picked me up and took me home.

The last time I was in this room, it looked exactly like this. Stuffed toys are still thrown around the room. Books are off the shelf and out of place.

I didn't care so much about order back then.

But I do now.

When I turn to face Ryder, he simply looks at me. He knows how much I hurt in this room. He listened to me cry for my father. He woke up every few hours when I jolted awake only to start crying again.

I never came in this room again after that.

I get Ryder's message loud and clear: I invaded his privacy, he's invading mine.

I'm more vulnerable in here fully clothed than I was standing in the dining room in my underwear.

Memories threaten to return, and I hang my head, taking a

step to the side to walk around Ryder and out the door when he stops me.

"You'll sleep in here tonight." He steps into my path, and his words confuse me for a moment before I try to keep walking, now with a little more urgency.

I can't stay in here.

His arm pushes against the back of the door, slamming it shut before I reach the handle, and I recoil as panic hits me.

"You can't do this. I want to go to my room."

More than anything, I want to run down the hall, close myself away, crawl into bed, and cry myself to sleep.

"This is *your* room, Amara." His answer is firm, and I feel the tremble in my lower lip as I look at him for signs of mercy.

I look back to the items on the floor. If it were any other room, I could bide my time sorting and organizing, but I don't want to touch anything in here. I don't want to remember any more than I already do.

The word is on the tip of my tongue, forcing its way out of my mouth and into our space.

"P-please." A dizzy wave sways with me as I leave my pride behind and beg to be let out of the room.

"Good night, Amara. I will see you in the morning."

That's it. He's not even asking me to apologize, and that's because I haven't completed my punishment yet.

He's going to leave me here.

He turns, reaching to the side of the door, where a key dangles on a hook I hadn't noticed until now.

No.

"I-I can't. You can't." He turns to look at me when I dare tell him what he can't do, and I bow, pleading for him to change his mind.

My first fat tear rolls out as he takes another step away from me.

"WAIT!"

He doesn't stop walking away.

"Just wait. Please. Um, you can—spank me."

He stops, taking a deep breath before turning to face me. "The next time I punish you like that, it will be with my belt, and it will hurt." He says the words as though he's saving me from the worst possible punishment, and he turns to the door, expecting this is the easy way out for me.

He has no idea.

"I'm okay with that."

He takes a half step before he stops, dropping his head then glancing up in my direction. His body is still turned away from me.

Relief bubbles up inside of me at the thought of this new punishment.

While he looks at me, he takes another step, but it isn't in my direction, and I look at him quizzically.

When he reaches the door, he's made his decision.

"The fact that you would welcome the pain from my belt over being forced to face one night in this room makes me confident I chose the right punishment. I won't tolerate your disobedience, Amara."

Before I fully process his words, he's gone, and the lock on the door clicks.

I can't be in here alone. The only reason I made it through last time was—

Ryder.

He was with me. He never let me be alone.

And now I'm alone.

In the quiet, I scan the room. Everything is a chaotic mix of happy and sad. There is no place in this room where I can separate myself from my past.

Off the bedroom is a washroom. I could barely fit in the

small bathroom as a child. I won't be able to stay lodged between the toilet and sink overnight.

My fear, pain, and anger bubble over, and my body slams against the solid wood door before I realize I've launched myself at it.

My fists ache as I bang them on the unforgiving surface, and tears pour out of my eyes, soaking the neck of my shirt.

This is everything I tried to protect myself against.

I was alone before Ryder came back into my life, but it was my choice, and I was in control of that choice.

When Ryder's mother first showed me this room, I thought it looked like a castle. Now it feels like a dungeon.

My throat burns when I try to yell. I must have been screaming, begging all this time for Ryder to come back and let me out.

But he won't.

Not until I learn his lesson.

And the lesson is that any illusion I have of power and control under Ryder's roof is just that—an illusion.

14

RYDER

Amara pounded on the door well into the night. After I locked her in her room, I stood outside in the hall, listening to her yell, then plead, then cry.

The key burned in my hand. I ached to open the door and go to her, but the punishment needed to be complete, not just for her.

I was punishing both of us.

I can't allow her to go rogue and pull this shit. Amara may think she has some standing with my family, but, when it threatens our own, there are some who will take matters into their own hands.

If I don't reign Amara in, I could lose her forever. She could become a liability, and I don't know if I have enough standing to protect her. I don't even know which of my brothers I can completely trust, thanks to our fucked-up family dynamic.

Family dysfunction ran rampant in our neighborhood.

Grayson and Amara were often left to fend for themselves. Their parents failed them miserably.

When Amara first pulled her little stunt at dinner, I knew I was going to take her up and show her her old room, but it was never my intention to lock her in there overnight.

No, I made that decision when she accused me of treating her like a possession. The moment she said the words, I felt rationality leave me. Indignation replaced it.

How dare she?

With Grayson gone, I'm the only one left who is trying to protect her.

Her own parents put a price on her and sold her to my family without her knowledge, and her mother just tried to sell her to me a second time.

Amara has always been mine, but that doesn't make her a possession. It makes her a treasure. She once knew this, but she's chosen to ignore it, and hearing her forget how valuable she is to me set me onto a dark path last night.

I left her in that room because I wanted her to remember who was there for her when her father passed away. I wanted her to remember how her mother left her alone, because she's pushed it all down and made me out to be the monster.

And maybe I am, but I can't afford not to be.

Now it's morning, and I've had three hours of sleep.

I leave my room and stand silently outside her locked door, listening for movement. The room she's in has a small washroom with a toilet and vanity, so I know she was okay through the night. My mother thought Amara might like her own privacy away from us boys when she designed the spare bedroom.

There is no sound, and I'm hopeful she found some rest.

When I threatened Amara with my belt last night, I was certain she would back down. I never got to use a belt on her before, and she was always afraid of the unknown.

But she welcomed it without hesitation.

Was she so desperate to avoid her past that she was willing

to take any pain? Was she that certain it would pale in comparison to the agony of facing those demons?

A more sinister thought nags at my mind. What if the pain of being whipped by a belt is no longer unknown to her? What if someone else had the pleasure of sharing that with her?

With that little nugget of sunshine eating away at me, I leave her to get some extra sleep and head downstairs to look for Sloane.

"Well, you look like shit." Cole greets me from his seat at the dining room table.

I ignore his observation and head for the coffeepot. "I thought you left last night."

"It was a long day. I didn't want to drive back to Portland so late." Cole's voice gets louder as he joins me at the hutch, picking up the pot I just set down and pouring himself another cup.

"Did you stay in your room?" I wonder how much he heard last night. Cole's old room is just down the hall from mine.

I'm not worried about me, but I feel protective of Amara's pain. She was extremely vulnerable with her fears, and I imagine she would rather keep them private.

"Naw, man. I stayed in the guesthouse. It sounded like you both needed to work some things out." His expression is somber. "Sloane stayed out there too. We both thought you needed some space, and it's none of our business."

His words make me chuckle, and Cole snickers at the irony too.

Sloane is my fiancée. It should be her business.

Except it is all for show.

Our engagement is a lie, and only a few of us know.

Cole faces me, lowering his voice. "How is Amara?"

I know my brother pretty well, and his question is genuine. His concern for her is oddly comforting.

I take a seat at the table and give Cole a shortened version of our night, then tell him she is still locked in her old room so he knows we won't be disturbed, and his voice returns to a regular level.

"That girl has a fire in her." He shakes his head, taking a sip of his coffee before setting it down. "I wasn't expecting her to come out swinging like that in front of everyone. And here we are, sneaking around." Cole is referring to all of the investigating we've been trying to do on our own. "She makes me feel like a fucking coward in all of this," Cole mutters to himself.

And maybe we are cowards.

My father, my brothers, and the people in our organizations are not to be messed with. It doesn't matter how connected we are. The right people can always make you disappear.

Amara is brave. It's one of the things I love about her, but her bravado is going to get her killed, and I need to work it out of her before the right people come looking for her.

"You know why it was you, right?" I ask Cole.

I saw the look on his face when Amara questioned him about Grayson's death. He went from thinking this was all funny to ready to put her in her place himself.

But I know Cole. He was hurt that she would think he could do that. Grayson was his friend too.

"It was me what?" He shrugs in confusion.

"Why it was you she asked about Grayson's murder?" I pique his interest, and he shakes his head, asking me to continue. "Out of everyone at that table, you were the one she felt safest with, and I'm including myself in this." Cole looks like he doesn't believe me. "Think about it. Dad and Lennox have earned everyone's fear, she never knew Dagen well enough growing up, and I'm not exactly winning her over. She tried to send a message to all of us through the safest channel she knew."

"It's fucked up that she thinks I'm the safest person she knows," he grumbles, taking another sip of coffee. "Why did you decide to bring her back here so soon?"

In a rare moment of weakness, I confide in my brother. "I was selfish. I wanted her here. The second I saw Grayson's video and Sloane made the suggestion to go get her, I knew I wanted her back. I wasn't going to approach her until I knew I could protect her, but then I saw her." I pause, remembering the first time I saw her after four years.

"You saw her here? In Seattle?" His eyebrows are pinched in confusion.

I'm already shaking my head. "No. I took a drive down to Portland, on my own. I just—wanted to see her. I needed to know she was okay."

"What happened then?"

"Then I saw her, and I couldn't—"

The moment I saw her, after all those years, I knew I wouldn't let her go again.

When I make eye contact with Cole, he nods in understanding.

A throat-clearing at the door catches my attention, and Sloane enters. She makes a beeline for the table and joins us without taking any breakfast.

"Is Amara okay?" She levels her gaze on me, and I get the feeling she's already taken her side in all of this.

"I'm going to talk with her shortly. She'll be fine." My answer is clipped.

Sloane shifts her attention from me to Cole, then back again.

"I like her." Sloane's eyes pin me in place. "A lot."

I know why she's saying this. Amara and Sloane have the

same fire. They are both strong women in their own right, and I'd admire that quality in them if there wasn't a good chance it could lead to their deaths.

I change the subject.

"I noticed Lennox watching you last night. Anything happen?"

"It's nothing I can't handle." She leans back, crossing her arms, as Cole shakes his head with a grin.

The Saint men are not to be underestimated, and that includes the two of us sitting at the table.

I catch Cole's attention. "Any word on the Luccianos?"

Cole nods, taking a gulp of his coffee, and Sloane takes the pause to pour a coffee for herself while Cole updates us.

"They're looking for his heir. Word in the Lucciano family is that everyone is looking closely at males born within a specific three-year range to the women who were—um, employed by their organization during that time frame. They're looking close to home." He hesitates for a moment as Sloane joins us. "I don't want to say it, but we both know what Mom did before she met Dad. I mean, it's possible, and the year ranges they are looking at would put both me and you"—Cole points between the both of us—"on his list of possible heirs. Dagen also makes the list, but only narrowly."

This new development is wild.

I think out loud. "I mean, it is possible, but it's doubtful it is either of us. Mom and Dad already had Lennox together. I don't think he would have allowed her back into that lifestyle after he had taken her out of it, unless she had no choice, but you do raise an interesting point. It would put Grayson on their list as well. Amara's mom wasn't the angel she leads her daughter to believe she was."

I look at Sloane. The implications of what I've just said settle into her, and she tenses.

If Grayson was the heir to the Lucciano family fortune, it could be why he was killed. Or he could have been killed because he found out who the heir was.

I tap my fingers on the old wooden table in frustration. Every time we find a piece of the puzzle, more pieces go missing.

"Stay on it," I tell Cole. "Whatever this is, we need to know before everyone else, but it stays between the three of us and Dagen."

Dagen is fairly removed from the family business. He chose instead to go into business for himself, and he's been very successful. He's been using his expertise to help us dig up anything we can on Grayson's death, but so far all we've found are dead ends.

"I'm heading out." Cole stands, squeezing Sloane's arm and excusing himself.

Less than a minute later, the front door opens and closes, leaving Sloane and I staring at each other.

"What if it's Grayson?" Sloane looks worried.

"The chances of it being any of us are slim. A lot of women worked for the Lucciano family, and Elia Lucciano was a womanizer in his day."

"You know what I mean, Ryder. If it is Grayson—" She lets our reality linger, and I settle her nerves.

"If Grayson is the heir, then it ends because he passed away. You are engaged to be married, and Henry is our son. He's *my* son. And no one is taking him from us. That's all anyone needs to know until we figure this out."

Sloane nods, but there's no confidence in her expression. She's worried for Henry.

"I'm going to talk to Amara now." I stand to leave, and Sloane grabs my hand, pulling my focus to her. She has tears in her eyes.

"Thank you, Ryder."

Squeezing her hand, I leave and make my way up to the room I locked Amara in.

Sliding the key in the lock, I let myself into the room.

The area is brightly lit, and I expect to find Amara lying in her bed like I found her just over four years ago, but the bed hasn't been slept in.

Amara is curled up on the floor in the center of the room. She's lying in a ray of light like an angel. Scanning everything around her, I realize this is the farthest away she could get from the rest of the room.

She couldn't sleep in her bed, and she couldn't bring herself to touch anything that reminded her of a happier time because those times ended in such sorrow.

This is going to get worse for all of us before it gets better, and it pains me to know I can't be entirely honest with Amara yet. There are secrets that will destroy innocent lives.

I promised Grayson I would keep his family safe, and that includes Amara and Sloane.

And the son he never knew he had.

15

AMARA

The night we found out my father died, I was unceremoniously dumped here, at the Saint home, while everyone went on without me. I remember Mrs. Saint met me at the door and took me in. Her hand held mine, but I didn't feel her touch. Her smile was sad as she spoke to me, but I couldn't understand anything she said.

I don't think I spoke to anyone. Nothing seemed important enough to say out loud.

Then I was placed in this room to sleep.

I tried to crawl into the bed and pretend we were at another one of their parties and if I could just fall asleep, then my mom and dad would come and get me when it was time to go.

But no one came to get me, and as the night went on my sadness seeped into my soul and the tears came.

I thought I was being quiet. I didn't want everyone to know I was in here crying like a baby, but I couldn't stop.

I was so wrapped up in my grief that I didn't hear the door open or the footsteps crossing the room. I felt the covers lift and the bed dip, and then he was there.

Ryder slid in quietly beside me, pulling my back into his front and wrapping himself around me.

He didn't say a thing. He didn't try to tell me everything was going to be okay. He didn't try to make me go to sleep. He just held me as though he wasn't going to let anything else hurt me.

He was going to let me fall. He was going to let me feel.

And I cried.

I soaked my pillow with my heartache, my body heaving with sobs as he held me tight and ran his hands through my hair and over my skin while his lips kissed the back of my head.

Ryder once told me I would always be safe with him, and that is the memory I wake up with as a bright ray of light blinds me.

I grunt as I attempt to sit myself up, remembering I fell asleep on the floor last night.

The bed doesn't look as scary as it did last night, but I still don't want to spend another night in here.

When I rub the sleep out of my eyes, my fingers come away wet.

I've been crying.

No.

I wasn't crying, but my tears were falling. My tears are my body's natural reaction to the stress and everything else I am feeling, and I have no control over whether I produce them or not. But I do have control over my emotions, and I refuse to cry.

When I've wiped the last of the wetness off my face, I stretch, and my skin prickles with the feeling I'm being watched.

Without turning to look, Ryder's presence settles around me. I hate myself for how he affects me. I know in my heart Ryder didn't kill Grayson, but what if he knows who did? My heart is betraying myself and my brother.

I need to know.

"Did you kill Grayson?" I ask without turning to see who is with me. I already know. I don't react to anyone else like this.

"No." He doesn't sound angry that I'm asking him. He sounds tired.

"Do you know who did?"

"No."

I sit in silence for a couple of minutes, and he doesn't make a move to join me.

Just like that night four years ago, he's allowing me the space to process.

My limbs ache, my face feels puffy. A sharp pain behind my eyes makes me wince, and the sunlight is too bright.

I cradle my head in my hands, wishing away the pain of the last twelve hours.

It was a mistake to accept Ryder's terms. I'm coming to see that finding Grayson's killer may result in me losing the pieces of myself I thought I had fixed.

A shadow creeps across the morning light, and I look up to see Ryder standing over me, the sun's rays bathing him in light like some kind of angel as I sit here on the floor, fittingly at his feet.

"You aren't as strong as you pretend to be, Blossom." I used to love it when he called me that. I was his flower. It made me feel pure and right and—loved.

I don't answer him.

Kneeling down so his eyes are level to my own, he continues, "I know you're putting up a front. I know you're struggling." He reaches out, combing his fingers through the hair near my cheek, and I instinctively lean in to his touch before I catch myself and pull back. His smile is triumphant. I've just confirmed what he's saying, and he keeps going. "Just know, every time you fight me, every time you challenge me"—he leans close, his lips brushing against the shell of my ear—"I know. I know you're scared. Your fear is all around you, and I recognize it." He pulls back, demanding my focus. "I see you. You can't hide from me."

My heart wants me to cry, but I won't. Piece by piece, he's taking me back. I feel it in my bones. The worst part is, in the end, I won't be fighting him. I'll be fighting my traitorous heart.

At the risk of him hurting me all over again, I want him to want me, but I don't see how this will end in anything but my already fractured heart laying shattered around me.

"Why am I here?"

He looks confused for a second. Like I've asked something ridiculous. His eyes shift between my own.

"You're here because it's where you belong." His answer is final. It's comforting yet devastating.

I know enough about myself to know I need to gather my thoughts on my own. Right now, I'm in a room that brings all of my raw emotions to the surface, and I'm going head-to-head with Ryder, who is in top form this morning.

"I'm sorry I went into your room and looked through your things." I mean my apology, and I look him in the eyes.

While I am trying to get out of this room, I mean what I say. I shouldn't have overstepped Ryder's boundaries.

He hesitates before answering, and I realize that I've lost a bit of his trust because of my actions. I should be proud of myself for sticking it to him, but I'm not. I've disappointed him, and the knowledge hurts me.

"I expect you to fall in line while you're here, Amara. You can't go around accusing powerful people of something you can't back up. Even if you can, things are done a certain way." Standing, he extends his hand to help me up, and I take it. "If you know something, come to me. We want the same thing." His gaze drops. He licks his tongue over his lower lip as he lands on my chest, and I feel a shiver run through me at the double entendre in his last sentence.

Hooking his finger under my chin, he lifts my attention from his mouth to his eyes. "Defy me again, and I'll show you what you're afraid of."

A dark desire passes between us, and the hairs at the back of my neck prickle with fear. It isn't anticipation. Real worry settles into my bones.

I'm terrified because I don't doubt he's already figured me out and he's holding on to that information until the perfect opportunity to use it against me arises.

Out of everyone, Ryder is the one person who can unravel everything I worked so hard to build up around me.

"Get dressed, Amara. I'm taking you into the office to get you set up." He takes a step away, and I nod and spin on my heels to get out of the room I never want to step in again.

My fingers touch the cool metal of the handle when Ryder catches my attention.

"One last thing." I look over my shoulder at him. "If I catch you in my room without my permission again, you will be sleeping in there with me from then on—and you will be naked."

I nod my head. Noted.

Turning to leave, I fumble with the door as visions of sleeping with Ryder fill my thoughts and confuse me.

I don't look back as I hurry down the hall into my room to gather my things before heading to the main bathroom.

There's only one shower down this wing on the floor. I don't know how all of the brothers shared it without killing each other when they were growing up.

Pulling the curtain closed on the world, I step under the shower and breathe a sigh of relief at being out of my old room.

The hot water soothes my sore back from lying on the floor all night, and my muscles begin to loosen.

Ryder's threats and innuendos play back in my mind as I wash my hair. My skin feels more sensitive than normal, and I glide my hands over my body as I picture his face, stern and demanding.

I'm too wound up to focus. I need a release. My conscience, and all that would come after, stops me from wanting to climb Ryder and ride him until I can't move, but it doesn't mean I can't use the image of him to get myself off. Just enough so I can think straight.

My hands slide easily over my soapy skin, and I move lower until I'm gliding between my lips. I grab onto a bar in the shower to hold myself up.

Memories of Ryder mix with my fantasies, and they swim around in my head as I close my eyes and focus on the building tension, searching for my release.

My body goes rigid, chasing its orgasm. Images of Ryder's hard body pounding into my own. That look of wolfish domination etched across his face as pure need rolls off him in waves and he takes everything he wants, using my body to please him.

I suck in a deep breath, ready to toss myself over the edge, when a loud bang on the door throws me out of my thoughts. My heart lurches into my throat.

Ryder must be ready to leave for work.

Was I loud? I was pretty sure I was silent.

What's wrong with me that I'm getting off on all of this?

I turn off the shower and squeeze out my hair, quickly wrapping it before drying off and running to my room in a towel.

I'm wound even tighter than I was before. Not only could I not make myself come, but I just edged myself after only getting a few hours of sleep and having it out with Ryder. Now he's taking me somewhere new, and I'm wound up.

Nothing is better, everything is worse. I chastise myself as I dry my hair before straightening the waves out of it.

I'm able to cover my blotchy skin and my puffy eyes, and I pick out my favorite outfit. I may as well look good on the outside. I feel like shit on the inside.

I reach for my phone and flip it over to see a number of text messages from Penny. They're all about work. A call comes in, and I take it without looking at the ID. I'm shocked to hear the voice on the other end of the line.

"There you are, honey. I was starting to get worried about you."

I pull the phone away from my head and look at it as though she can see my shock through my phone.

"Mom?"

I can't remember the last time she called me. I was sure she didn't have my number.

"Of course it is. I wanted to see how you were settling in back in Seattle. I have to say, I was shocked when you emailed to tell me what happened. Are you doing well there?" My cheeks stretch with a smile. I'm touched she thought enough to call and check up.

I know she's been busy, and I'm an adult now, but it's nice to know you are on someone's mind, especially your own mother's.

"Mom. Thank you for calling. Um, I'm just getting settled here. I start at the new office today. I'm a little nervous."

There's a lot I want to tell her, but the memory of Ryder's impatient knock on the bathroom door reminds me I should move it along.

"That's good, sweetie. Well, I won't keep you long." My heart sinks a little. She's already trying to say goodbye.

"I mean, I could talk later if you'd like. I should be around tonight. Maybe we could catch up," I offer.

"I'm going to be out tonight, but I'll call again." There's a pause. "Amara?"

"Yes, Mom?"

"Can you tell Ryder I said hello?"

The request is odd, but I tell her I will, and she says goodbye.

It isn't much, but maybe me being away from Portland has made her realize she misses me. The thought makes me smile.

After the morning I've had, being in an office can't be worse than sitting around here, so I gather my things, hoping to turn this day around. The only problem is false hopes are more dangerous than fears, and the sinking feeling in my stomach is warning me to tread lightly today.

16

RYDER

The ten minutes I waited in the car for Amara tested my patience, and she knows this. Tardiness is disrespectful, and she's walking a fine line in pushing my leniency, especially after what she pulled last night.

A reminder of her place may come sooner rather than later if she keeps this up.

When Amara finally joined me in the car for our drive into the office, she averted her gaze, and I caught her glancing at me sheepishly as she buckled herself in.

Nash sent me a text to tell me she had a call, and I assume this must be what is making her react strangely. I wondered if she would share her conversation with me.

Before I had the chance to pull out of the driveway, she informed me her mother called. I was pleased she confided in me, however, she added that her mother asked her to say hi to me.

My mood turned sour knowing Alicia only called to fulfill our bargain. Amara was nothing more than a to-do list item she just ticked off.

Once we got into the office, I set Amara up with my assistant, who showed her to her office and set up all of her clearances and passwords.

We had one meeting, then Amara picked up her new position like it was always meant to be hers. I sent her a list of everything I needed to be addressed about the takeover, and updates started coming in within the hour.

I see why her old boss considered her his most valuable employee.

"Mr. Saint is here to see you." The tinkly voice of Constance, my assistant, comes through my phone. She's usually more specific since there are a lot of us Saints, but this is my two o'clock with Dagen, and I tell her to send him in.

Dagen casually saunters to one of the chairs in front of my desk. He sits down and leans back, crossing one ankle over his knee like we're about to order drinks in a lounge.

"So that was a fun dinner." Dagen smirks, and I flip him off.

He acts aloof, but the guy is innately aware of what is happening around him.

I change the subject.

"Cole fill you in?" I unbutton my jacket and lean back as well. I haven't taken a break since I got here this morning.

Dagen nods. "Yeah. It's fucked up, for sure. The Luccianos are even looking into Ma, but I've been told she isn't high on their list. Cole says we need to make good with Elia's second."

I take a moment to consider what Dagen is saying. When Elia Lucciano dies, the organization will fracture if they can't find their heir. If we need to get in good with his second in command, it means they already know where the line is going to be drawn.

A seedy underbelly has been infesting the Lucciano family for years now. Most business is illegal, however, it isn't entirely morally corrupt. Elia ran his business on the willing backs of others. The whores in his sex clubs were there by choice. Gamblers chose to indebt themselves to the organization.

More recently, though, there have been whisperings of sex trafficking and forced fighting, not to mention some unsanctioned killings that happened without Elia's blessing. Those closest to Elia, including his second in command, Credence, who goes by Creed to anyone who doesn't want a bullet in their head, have been good at putting a stop to everything they deem crosses a line, but they've never been able to cut it out completely.

Now it's coming back to bite them in the ass.

"Any idea how we do that?" I ask.

"Yes. I've invited Creed and his group out to Eros on Saturday. Lennox is throwing an exclusive masquerade party, and they've already said they'll be in attendance. They are interested in talking to all of us. It's a good idea to make an appearance, and bring Sloane along. I think it'll go a long way toward relations. A couple of them will have their women there as well."

I'm already wincing at the thought.

"I don't think it's a good idea to put Sloane and Lennox together in a place like that." I reject his idea, and he shrugs. He knows Sloane and Lennox have a history. "Besides, we both know this engagement is a sham, and I don't want to put Sloane in a position where we need to test our devotion in front of others."

"Do you still think Lennox could have killed Grayson?" Dagen asks.

He's always blindly assumed Lennox wouldn't have killed anyone like that. I think it's because they're closer in age. They are the oldest, and they've been together the longest, but even he can't deny we've had a deep wedge between us for a long time now.

"You don't?" I test the waters.

"I don't know, man. I still don't think he could."

Before either of us argue our cases further, the door opens, and Amara walks in with some files, heading straight for my cabinet. Her back is turned to us as we watch her quietly, and her head is down, looking at the tabs on the folders in her hands.

"Hey, Sloane." Dagen greets her, and she startles, spinning around with her hand on her heart and gasping for breath. "Oh, shit. Sorry. I thought you were—" Dagen cuts his sentence short when he realizes who he's talking to. Then he turns to me, lowering his voice to explain. "From the back, she looks just like..."

He doesn't say her name again.

Amara quickly excuses herself, saying she thought I was out of the office and she'll come back to file later before running out of the room.

I don't respond. Instead, I let her go as I examine her, seeing what Dagen just saw.

Amara straightened her hair today, and from the back she looks just like Sloane.

"You said it was a masquerade?"

Dagen slowly nods his head.

If I take Amara, I'll be able to keep her under my thumb. She'll have a mask on, and the club is dark. Sloane will be able to avoid Lennox and stay home with Henry.

My decision is made. "My guest and I will be there."

"I'll set it up and let Cole know. See you Saturday then." Dagen stands and reaches into the bowl on my desk, taking a fistful of mints before excusing himself.

I wait until the elevator dings before leaving my office and walking to Amara's down the hall.

The door is open, and I enter to find her typing away. She looks up instantly and holds up a finger, asking for a minute before returning to her keyboard. I take the time to look around.

I saw this office yesterday, and it did not look like this. Everything looks like it has been moved around to reflect anything but what it was originally set up to be.

Even the reference books on the shelf have been rearranged by size. I've been monitoring Amara's work today, and she shouldn't have had enough time to also do all of this.

She finishes typing and turns to me, hiding any emotions behind a reserved expression. She only offers me a terse smile.

"I need a pen and a piece of paper." I point to the three pens she has placed side by side in a perfect line, and her fingers hover over them nervously.

Yes, I think, *I am telling you to disrupt your order.*

She chooses the one closest to me and opens her desk drawer for a notepad.

I smile as I take it, then look intently at the pad of paper before scribbling absolutely nothing on it. I doodle a circle, a hashtag, and the number forty-two before tearing off the paper and placing it in my jacket pocket.

Instead of handing the pen back to her, I lean over her desk and make a point of placing it at an angle, knocking the other two out of their place.

I stand back to my full height to thank her, and I wait for a moment to see her reaction.

She glances at the pens, then back to me before clasping her hands together in front of her.

I walk over to the window to look over the city. The day is overcast, and a light dusting of snow fell last night. It melted to slush on the ground, turning everything an odd shade of dull.

When I turn my attention back to Amara as she tells me everything is fine, I see the pens have been straightened and placed back in their spots.

I decide to let it go, as many people like to have neat desks, and I glance around the office when a picture catches my eye.

"I remember when this was taken." The memory leaves my lips as I pick up the photo of a smiling Grayson. He's holding an award in one hand, his other wrapped around his little sister. It was a track and field ribbon. I remember how proud Amara was of her brother.

I think it was the only time his parents came to any of our events. Grayson told me it was because Amara heard them talking over dinner, and she begged her parents to take her to watch her big brother win. I don't share that part of my memory with Amara.

But there she is, in the photo with him. She's looking up at him like he's her superhero. He's grinning from ear to ear, and it isn't because he placed.

It's because of Amara.

She was his biggest fan, and she made him feel like he could do and be anything he wanted because she believed in him enough for the both of them.

"Do you need anything else from me?" Amara sounds tired.

When I look back, she has a sad smile on her face, and I realize I've hit her with too much in the last day.

I place the photo back on a different shelf, then excuse myself. There is one thing I need to know.

Stepping into the hall, I close the door behind me and slowly count to ten. Then I open the door abruptly.

Amara startles, and she's right where I thought she'd be: standing in front of the shelf, holding the frame, and putting it back in its proper spot.

She looks stressed. The weight of everything is pushing her down. Something Sloane said earlier registers.

Amara does need a friend. She needs something outside of all this. Someone who shares her pain. Someone who isn't me.

"Um, did you forget something?" She sets the frame down and brushes her hands down her skirt.

"I did, actually. I won't be home tonight, but Sloane will be. Maybe you can have dinner together," I offer, and she looks at me with wide eyes.

"You want me to have dinner with your fiancée?" She speaks slowly, like English isn't my first language, and it only now hits me how odd the suggestion is.

"It was just a thought. I know Sloane doesn't like it when she's in the house all alone," I reason, hoping it sounds like an afterthought.

The look on her face tells me I've said something wrong. She looks hurt, and I realize I made it sound as though it was in Sloane's best interest and not hers.

"I thought you might like to talk to someone." If I had a shovel, I'd be all the way to the basement at the rate I'm digging myself in.

"Tell me, Ryder. Exactly what am I going to talk to your future wife about?" Her defiance looks like it's about to make a comeback, and the blood from my racing heart makes a beeline for my cock.

I should have just walked out of this office and not come back. The tension growing between us is close to bubbling over. Amara looks agitated, I feel tense, and we can't stop pushing each other's buttons.

And fuck if that tight skirt of hers doesn't hug her ass just right.

"Forget it. I just thought you wanted a friend. I mean other than me." I sound like a preteen all over again, asking a girl out for the first time—except I'm not asking her out. I'm asking her to be friends with the woman she thinks I'm going to marry.

The look on Amara's face says it all.

"Sure. Um, okay." Our eyes meet, and I swear she can tell I want out of this office just as much as she wants me to leave.

And this time, when I leave, I don't go back.

17

AMARA

Knowing Ryder is out of the house for the evening should be a relief. Instead, I'm hiding in my room—yet again.

I made my way into the kitchen as soon as I got home, startling most of the staff. Grabbing an apple and a few packaged items from the pantry, I smiled sheepishly as I ran out of there and up to my room before anyone else saw me.

By "anyone," I mean Sloane.

I know Ryder wanted me to hang out, maybe have dinner with her and their son, but I don't have it in me tonight.

Plastic wrappers from packaged cookies, an empty bag of chips, and a half-eaten granola bar cover my bed. And I wonder why I have a stomachache.

The disorder bothers me.

Crumpling the empty items in my hand, I swiftly toss everything in the trash before returning to the bed to brush the crumbs off my covers.

It's too early to go to sleep, and I have no one left here to meet up with.

Maybe Ryder is right; I do need to find some friends.

I know he thinks I didn't have a life back in Portland. I might not have had close friends, but I did have a life. I had a schedule. I had hobbies and things I looked forward to every week, and I know Ryder doesn't know about them yet, or he would have mentioned them.

He definitely would have mentioned my secrets if he knew them.

A sly smirk spreads across my face.

I like having secrets.

Little pieces of me that no one else gets to have. Something just for me.

One of my bags sits by the dresser, only half unpacked. It's my way of keeping one foot on the ground. A reminder that I won't be staying long.

I have a purpose here, then I will leave.

I can only be discarded if I want to stay. Ryder can only let me fall if I choose to jump.

My gaze lands on my broken butterfly. Once pretty and whole, its jagged edges are a reminder of what happens when I allow someone else to care for the things I hold dear.

I gather the pieces in my palm, then gingerly spread them out on the bedspread in front of me. I'll have to find some glue and fit the pieces back together before any of them go missing.

A squeal catches my attention as little footsteps thump down the hall, and I tiptoe across the room, pausing behind my closed door.

Holding my breath, I turn the handle and pull the door open a crack, just enough to see through.

Henry stands barefoot and wrapped in a towel as big as he is. His hair is wet, and puddles shaped in little footsteps lead from him to the bathroom as he reaches up, trying to open the door to one of the bedrooms.

I take a small step back and close the door an inch as Sloane catches up to him. She laughs softly as she opens the door for him, and he races into the room.

Once Henry disappears through the door, I steal a glance at Sloane, and her eyes meet mine. She caught me staring. She tries to smile, but I'm suddenly aware I must look like I'm stalking them, and I retreat into my room, closing the door behind me to hide away once more.

I return to my shattered glass puzzle sitting on my bed. I pick up the pieces and fit them into their spots.

I've become adept at picking up the pieces.

Under different circumstances, I think I would have really liked Sloane.

She has a strength about her that she doesn't flaunt. She's not aggressive or demanding. She's kind and understanding, and this is what hurts so much.

Grayson spent most of his time with her. He adored her. I thought she felt the same.

The life I once wanted now tastes bitter on my tongue. It wasn't so long ago that I imagined I would be the mother of Ryder's children.

I took it for granted, really. Nothing is set in stone.

Ryder dropped me once, and cracks formed but they were buried deep under the surface. I widened them over the years by closing myself off. I know I did, and I knew what I was doing, but not feeling was better than hurting. I learned that after a few months of the so-called "therapy" my mother insisted I sit through.

A knock on the door catches my attention, and for a moment I hope it is Ryder.

"Come in." I busy myself with picking up the glass shards and the door opens to Sloane.

"Hi, Amara." She glances around the room before making

eye contact again. "Can I join you for a bit?"

"Um, sure." I set the pieces on the nightstand beside me to clear some space, and Sloane walks in, taking a seat on the edge of my bed.

"Thanks. It gets quiet in the house after Henry goes to bed, and no one else is here. What is that?" Her eyes focus on my glass butterfly.

"Oh, it's nothing." I don't have it in me to share any of the sad memories this little thing conjures up for me.

"Are you settling in well enough?" Sloane clasps her hands in her lap. It's a coping mechanism I use to settle my nerves, and I wonder if she's doing the same.

I nod, and she continues with the conversation

"I know Ryder isn't the easiest person to work with." She huffs the hint of a laugh, as though she's trying to lighten the mood, and I don't respond.

I can't tell what she's getting at. Did Ryder ask her to be my friend too? Or is she trying to figure out if I'm sleeping with her fiancé?

I hate that I wish Ryder would come home right now and end this awkward conversation.

"The house feels empty without Grayson here." I can't bring myself to say it louder than a whisper, and her face falls at the mention of his name.

We sit for a minute, looking at anything but each other, before she breaks the silence.

"Grayson talked about you all the time, Amara. He was so proud of you."

Our eyes meet, and hers are glassy.

"I'm going to find out who killed him." I deliver my threat with conviction.

Her gaze shifts between my eyes, and she leans over and

places her hand on my own. "I hope you do." I search her for a hidden message, but there is none.

I sense she really means it, and I press on. "Even if it's Ryder?"

I'm testing her.

I know they were best friends. I know there couldn't have been anything that Ryder would have killed Grayson over. I'm staking my own life on it just by being here.

"It wasn't Ryder," she answers flatly.

"How can you be so sure?"

Sloane examines me, and I sense there is something she wants to say. Her breathing deepens, and she takes her time considering her response.

"Ryder was with me the night Grayson died."

Her confession rattles me to my core.

The answer is bittersweet.

Ryder didn't kill Grayson, but he was with Sloane.

He *is* with Sloane.

I thought Sloane was Grayson's girlfriend until his end, but maybe I don't know everything.

I'm sad for my brother all over again. "He loved you, you know."

Sloane had to know Grayson thought the world of her, yet she was with Ryder during my brother's final moments.

"I loved him." The sadness in her tone pulls me from my thoughts.

I want to yell at her and ask her how she could do that to him, but it will get me nowhere. My questions won't get answered, and I'll most likely end tonight with another punishment once Ryder gets home. Right now, I don't want anything to do with him.

"I don't understand any of this." I think out loud, hoping

Sloane will set me free and give me some of the pieces I need to complete this puzzle. "I see the way you look at me," I tell her. "You know what Ryder's plans are for me." I don't say it as a question. I'm not sure I want the answer. "You said it yourself: this was your idea. Ryder is your fiancé. I don't understand, Sloane. Why am I here? If you loved Grayson, why are you doing this?"

Her fingers squeeze my hand, and I consider pulling it away for a moment, but I like the fleeting comfort.

After a moment longer, she breaks our connection.

"People get married for many reasons." Her eyes search my own. "Love is sometimes very far down on that list." Her cryptic answer doesn't sit well with me, and I push a little more.

"But you have a son together." At the mention of Henry, she straightens. She is what I wish my own mother was: protective. "I see it written all over your face, Sloane. You know the damage Ryder caused. Either he told you or Grayson did. You know he sent me away and hurt me. Why are you doing this?"

Sloane turns her head toward the door, no doubt regretting her decision to come in to talk with me. When she turns back, there is something different about the way she looks at me.

"I did it because he's hurting too."

What?

Sloane's answer rattles around in my head like the punchline to a joke that doesn't make any sense.

I open my mouth to ask her to explain when my eyes catch movement just over her shoulder. Sloane turns, following my line of sight to Ryder, who is standing at the door.

He looks cautiously between us, and Sloane takes advantage of the interruption. Standing, she smiles at Ryder before excusing herself.

When she reaches Ryder at the door, she turns back to face me, and Ryder watches her carefully.

"I enjoyed our talk, Amara. Could we maybe hang out again—another time?"

Ryder looks away from her, and my face heats under his attention. I nod before she leaves us alone.

I wish so many things were different. I wish I truly did have a friend like Sloane.

"I'm happy you decided to talk to her." He steps into the room, stopping a few feet from my bed. He looks at the edge where Sloane just sat, but seems to think better of taking her place.

I stay quiet. There's no point in telling him I actually spent the night hiding out in here and it was she who sought me out.

He takes my silence as an invitation to ask another question.

"What were you talking about?" He tries to sound as though he's just making conversation, but I feel like he really wants to know.

"Sloane just stopped in to say hello and see how I was settling in." He stares at me in silence, weighing my answer.

Technically, she did ask that, so I'm not lying, and I wonder if he'll ask her what we spoke about. I wonder if she'll tell him everything.

His gaze drifts around the room before settling on my nightstand, and I know without looking to confirm he sees the glass pieces.

Good. Let him see the damage he's done.

Maybe I won't be so quick to glue the shards back together. This will serve as a physical reminder that his actions have consequences too.

"There is a masquerade ball this weekend at my family's club, Eros. It's a—"

I hold up my hand, cutting him off. "I know what Eros is."

He raises his eyebrows in response. I know he wants to ask how I know, but he doesn't, and I won't elaborate.

I found out Eros was owned by the Saint family when I was researching BDSM clubs in Portland, and I learned they also have one in Seattle.

I'm sure Ryder hasn't yet figured out that I've been a member at a competitor club for a couple of years now.

Back when my therapy wasn't working out, I needed to find my own way of controlling myself and managing my anger and hurt. In short, I needed an outlet, something I had control over. Something I could access in private and use to curb my needs.

He tries to start again. "You will be joining me as my guest. I will arrange for your dress and mask."

I nod, showing the compliance I know he wants from me, but inside my stomach knots in uncertainty.

Ryder turns to walk out the door, pausing when his hand rests on the handle.

"And Amara?" He glances at me over his shoulder. His gaze lingers on my pajama shorts and top a little too long, and my stomach tenses as my core heats. I shift to clench my thighs to control my response.

His stare drops lower. He notices the effect he has on me, and I know he loves it.

"Y-yes?" I stutter. My cheeks flush, and goosebumps prickle along my arms.

A wolfish grin tugs at the corner of his lips. "Sweet dreams, Blossom."

As the door closes behind him, I release the breath that was burning in my lungs.

I'm not so sure I'm going to survive a night at a sex club with Ryder. He'll be in his element, in the club his family owns, and I'll be at his mercy.

And, worst of all, I'm starting to want it that way.

18

RYDER

It took me a couple of hours to settle down enough to fall asleep last night. I couldn't get the image of Amara out of my head after I told her I would be taking her to a sex club.

My little flower can't hide her emotions from me, and her reaction awoke a dark side of me, one I've been holding back because I didn't have the one thing I needed to let loose—her.

My excitement quickly turned into nervous energy, and I left my room with the intention of taking a cold shower before falling asleep. But it didn't quite work out the way I planned.

The hot water ran over me as I pictured the glint in Amara's eye when I told her I would be taking her to Eros.

I'd say she looked "receptive" if I was being a gentleman. But I'm no gentle man, and Amara looked hungry. She looked like she was just a nudge away from surrendering to all the depravity building inside of me.

The thoughts of what I could do with her in one of those rooms had me fisting my erection while my free hand propped me up against the wall.

My Blossom, on her knees in front of me, her mouth open, head tilted back as she stuck out her tongue to lick the first drop of precum from my cock.

How did she know what Eros is?

The thought of her being chained to a bench, my cum dripping from her puffy lips as I spread her wide and fucked her until she cried for her release set me free, and I came harder into my own hand than I had in a woman in a long time.

Since her.

After that, I slept like the fucking dead, and I woke up this morning feeling more rested than I have in years.

It's still early, and I decide to let Amara sleep a little longer. I make my way into the dining room to get a bite to eat, and Henry waves at me with a big smile on his face as he picks up some cereal from his bowl and shoves it into his mouth before grabbing a strawberry.

Sloane smiles and takes the break to drink her coffee. One of our servers enters from the kitchen, pointing at the coffeepot, and I nod. She makes my coffee for me and meets me at the table with it.

I haven't had a chance to talk to Sloane since I found her with Amara, and my curiosity has been eating away at me.

"So you had a nice conversation with Amara last night? What did you talk about?"

The pipes make a soft creak when the showerhead from upstairs is turned on, and the sound catches our attention.

Sloane finishes her gulp and pats her lips with a napkin before she answers.

"Before I forget, Cole dropped by wanting to talk to you about something, but you were asleep, so he said he's taking a shower." She points to the floor above us.

My attention instantly shifts to what could be so important

that Cole would drive the few hours from Portland this early in the morning, and I set my coffee down. "Did he say what he wanted to talk about?"

Sloane shakes her head. "It sounded important, but he didn't say."

"I'll be right back." I mentally list all of the things that would warrant Cole to drive up here, and I decide to talk to him before Amara wakes up. I leave Sloane and head up to the bathroom on our floor.

It's not unusual for my brothers to use the shower. We technically all own this house together.

Making my way down the hall, the sound of the pouring water gets louder, and I open the door and step inside. The room is full of steam.

I turn to ask Cole what is so important when the door to the shower opens wide, and I stop dead in my tracks.

Amara stands in front of me, frozen in place, with water glistening down her naked body as one arm reaches out, grabbing for a towel that is just out of her reach.

I know every inch of Amara's body, yet I am still stunned in awe at how beautiful she is. Droplets round her full breasts and continue to roll over her taut abdomen and down to her—

Holy shit.

I spent hours mapping out every curve. I would commit every sensitive spot to memory. The sound she would make when I sucked on her *there* drove me wild and made me instantly hard.

Spit fills my mouth at the thought of everything I want to do to her, and I clamp my lips shut, swallowing my desire down with the lump in my throat.

Amara stumbles and grabs for the towel, snapping me out of my daze. She wraps it around her, hiding what's mine.

I forget myself.

"You won't hide yourself from me. Take it off." My low, demanding growl surprises both of us.

She lifts her hands to the towel and slowly untucks it. She obeys me, and my head swirls with need and possession.

My eyes travel to the shower, to the place I stood last night, gripping the wall and jacking off to the thought of her taking all of me.

"Fuck." I'm not sure if I cursed out loud.

Last night's release is a distant memory. My tension is back, and it's choking the air out of the room.

"Wait." I pull a second towel from the rack and cover her. "I mean—I shouldn't have barged in. I thought Cole was here."

Tilting her head to the side, she looks like she doesn't believe me.

As soon as I say the words, I know what happened.

That meddling little—

"I'll see you downstairs." I turn and leave Amara in the room, watching me with wide eyes.

I make my way back to the dining room in record time to find Henry finishing up his meal and a guilty-looking Sloane, who refuses to look me in the eye.

Circling the table, I stalk over to my seat and plant myself in front of her, waiting for her to look up, but she doesn't.

After an awkward minute, I break the silence. "You said Cole was in the shower."

While I wait for her reply, I take a long sip of my coffee. There is not enough caffeine in the world for this shit today.

She looks at me quizzically. "Did I?" She tilts her head to feign ignorance. I don't respond. Instead, I let her dig her own grave. "Oops, sorry. I meant Amara is in the shower and Cole *called* earlier. He wants you to call him back. I must have gotten that mixed up."

"Sloane," I warn, shaking my head.

This is a very dangerous game she's playing, and she knows it. She knows what's at stake.

Henry giggles, and I smile at him before leaving Sloane in the dining room with him once again. It isn't lost on me that not only did she send me up to see Amara, she also didn't answer my question about what they spoke about last night.

I walk across the main area and into the office, shutting the door behind me before making myself comfortable in one of the leather chairs and returning Cole's call.

He picks up on the third ring.

"Hey, man. I finished looking into your girl. I know I'll see you on Saturday, but Dagen tells me you're bringing a date, so I might not get the chance to talk to you." I imagine the smirk in his tone.

Of course Dagen told him I was taking Amara. My brothers gossip worse than my mother and her friends during tea.

"Did Dagen tell you why I'm bringing her?" I want to make sure that they don't let it slip that it's Amara who's with me. I need Lennox and everyone else to think it's Sloane to keep our charade up.

"Your secret is safe with me. Anyway, I thought you'd want to hear this sooner rather than later. I know how impatient you can be."

"Fuck off."

He chuckles. "This is too easy."

"Tell me what you've got." I'm not normally this impatient, but there's something about Amara that makes me want to know everything.

"Her life was simple yet regimented. She went to work, she went home. Once a week, on Wednesdays, she attended a yoga class for an hour and a half around the block from where she lived. When she was at home, she watched a lot of cooking and travel channels. Amara never had a long-term boyfriend, or at least one I could find, and she pretty much kept a strict yet boring schedule—um, with one exception."

He slows his words at the end of his sentence. I wish he were giving me this information face-to-face so I could strangle him for drawing it out.

"What's the exception?"

Another pause, then a sigh. "Well, it turns out your little hellcat attended a BDSM club in Portland once a month."

I don't think I heard him right.

"Eros?" I ask through teeth clenched so tight my jaw aches. Eros has a sister club in Portland.

"No. It wasn't one of ours, which makes me wonder if she purposefully went to one that would be off your radar. I mean, Eros has the best reputation among those in the lifestyle—"

I cut him off. "Give me a second."

The line goes quiet, and I'm left to deal with the screaming in my own head.

Amara knew what Eros was.

She attended a BDSM club on a monthly basis.

Did she play?

Does she have a partner?

Something deep inside me snaps at the thought.

"Continue." I need to know everything.

"It's not one of our clubs, but I have a connection. One of the guys who works there has been asking about a job at Eros, and I did a little trade. A job for information. It turns out she attended as a member, and she has a sheet." My heart sinks into my stomach. If she filled out a sheet, she shared her limits, which means she was exploring her boundaries—without me.

"What was on it?" My eyes sting as I ask the question, and I clear my throat to calm the pounding behind my eyes.

A piece of paper rustles on the other end of the line, and I wonder if Cole is looking at her handwriting now. Can he see all of her sins on the page in front of him?

"Amara always requested a different Dominant." My fingers tighten around my phone as I imagine them taking what belongs to me—many "thems," apparently. "She never saw the same person twice, even though many of them sent requests through the club to play with her again."

My mind wanders back to the night of her CEO's going away party, when she told me she had slept with many men, and I'm angry all over again as Cole continues talking. "That isn't even the odd part. She had strict rules in her file about aftercare. Specifically, she was adamant she did not want any."

"What?"

"She listed aftercare as a hard limit." Cole sounds as confused by this discovery as I am.

I've never heard of anyone denying themselves the care they should have after they scene, and I can't believe a club wouldn't question this.

I tell Cole to repeat everything he just told me.

As he rereads her file, I think about the night I punished her for disobeying me. She gave the impression she wanted to feel my comfort once it was over, but she pulled away suddenly before asking to be excused, and I let her go.

She didn't just deny herself aftercare.

She denied me the opportunity to provide aftercare.

Amara sought out that club in Portland to fill a need. That's why we all go.

What we deny ourselves is just as telling as what we allow.

She chose a club my family does not own to keep her secrets hidden from me, and she did that because she knew this was something I would use against her to make her mine.

And I intend to.

But first, I'll find out exactly why she won't allow herself support after a scene, and I'll do it at the club this weekend.

19

AMARA

After the shower incident a couple of days ago, I've taken extra precautions to make sure the bathroom door is locked when I'm in it.

I'd gotten used to being the only one in my apartment, and my mistake can't happen again.

Ryder's eyes exploring my naked body while I stood there, too stunned to move as I slipped into a past that welcomed me back with open arms, still makes me shudder two days later.

Even after I wrapped the towel around me, I felt like I had nothing on. The way he devoured me with his eyes left no doubt between us. His hunger was written all over his face.

Then I put the towel on, and everything tilted on its axis. Everything shifted when he told me to remove the towel and I did so without thought or hesitation.

I responded to him, and my capitulation was instinctual. My stomach knotted on itself, and I clenched my thighs together to ease the building tension I couldn't control.

So that is why I'm checking the door for the seventh time in half an hour to make sure it is locked.

A black box with a red satin ribbon arrived for me earlier today, and I haven't opened it yet. It's sitting on my bed like a Christmas present, and I have the same jitters I used to get when Grayson and I would unwrap our gifts around the tree.

I shouldn't entertain these desires, not with Ryder. My level of anticipation will only be matched by the sting of disappointment, and I wonder for a naive moment if the flight is worth the fall.

My soft robe hangs by the door, and I slide it on, making sure it is wrapped and tied securely around me before leaving the bathroom to walk to my room.

Glancing to the left, I see Ryder's door wide open, and he doesn't appear to be inside. I haven't seen Sloane since dinner.

I breathe a deep sigh of relief.

The last couple of days have been uneventful. While Ryder never left me alone with Sloane again, I haven't seen much of either of them around the house outside of our dinners, which have been pleasant. Ryder sticks to work topics, and Sloane keeps asking me if I'm settling in well. She looks like she wants to say more, but she doesn't. Instead, she steals a glance at Ryder, who often changes the subject without acknowledging her obvious discomfort.

I use the time to watch Henry. He feeds himself, and I've learned he doesn't like his vegetables, so we make faces at each other when Ryder and Sloane aren't looking. Then we giggle while we eat them down.

Henry is innocent in all of this. Whatever our situation is, I won't attach him to it.

I rather like him.

The box is sitting where I first found it, in the middle of my bed.

I drop my clothes in the laundry and plug in my flat iron.

Ryder asked me to straighten my hair tonight, and I like the look, so I tell myself I'm doing it because I want to.

I pull open the top dresser drawer, pushing aside my cotton panties for the little black lace ones at the back with the matching bra. I'm going to a sex club; I'm sure my mismatched, generic bra and underwear isn't going to cut it.

Speaking of "it," I'm putting this off. I'm stalling because my fear is battling with my curiosity, and it's culminating in one giant stomachache. I should get it over with before I make myself nauseous.

I take the sexiest underwear I own and return to the bed, dropping them beside the box before tugging at a loose end on the ribbon, and the bow falls away.

Lifting the lid, I audibly gasp in surprise as a face looks up at me from the tissue.

The masquerade mask won't just cover my eyes. It will conceal most of my face, and I'm relieved.

I know I hide pieces of myself away. It's a comfort to know people don't really see me. I feel like I can't lose any more pieces of me if no one can find them to begin with.

My anxiety settles a fraction as I lift the mask to examine it more closely. It's made of a lightweight material, so I shouldn't have any problems breathing through the silvery mesh.

There is no doubt in my mind who chose my outfit tonight.

Half of the face is accentuated with rose gold flower petals. Although they're made of metal, they grow seamlessly out of the mask and blend in. The rest of the mask gives me pause. A silvery white butterfly wing spans the other half of my face, with my eye nestled in between the top and bottom of the wing.

My fingers tremble as I run them along the indents and ridges.

No one will know it's me.

Carefully setting down the mask, I return my attention to the box, lifting the black fabric up and letting it flow open in front of me. The silk wraps around my fingers, caressing my skin.

It's a full-length piece, but I wouldn't call it a gown. It looks like something a virgin would wear if she were about to be sacrificed in some kind of erotic ritual for the king of demons.

I snort as I realize I'm probably not far off the mark...except for the virgin part.

I haven't put this on yet, but I already know I've never worn anything this sultry. Even the outfits I wore to the club back home paled in comparison to this.

I drop the fabric on the bed, and my hands are on the belt of my robe before I remember my surroundings.

I hurry to the door, lock it, then unlock it and lock it once more, just to make sure, before returning to the bed. But it isn't the dress I pick up.

The mask fits like it was designed for the shape and size of my head. I walk to the full-length mirror and look at myself, tilting my head to the side and waving just so I know for sure I'm still in here.

My hand drops to my belt once more. I'm alone now. Pulling the tie loose, my robe opens, revealing a three-inch gap where I can see myself, but it isn't enough.

Sliding the fabric off my shoulders, I let it fall to the floor, and I stand staring at the woman I've missed. She may have a mask on, but she's more real than I've felt in a long time.

I trail my fingers along the path Ryder's eyes took when he found me naked in the bathroom.

The woman staring back at me is bold. She's strong, and she knows what she wants.

My fingers circle around my breast before pinching my nipple until the bite of pleasure makes me wince.

Under this mask, I can be anyone, and I desperately want to be myself. I want to be that girl who was abandoned. I want her to have the happily ever after she deserves, but I won't risk hurting her again.

I turn and kick away my robe and step up to the bed. Sliding on my own lace panties and bra, I open the top of the dress and step into it, pulling it up my body and pushing my arms through the open top.

I know my bra is noticeable without needing to look at myself in the mirror, but I do anyway. The dark fabric circles my neck and hangs over my chest, leaving the back entirely open. I follow the line of two inches of exposed flesh that reaches from my neck down the middle of my breasts and all the way to the waist of the dress.

This won't do. I reach my arms around to my back and unclasp my bra, pulling it down my arms and tossing it on the bed.

Thankfully, the material is opaque enough that you can't see through it unless you are up close in a bright room, which we definitely won't be once we get to Eros.

I've never been in their club before, but if it is anything like the club I went to in Portland, it will be dark and private.

Two slits run the entire length of the dress from the floor to my hips, and I have to tug the sides of my lace panties up half an inch to keep them hidden. I'm satisfied with the way it looks because I really don't want to go anywhere with Ryder and without panties.

Together with the mask, the outfit is breathtaking. I feel like a goddess, and I haven't finished getting ready yet.

Pulling the mask off, I turn back to my dresser and plug in the hair dryer beside my flat iron. As I dry my hair, I steal glances at myself in the mirror.

I'm worried about the person looking back at me. I've

changed so much since I left her four years ago, and I don't want to go back to that dark place, yet I'm scared that I am doomed to end up there.

I've been dressed up, and I'm going to a sex club with Ryder. I don't know what to expect from tonight. I know his whole family will be there—with the exception of his mother, of course. The last time I saw them, I basically accused Ryder and his brothers of killing Grayson, and at least three of them didn't deserve it. But I'm positive one of them did.

Then there's Ryder. I need to stay in control tonight. Not of my surroundings, but of me. I can't allow myself to be pulled down in his undertow.

I reach out to touch a piece of the glass butterfly sitting near my bed. Grayson gave it to me for my birthday. As soon as I get my boxes from Portland, I will pull out my photos of the two of us and put them up all over this room. I miss having those reminders around to ground me.

Running my stray strands through the flat iron, I straighten my hair until it is shiny and soft. I unplug my dryer and iron and push them to the side to make way for my makeup. Opening my eye shadow palette, I go to the colors I usually overlook, as they are too bold for work. They are just right for tonight.

I choose a shimmery, smokey black for my eyelids then line my eyes with a jet-black liner before trying the mask on once again. The shade makes my eyes look fierce through the disguise.

I can do this.

My mouth is covered on one side by the butterfly wing and some jewels hang down on the other, so I choose a subtle lipstick to round out my look. I want Ryder looking at my eyes. I want him to know that I see him just as clearly as he sees me.

While I straightened my hair for Ryder, he didn't say I

couldn't do anything else to it, so I dig into my dresser and pull out a clip to pin it loosely at the back of my head and off my shoulders.

I scan the room for anything I might have forgotten.

There's no point in taking anything with me. I have nowhere on me to carry it, unless you count the little strap on my underwear. I leave my phone where it is on my dresser and open the door. The black heels I found beside my bed fit nicely, and they clack against the hall floor as I strut with purpose toward the stairs.

Ryder is the only one who knows how much my butterfly figurine means to me, and no one knows he calls me his flower. I know it was him who got me this mask and this outfit, and I'm sure he did it to try to throw me off balance.

He's been testing my control. I know he thinks I don't notice that he's been moving things around on me on purpose. He's been mentally circling me since he came back into my life, and he's closing in.

He got this outfit to assert his dominance, and I'm determined to make him regret it by the end of the night. The thought makes my stomach flutter with nervous energy. I hope this doesn't backfire. If it does, Ryder will take full advantage of the fallout.

20

RYDER

The delivery arrived for Amara just as dinner was finished. Sloane grabbed the package as I signed for it and ran upstairs to deliver it to Amara's room. Then she made herself scarce, and I think I know why.

After I saw Amara naked in my shower, I didn't trust myself to pick out a dress for her. I waffled between covering her all the way up and making her wear something entirely too slutty. There was no in-between.

This is what having Amara in my physical and mental space is doing to me.

Now I'm pacing between the dining room and the front hall, and my composure is crumbling. I'm second-guessing the decision I made to ask Sloane to pick out Amara's dress for me.

My mind is going crazy with thoughts of what Amara might look like, and Sloane wouldn't describe the outfit so I could prepare myself.

I did, however, design the mask she's going to wear, because I want to look at her tonight and see everything that belongs to me. I want to see all of her weaknesses and her strengths etched into the mask she is hiding herself behind.

The muted thud of the back door slamming catches my attention, and Henry's faint squeals of laughter echo down the hall. I should have known Sloane would take him outside to play. I take a step toward the voices when footsteps from upstairs stop me from going any further.

I turn my attention to the top of the staircase, and my brain short-circuits.

Sloane was right to hide from me. If she knows what's good for her, I won't see her until sometime next month.

Amara stands tall at the top of the stairs, looking down at me from behind her mask like the sexiest fucking angel I've ever seen.

I don't deserve her. But that's not going to stop me.

With one hand on the railing, she looks down on me in silence, and I can't tell whether she is smiling or not.

Her dress is the definition of seductive. It hugs her curves and flows over her hips all the way down to the ground in a waterfall of sleek fabric.

She descends the stairs, her naked legs making an appearance with each step, and I feel the sudden need to have her as close to me as possible. I want to climb the stairs and meet her halfway, but my legs won't cooperate. Unfortunately for me, my dick is fully on board, and if I don't adjust myself soon he'll start pointing the way to her.

Passing the middle of the staircase, the steps round to give me a full view of her body. Under the bright hall lights, I see everything, and I'm not talking about the dress. To stop my jaw from hitting the floor, I clench my teeth together until I hear vibrations from the tension thundering into my ears.

There is little room for the imagination from the waist up.

It looks like she only has a scarf draped around her neck and over her breasts, and she isn't able to wear a bra with the dress, which is unfortunate for the first asshole who gawks at her—other than me.

Her heels land on the floor a few feet away from me, and her hand comes to her midsection. I can't see her face, but the motion carries an aura of insecurity.

I take a step toward her. "Let me see you."

Her hands go to the bottom of her mask, and she lifts it off her face. I take it from her and set it on a table to the side. When I turn back to her, her intense eyes, which are surrounded by dark eyeshadow, draw me in.

I stare at her for a moment too long on purpose, and she sucks her bottom lip in, dragging her teeth along the plump flesh. My thoughts snap to a fantasy of her mouth wrapped around my cock.

Stepping into her space, I slide my hand around to the back of her neck, pulling her face close to my own and locking our gaze. "If you understood you were mine, I'd make you open those pretty lips for me. Then you'd suck on my fingers, making them wet before I fucked you with them to take the edge off before we left tonight." Her chest heaves with deeper breaths as she looks from my eyes to my lips then back again. "All you need to do is say the word, Blossom," I taunt her.

I know she won't give in easily. She's spent years fortifying her figurative armor. Finding my way back to her will take time, and, lucky for her, I am a very determined man.

But there is one thing I need to deal with before we leave tonight.

I tilt my head, bringing my lips to the shell of her ear, and her body shudders as I whisper, "Take off the panties."

I hold open my free hand, waiting for her obedience.

When I pull my head back to look at her, she doesn't make eye contact, but she does listen to me. Still in my hold, she slides her panties down her hips and leans forward. I loosen my grip, allowing her to shimmy out of them before she balls them up and places them in my palm as she rises.

I reward her by releasing her, and she drops her gaze and takes a step away.

I close the distance with a step of my own, dropping my head in an attempt to recover her attention, but she doesn't look up. Her chest and shoulders still rise and fall with prominent breaths, and I lift the hand holding her lace underwear to her face. I run my finger along her jawline and down her exposed neck, and I wonder if she can smell herself on the thin lace fabric she gave me.

The hint of a smile crosses my lips as I draw my free hand back up the length of her neck and around to the back of her head. I release the clip and let her hair fall down her back the way I requested it. Wrapping the clip in her underwear, I slide the items into my pocket.

She struggles to swallow, and I brush her hair off of her shoulders before I comb my fingers into her soft strands. I capture the back of her neck again and tilt her head up to make her look me in the eyes.

"I love seeing you like this." My voice is low, restrained, and dangerous.

Her cheeks blush, and her skin feels hot under my touch. "Like what?" Her lip quivers; her fear is endearing.

"Flushed, panting—and all mine, whether you're ready to admit it or not."

She shudders in my hold and shifts her weight from one foot to the other.

I smirk at her, letting her know that I know I got to her just now. Then I release her and straighten my suit. "There are rules you must follow tonight, Amara, and, for your sake, you would be wise to. I will remind you of where we are going. I have no problem with punishing you in public." Her eyes dart quickly from me to the floor, and surprise catches me off guard at her response, but I keep my expression firm. By the look on her face, this may be something she wouldn't consider a punishment under different circumstances, so I add to my threat: "In front of my father and brothers."

Yup, there's the look of horror I was hoping for. Now we are back on the same page.

"No one uses names at the club to protect those who wish to remain anonymous. You are to call me Sir." Amara's eyebrows crease together, and she opens her mouth to object, but I keep speaking. "It's Sir or Master. The latter will tell me you wish to challenge my authority, and you should think long and hard before you use that title." I pause only long enough to tell she has decided not to fight me on this, and I move on to the next one. "The second rule is that submissives are to keep their masks on. Most Dominants will as well, but it is a choice for us. It is mandatory for you."

"I'm no submissive." She straightens, adding an inch to her height as she glares at me, and a muscle in my cheek twitches at her defiance.

"You will not lie to me. I know exactly who and what you are. Don't force me to show you what we both know is true. Want to try that again?" I hold her attention as I speak, and with each word her face falls a little more until she sheepishly shakes her head, backing down.

There's my good girl.

"The last rule is: you are only permitted to talk to me once I grant you permission. You will be given a collar in a color that will indicate you are spoken for and not to be approached by anyone. If someone speaks to you, you will defer to me for an answer, no matter how badly you want to respond. Do you understand all of these rules?"

"Yes," she answers with a snarl on her lips.

"Yes what?"

"Yes, I understand the rules, Sir." I'm not sure how she did it, but she just made "Sir" sound an awful lot like "asshole." I decide not to push it, as I have more than enough ammunition to work with tonight.

"Good. The car is out front. Wait for me inside." I step to the side to allow her to pass. As she reaches the door, I think better of my instructions and add an amendment: "In the passenger seat, Amara."

Knowing her, I'd end up finding her ready to drive me to the club.

Amara lowers her head and opens the door, letting a gust of cold wind into the room. The shocking change in temperature hits her, and she walks down the stairs to the waiting vehicle at a steady pace, her ass swaying from side to side with each step. I'm momentarily thankful I didn't ask Nash to drive us tonight. I would have had to fire him for laying eyes on her.

Once I hear the car door close, I cross my arms and speak loudly into the room.

"You can come out now."

I wait for a few seconds before soft footsteps fall behind me, and I turn to see Sloane smiling. It isn't lost on me she won't come any closer than two steps into the room.

We stare each other down before she asks, "So? What did you think of the dress?" She swings her arms and rocks back on her heels, trying to make herself look more innocent than we both know she is.

"Are you fucking kidding me?" I raise my voice. "I can see right through the fabric." I shove my hands into my pockets to keep myself from walking over and strangling Sloane. My fingers wrap around Amara's lace panties as I ball my hands into fists. The reminder of her fully naked under that little dress makes me horny and angry all over again.

Why did I ask her to take these off? What the hell was I thinking?

"Relax. You know it's dark in there, and it's nighttime. No one will see anything you don't want them to." She shoots me a sly wink, and I shake my head.

"I don't know if this is a good idea anymore. We're risking a lot, and this"—I point toward the car—"could ruin everything."

Her face softens, and she comes a few steps closer to me. "We all lost so much when Grayson died. Whoever is responsible will pay. I just don't want anyone to suffer more than they already have—and that includes you and Amara."

"Fuck, Sloane. I know your heart is in the right place, but one wrong mistake could put more bodies in the ground. That includes mine and Amara's, and—" I glance over her shoulder toward the back of the house, and she turns to follow my train of thought. She knows I'm talking about Henry.

When she looks back, she pinches her lips together and nods in agreement.

I know what our family is capable of when we are crossed. What I don't know is what we are capable of when it is done by one of our own.

"I just wanted—"

"I know."

I won't tell her she's right or wrong in the choices she makes. That is up to her. I will only admit to myself that I finally feel like I'm in my place. I feel like I'm at my best, my strongest, when I have Amara with me, but I don't know what new hell this will bring to our doorstep.

First, we have a few things to work out. Then, depending on what goes down over the next week, and what information Cole is able to find out about Grayson's murder, I may be able to bring Amara into our plan. I can only hope doing so won't risk the lives the people who are relying on me.

21

AMARA

My nipples swelled against the sheer fabric of my dress as Ryder opened the passenger door and helped me step into the alley in front of Eros.

Before we entered the club, Ryder rounded on me, pulling a black leather collar out of nowhere. For a moment, I was sure his fingers were trembling as he locked the clasp around my neck, but I shook off the thought. I'm sure it was me who was doing all of the shaking.

The grip from the collar and the pressure building in my pebbled nipples from the cold added a level of sensitivity I wasn't prepared for. My stomach clenched, and a wetness pooled in my core, slicking the tops of my thighs as they slid against each other with each step.

Saying Eros is the best sex club in the city is an understatement. The word "impeccable" doesn't do it justice.

Even with the dim lights, the place reeks of luxury. Judging by the lack of a line outside and the clientele sitting casually around the main room, this is a VIP-member-only event.

The man behind the bar smiles at us as we approach. Ryder

rests his hand on the skin at my lower back as he pulls me in with him while he orders two drinks, and I watch the gentleman beside me taking his order away without any exchange of money.

The bartender pours Ryder's drink close to me, and the heavy spice smell reminds me of the drink his dad used to make when he had mine over. The scent fills my nostrils, and the tickle of tears stings my eyes. I imagine it would burn going down.

He places a wineglass in front of me and watches as I reach out to take it, smiling my thanks.

I know I'm allowed to ask to speak to him, but I don't want to take advantage of the privilege. I don't really care about the formalities, but I do care about disrespecting Ryder in front of his peers. I know his family and associates have their limits, and I don't want to test any of them—especially not here, wearing a see-through dress with nothing on underneath.

"One drink only. Make it last." Ryder lowers his voice and turns me away without paying. I pause, looking between him and the bartender for a moment too long, stopping Ryder in his tracks. "You want to say something."

I shake my head, and Ryder furrows his brows in displeasure before someone catches his attention. I follow his line of sight across the room to where Ryder's father is standing with a group of men. Ryder lifts his glass in cheers, and his father returns the gesture before turning his back to us and returning to the men standing around him.

As I scan the rest of the room, I notice most of the men don't have their masks on, but the women do. There are only two women I notice without, and, judging by the stance and dress of one of them, I would guess she is a Domme.

"Say what's on your mind, Amara. We all know what happens when you hold things in."

"I just noticed no one is paying for their drinks."

He takes me in with a quizzical expression. "You're standing in the middle of a sex club, wearing my collar, and I have your panties in my pocket, and *this* is the question you have?"

I blink at him a few times.

There were probably better questions.

"Well, now that you made me say it out loud..." My voice trails off, washed away with my embarrassment.

He considers me for a moment longer before he breaks the stern grimace on his face and chuckles at my expense.

I grimace.

The motion eases some of my anxiety, and my muscles relax as my attention wanders over Ryder's shoulder and lands on a man standing in the corner. His body is squared in our direction, and it is too dark to tell, but a shiver runs up my spine as though he's looking right through me.

A moment later, a club light shines across his face.

It's Lennox, Ryder's oldest brother, and he is glaring at us.

No. He's glaring at me.

My skin prickles in agitation, and Ryder's voice pulls me back to the present.

"Tonight's event is exclusive. The price of membership for elite access covers the drinks and the tips."

I nod. I know this isn't the time to have a conversation with Ryder, and I'm done asking stupid questions for a while.

"There they are." Ryder nudges me, and I turn toward the area he's looking at. With his hand at my back, he guides me across the room. Like most of the others, these men aren't wearing masks. They are all set down on the table and the seats beside them. The first person I recognize is Dagen, and I'm sure I don't know any of the other men with him.

If I thought the Saint family wasn't to be crossed, I'm sure this new group of guys with them are capable of making someone disappear in broad daylight. The smiles on their faces contradict the warning bells, and I take a second look at Ryder and Dagen.

Have I always assumed the Saint brothers are not as scary as the men sitting around the table with them because I grew up with them? The question sends shivers down my spine.

"Gentlemen." Ryder greets the table as a collective, and they all give him their attention as he turns to take a seat on the couch. The men return to their conversation.

I guess introductions are out since we can't call anyone by their name.

I feel awkward standing at the table while everyone is seated. There's a small space beside Ryder on the couch, and I take a step toward him when his hand touches my leg. His gaze captures mine as he curtly shifts his head to the left, telling me no without drawing attention. The sensation makes me still, and he draws his finger in a line up my calf, around the back of my knee, and circles my inner thigh.

He extends his hand to me, and I take it, then he tugs me down to the floor. It's now I notice there is a cushion at his feet, and I am meant to sit on it.

When I attended the club in Portland, I was never there as someone's submissive, so I don't know the etiquette. I only showed up for sessions. My times were scheduled, and I never hung around the mingling area.

My body rebels for a moment, and I scan the faces of the other men at the table. Only Ryder and Dagen are watching me. Dagen leans back in his seat, crossing his ankle over his knee as he watches us with great interest and a smirk on his face.

Had I been the only one kneeling, I might have made a different choice, but there are a couple of other women seated on cushions around the table, and I don't want to disrespect anyone here. I decide not to give Dagen the show he's looking for, and I follow Ryder's pull down to the cushion, tucking my legs under me and leaning myself against the couch.

With one hand, I pull the beads that hang down from my mask and over my mouth out of the way so I can take a sip of my wine.

"It's nice to see you here with someone." One of the men tilts his glass in my direction, and Ryder's hand settles on my shoulder. I keep my eyes cast down and smile into my drink.

Knowing Ryder either doesn't come here or shows up alone makes me happier than it should. I shouldn't care, but the quirk of my lips tells me I do.

Ryder doesn't answer the question, but he does massage the muscles at the base of my neck.

Another man chimes in, pointing at Dagen. "Now it's only this one we've never seen in here with anyone." The men all chuckle, and I steal a glance at Ryder's brother while Ryder answers.

Like Lennox, Dagen is a bit of a mystery to me, and I get the sense he knows a lot more about my life than I'll ever be told about his.

"Ah, my brother will be forever pining for the one that got away." Ryder captures everyone's attention. "Literally. She got away from him, and he hasn't been able to find her." Everyone laughs but Dagen, who motions to a waitress and orders another drink.

"They let anyone in here these days." My head whips around at the familiar voice, and I look up to see Cole standing over me. The men stand to shake his hand, and I get the impression that Cole is closer to these unknown men than Ryder is.

I turn my attention to the floor before I make eye contact

with Cole. I'm not ready to face him after what happened between us at their family dinner.

"Well, anyone with a hundred grand," the man beside Ryder answers. I choke on my gulp of wine at the price tag and cough to clear my throat.

My choking catches Cole's attention, and he looks down with a sly smile before crouching to look at me eye to eye. Ryder's hand tenses at the back of my neck.

"My, my, my. Don't you look good enough to—eat." His eyes flick to Ryder before returning to my own. "Don't worry, Sunshine. I know your master doesn't like to share." He lowers his voice to a whisper. "But I sure wish he did." Cole blatantly licks his lips and winks.

This is a side of Cole I've never seen before. He's always seemed confident, but I'd always looked at him like a second brother.

When he rises to take a seat on the couch across from Ryder, I breathe a deep sigh of relief.

Cole addresses the men around the table, but his eyes remain on me. "Guys, this is a friend of mine who came to check the club out."

The man with Cole shakes hands around the table without sharing his name. Then he takes a seat beside Cole.

When I finally see him, I realize no introductions are needed.

I know him. And he knows me.

Sitting across from me is one of the Dominants from the club I used to frequent. I saw him around the club often, but I only met him once, during one of my sessions.

My hand instantly flies up to my face to conceal my identity. When my fingers hit my disguise, I remember I'm wearing a mask.

My momentary feeling of relief is shattered when I return

to the conversation to see everyone talking intently except for Ryder and his brothers. All three of them are sitting quietly, staring at me in their own way.

They were waiting for my reaction, and I gave it to them.

My stomach sinks. They already know my secret.

I take a larger gulp of my wine while Ryder traces his fingers over my exposed skin. How can his touch be so gentle yet threatening?

The smug look on Cole's face tells me I walked right into whatever trap they laid. Dagen has started up a conversation with the Dom from my old club, and Ryder is waving down the waitress, his hand still on me.

I hope I'm getting more wine.

Cole taps his buddy on the shoulder and tells him he'll show him around, and they leave. The conversation around the table shifts to business. The other two women seated on cushions grow tired quickly, and they start talking quietly among themselves.

I guess their rules aren't the same as mine.

I keep my attention focused on the conversation, but I divert my gaze so I don't make it obvious I am eavesdropping. It sounds as though the men with Dagen are looking for someone, but I don't know who or why. Ryder and Dagen both offer to help in any way they can. By the sounds of the words being thrown around, I get the impression they are doing some kind of business deal, but I can't be sure.

Out of nowhere, a hand reaches across my line of sight, startling me. The waitress is back, and she's handing something to Ryder. Ryder finishes his drink and sets his glass on the table.

I try to follow his lead and drain my wine, but Ryder is too fast, and my glass is out of my hands before I get the chance. Then Ryder circles his fingers around my upper arm and helps me to stand.

Excusing us from the group, he leads me away, and I steal a glance over my shoulder. The men are watching us with approving smiles, and I catch a quick wink from Dagen as he wiggles his fingers at me to wave goodbye.

Ryder releases his hold on me and steps in front to lead me across the room, trusting I'll go with him, and I do.

Keeping my head angled down, I follow the outline of Ryder's firm body. His lithe, muscular build is evident even through his suit jacket. The music thrums on, and conversation flows all around us as we pass the bar and continue deeper into the club.

The room narrows into a hallway, and the sound gets quieter the farther away we get from the main room. When Ryder stops suddenly, I'm consumed with thoughts and curiosity, and I don't catch myself in time. I walk into his back and he turns, eyeing me suspiciously as he pulls something out of his pocket.

Returning to the door, he slips a key in the lock and opens it before ushering me inside.

The door is closed before my brain catches up, and I take in all of the items around the room as the rest of the sound is blocked out.

"What's this?" I spin around to face Ryder.

He tsks me before saying, "I told you: no speaking unless I allow it, Amara." Circling me, he loosens the tie around his neck and slides off his jacket. His dark shirt stretches tight across his upper body, and the outline of his muscles makes my mouth go dry. I almost miss his next words: "Why is it always the simple rules you have trouble following?"

He walks past me toward some of the furniture placed around the room—except it's no normal furniture. Benches, chains, tables, and a cross are some of the unique pieces spread all over.

His hand glides along a table that has leather restraints at all corners, and I shuffle in place to find a comfortable stance.

"You know what this is, Amara. You've seen one before," he challenges me.

"I don't know what you're talking about." Internally, I'm retreating. I'm mentally making a run for it.

That little voice in my head—the one that always seems to keep me safe—is screaming at me to get the hell out of here, but my heart won't let my feet take the first step.

"Do you deny you know what this room is? Are you really going to lie to my face?"

He knows. Without a doubt, he knows.

I backpedal. "I meant to ask, why did you bring me in here?"

His grin turns wicked.

Lowering his head, his eyes zero in on me, and I feel like feeble prey caught in his sights.

"But that's not what you said. So answer my question before asking another, Blossom."

I cross my arms in front of me in defiance. I'm not a scared little girl. I haven't been for a long time.

"No, I don't deny it."

A fresh wave of control covers his features as his smile softens at my admission.

"Good girl. Now, to answer your question, I brought you in here because you and I are about to go through some things, and we need to work our shit out. Now take off your mask."

My heart hammers into my rib cage at the authority in his tone, and I respond in surrender as I pull the mask off my face. The cool air hits me, and I take a refreshing breath as I set it on the table, glancing around for the mirrors.

There are none.

The rooms in the club back in Portland all had mirrors. I

would watch myself during those sessions. I was able to keep my focus on me, as though I was watching from afar. Here, I am forced to live any experience Ryder wishes me to have.

The other difference is the lights. Ryder hasn't turned them down. His eyes are on me, and he can see everything, including every expression I make as well as every movement my body makes.

Lowering my gaze, I see the dark circles of my areolas peek through the see-through fabric.

Ryder takes advantage of me staring at my own tits, and I look up a second too late. He's already in my space.

"I won't fuck you." I step back and blurt the first thought I have, and he regards me like I'm a cute puppy.

"No, *I* won't fuck *you*...or play with you. Not tonight. No matter how much *you* beg *me* to." His arrogance stuns me, and I open my mouth to deliver a comeback, but I have nothing, so he continues, "It's been brought to my attention that we have a lot to talk about, and I have a feeling this is going to be painful for you. So I will allow you to ask the first question."

22

RYDER

Seeing Amara distressed like this sends a wave of gratification surging through my veins. She has no idea what to expect, which makes her vulnerable, and that's just how I like it.

She squints as she tilts her head to look up at me. The contrast of the bright lights against all the sins a dim room would hide away brings a restrained chaos to our space.

I really do want to fuck her tonight. I've wanted her ever since she refused to shake my hand in her conference room.

For now, I'll settle with the confirmation that she knows I know her dirty little secrets.

I've been a tempest of conflicted emotions since finding out she frequented a sex club, and I'm not sure which one to entertain at this moment, so I let her ask the first question.

She doesn't disappoint me. She always wears her heart on her sleeve. Her eyes lower to my chest as she considers what she wants to ask me. The question she chooses will be telling, and the anticipation is eating away at my patience.

"Why are you marrying Sloane?" She hears herself ask the

question at the same time I do, and she cringes. She knows she sounds hurt, and she startles, then tries to recover. "I mean, Grayson loved her, and...I thought you were friends."

My chest aches with regret. I don't want to cause her this pain, but this is a question I can't answer in its entirety.

"There is a child involved, and I made a promise that I would take care of both of them no matter what." My answer isn't a lie so much as it is a play on words.

Amara's eyebrows crease together, and she takes a slow breath as she processes my words before hanging her head in resignation.

I know what assumptions she's making. She thinks Henry is mine and the promise I made was to Sloane.

Everyone, including Amara, will remain safe if she believes this is true.

Now it's my turn.

"Take a seat, Amara." I point to the bondage chair, and she turns her attention toward it.

The heavy chair has leather-covered armrests and a tall back. It is comfortable to sit in, but it is clear by the placement of the bindings that one's legs will be spread open.

Her face falls, and I know by her expression that she understands what it is as soon as she sees it. She haltingly shakes her head. The gesture is inconspicuous, almost as though she's telling herself no. I step toward her until all of the space between us is gone and hook my finger around her strands to draw her hair off her shoulder.

She shudders, and goosebumps cover her arms.

I offer a sliver of mercy. "I've already told you I won't fuck you. The door is locked, and there are no cameras in this room." I bow my head. The smell of her fills my nostrils as I whisper into her ear, "Take a seat and let me bind you to it—or tell me what you're afraid of."

My challenge hits her, and she swivels her head. Her glare burns into me.

I've hit a nerve.

She straightens, pulling her shoulders back in defiance, and I stifle a smile.

Good.

I want her to sit her ass down and let me do what I've wanted.

She takes a few steps across the room. The thin fabric of her dress caresses her curves every step of the way.

Turning to face me, she lowers herself into the seat, and her stare remains set on me as I approach.

Lowering myself to one knee in front of her, I rest my palm on her leg. She startles at my contact but keeps silent. Her skin is warm to the touch, and her gaze pierces my own. Her luminous eyes look fierce framed by the dark color on her lids. But that isn't what holds my soul still for a moment while I appreciate her.

The warmth of her skin and the heat from her mask have taken their toll on her makeup. Smudges appear on her face, and they only add to her beauty.

I want to wreck the perfect image of her, smear that shade down her cheeks. I want to see her tears trail dark lines down her face and neck.

Wrapped up in my fantasy, I reach my fingers up and draw a line down the side of her throat where I want her tears to fall for me.

If I'm not careful, my control will snap.

I turn my attention to her clasped hands in her lap. I separate her fingers, lifting one arm onto the chair and binding her just above her wrist, allowing her hands to dangle off the ends. I repeat the process on the other side before moving to her legs.

She inhales audibly when my fingers wrap around her thigh, and I guide her leg open to the side. Her dress dips between her spread legs at the slits. I keep working to secure her thigh with a leather bind, but I steal a glance at her core. The outline of her pussy peeks through, and I swallow hard, fighting to retain control over my own fracturing restraint. I want to bury every bit of myself inside of her and make all of this shit disappear for the both of us.

Feeling the pain of what I'm denying us both is a reminder that it would be worse for everyone if we gave in to our desires, and I shift my focus to binding her calves just above the heels that make her legs look amazing.

After both legs are secure, I stand, hovering over her.

"I see you, Blossom. All of you." My voice sounds loud against the quietude lingering in the room around us, and Amara drops her head, looking down her front.

The trimmed patch of hair between her legs is noticeable through the fabric, and her legs jerk in their restraints as she notices what I see under the bright lights.

Stepping beside her, I wrap my hands around her shoulders, guiding her upper body back toward the headrest. When she slips into position, I brush her hair to the side and attach a clip from the chair to the back of her collar.

As I step away, she tries to look down again, but the clip at her neck keeps her sitting up straight, making it uncomfortable to look anywhere I don't want her to.

She has to look at me.

I return to the place between her legs and look down at her, examining her in silence as she watches me. I don't bother to hide my thoughts, leaving a look of pure lust on my face. I want her to imagine what we could be doing now, because those thoughts are driving me to the point of insanity.

I want to haunt her thoughts. I want her to feel what I feel.

I need to be the one she can't get out of her head, because it hurts to have her in mine like I do. I want her to masturbate in the shower at one o'clock in the morning to thoughts of me because she can't sleep.

Her labored breaths draw my attention to her hardened nipples. As though she can physically feel my eyes on her, she slouches inwardly to hide her chest as best as she can, but it doesn't work.

To heighten her discomfort, I kneel between her legs, my eyes level with her round breasts as her hardened nipples pebble further under my stare, and I smile at her.

It isn't a kind smile. It's hungry, piercing, and triumphant.

We both know where this will lead. It won't be tonight, it might not be soon, but it was always our destiny. There is no place, no time, no one who would take us off the collision course designed for us.

But first, I want answers.

I rise and step back from her to ask my first question. "Why is aftercare a hard limit for you?"

Everything soft about Amara tenses. The heat between us cools, and she balls her hands into fists, testing the security of her ties. She's not going anywhere.

"You have no right to invade my privacy."

"I have every right." My voice is angrier than I would have liked, and I rein myself in. "Especially since I think it's because of me."

"It isn't."

I could almost believe the anger in her voice, but she isn't looking me in the eyes as she says the words.

"I'll remind you not to lie to me." I punctuate my words with the threat I intend for them to have.

Her mouth snaps shut, but she'll give me her answers in another way. I watch the expressions on her face wage war with each other. She knows this is a test—a trap of sorts. She knows if she doesn't answer, it is the same thing as confirmation in my eyes, and my grin turns wolfish.

After a moment, she tries to change the subject. "So you're stalking me?"

She has no idea the dark path she's straying a little too far down.

"No." I rise and step close to her so I am above her once again. "Stalking implies you don't want my attention. But I know you do. You crave the way I touch you. You need the dirty things I used to do to you. The only thing I can't figure out is why you don't accept aftercare and why you insist on a different Dominant every time." Her eyes go wide, and I pause. I'm onto something, and she knows it. I sense her fear like a predator smells blood. "Unless—"

"You don't know any—" The fear in her voice tells me I'm close, and I raise my hand, silencing her.

I start to ponder out loud. "Is it a punishment? Is denying yourself aftercare a way of punishing yourself?"

She doesn't respond, but her eyes hold my own. That isn't it, but she's hoping I will think it is.

I muse out loud, "No. It's not that. At least not entirely." She continues to watch me as I assess her reactions. "Unless it's the care itself." One look at the worry on her face, and the answer hits me. "It's the connection, isn't it? A different Dominant and no aftercare means you don't surrender control. If you don't fully submit, then you don't allow anyone to have all of you."

Amara's bright eyes turn glossy with the tears she's trying to hold back. She won't even blink, knowing they'll spill out and confirm my suspicion, revealing her truth.

Her lips part as she releases a steady breath, and I realize she's been controlling herself. My gaze drops to her hands, fisted and trembling. I return to my knees in between her legs, gently twisting her arm and turning one palm up to pry open her hand. I brush my hand over her fingers, opening them to the deep red indents on her tender flesh. I open her other hand before directing a warning look at her not to close them.

"You said you wouldn't touch me." She chokes on her words. Her anger catches me by surprise, and I match her anger with a frustration of my own.

"I said I wouldn't fuck you and I wouldn't play with you. There's a difference." I wrap my hands around hers, holding her back from creating her own pain to offset the suffering we need to go through. "I'm not playing, Amara. I promise you, I'm going to break you down, and you'll give me all of that control you desperately try to cling to."

We've been waiting to combust since the moment we saw each other again after all of our time apart. All of this tension between us is threatening to ignite.

"That ship has sailed," she growls through gritted teeth. Her fingers dig into my hand, allowing me to feel the pain she inflicts on herself, and I clench my teeth to stop myself from showing any indication that it hurts.

I hold her hands tighter, pulling her attention to my next words as I get in her face. "No. That ship is lost at sea and searching for its home."

Her first tear falls, and I take a moment to admire her.

Amara is beautiful when she's strong and feisty, but she is breathtaking in those rare moments when she lowers her defenses.

I've allowed Amara to run away and regroup many times since she's been back, and that ends now.

This won't be the last tear she gives me tonight.

23

AMARA

A fat tear rolls over my cheek, and Ryder's irises break contact with mine to follow it down. There's nothing I can do about it, but I can hold the rest of them in.

"Let me show you the way back to where you belong." His vulnerable tone is a sharp change from the bitterness that charged between us a minute ago.

Ryder's proximity makes my heart pound into my chest. I shouldn't have come tonight. I should have set boundaries. And not because I don't want this—but because I do. His familiar scent scrambles my senses, and I tilt my head back toward the headrest to create a necessary space. Ryder fills it when he drops his head to my exposed neck. My body shudders as he takes a deep breath. His exhalation is hot on my throat.

I whimper without restraint when his tongue licks along my clavicle. He murmurs into my body, "It's just us, Amara." I respond to the groan in his voice. "Tell me you don't feel what I feel. Tell me you don't want me to bend you over once again. Just like I used to when it was our dirty little secret."

I want to clench my fists, but this time I remember he's

holding my hands. Like a real-life lie detector, he's waiting for me to face my ugly truth or dig my fingernails into his hands. I know how much my nails hurt, and I don't want to hurt him now, but I'm not sure I can put myself out there. Hiding my heart took practice, and it's become a part of me to the point where exposing myself is agonizing.

He doesn't stop.

"Tell me you don't close your eyes while you're being dominated by those strangers you'll never see again, that you don't imagine me in their place, needing to own you, wanting to bring you home."

A sting in my eyes tells me my misery is threatening to break free once again.

"Please. Don't—"

The expression on his face falls as an odd realization settles in his eyes.

"It's not just about control." He mutters to himself, and I wish I could hide away before he finishes his thought, but I stupidly agreed to being bound. I arrogantly thought Ryder didn't know all of me, but he does. He's the only one who does. "The aftercare is a way of healing, and you don't want to heal yourself because healing means moving on—and you can't."

The anguish in his tone when he uncovers the rest of my secret unravels me, and tears pour out of my eyes. They roll down my cheeks and fall in heavy drops onto my chest.

I could never let him go. That's why my therapy never worked. You have to want to heal, and I wanted to hold on to the pain because it was all I had left of Ryder. Then, when Grayson died, my sadness was all I had left. It was mine. It was the only remaining tangible piece of Ryder and Grayson I could hold on to.

I held on to it.

I nurtured it.

And now I don't know how to let it go.

Ryder leans his body into me, and the feeling of comfort is so unfamiliar that I push myself into the chair and fidget with his hands until he lets them go.

"I—can't..." The air is too heavy to take deep breaths, but I try anyway. I'm thankful I'm sitting down as a dizzy wave of fresh hell hits me.

Ryder's hands grip my upper arms, and he hovers his face in front of my own as I realize he's speaking to me. "Just breathe, Amara. You're okay. I should have known. I never let you go either." He says his last sentence as he pushes us into a hug, reaching around behind me to unclip my collar before tugging me forward. My head drops into his neck, and I sob into his shirt as his hands jerk at the binds on my wrists, freeing me.

This time, I don't push him away. I dig my hands into the sides of his shirt and cling to him, burying myself in his being. I don't care if he knows. I don't care if he's engaged, or if he has a son, and the guilt gnaws at me, but I need to hold on to something that doesn't hurt for once.

I told myself I would never fall again, but the truth is I've been free-falling for years. I just need someone to catch me because I'm tired.

Ryder leans back, pushing me in front of him, and holds me still while he scans my face. I drop my head, embarrassed that I gave in to my emotions.

"We are not done. This just isn't the place, and I want to get you home and let you rest." His eyes scan the rest of the room before stopping at the table, and Ryder stands up and walks over, retrieving my mask and returning to me to set it in my hands.

He's letting me put my mask on.

He's allowing me to protect myself and hide.

And I do.

Once the mask is in place, I feel better.

I imagine my eyeshadow must be smeared down my face by now. Ryder's black shirt doesn't show any signs of stains, but I see where my tears soaked through the fabric.

He frees my legs and reaches a hand out to help me stand, and we cross the room in silence. He stops at the door, tugging on my arm to stop me.

"I'll remind you of your rules while we are here."

I nod.

He opens the door, and I take a step to lead us out when a large, muscular body fills the doorframe, blocking my exit.

I crane my neck up, and Lennox's hard glare makes me cower internally. He looks like he's ready to tear right through the both of us.

I take a step back into Ryder, who wraps his fingers around my arms and pulls me to the side before Lennox charges in and pushes him backward into the room.

"WHY WOULD YOU BRING HER HERE?" Lennox yells as he fists Ryder's shirt and keeps pushing until he slams Ryder against the wall behind him.

My heart hammers into my chest as Ryder pushes his brother back and straightens his jacket as though the conversation is one-sided.

He stares Lennox down with a smug sneer. "I can do what I want with what is mine."

Everything slows down.

"Sloane isn't yours." Lennox loses what was left of his composure and punches Ryder, sending him backward against the wall.

Lennox looks like he's going to strike him again.

In a moment of panic, I rush toward them and place myself

near Ryder, taking my mask off to show Lennox he has the wrong idea and I'm not Sloane.

His anger morphs into disgusted shock, and he recoils from me.

The door flies open behind Lennox, and Cole rushes into the room. Everyone looks at everyone in stunned silence.

"Your face." Cole points to his own face and drops his gaze to my mask lying on the floor.

Ryder stands as he speaks. "Put your mask on—NOW!" The previous comfort in his tone is gone. Shame and guilt flood my system, and I reach down and slide the disguise over my head, hiding myself away like the dirty secret I am.

"Did you know?" Lennox stares Cole down. Cole doesn't respond, only shrugs, so Lennox raises his voice and repeats himself. "DID YOU FUCKING KNOW ABOUT THIS, COLE?"

The tension in the room is overpowering, and I stay still, trying to figure out what is happening between the brothers. They look primed to go to war.

Ryder speaks for him. "The arrangement I have is no one's business."

Lennox takes a hard look at me, and my knees feel weak. Staring me down, a wicked grin crosses his features.

Lennox keeps his stare on me as he asks Cole, "Not about any *arrangement*. Did you know Ryder was bringing her here to pass her off as Sloane?"

The room goes silent as his accusation settles on me, and neither Cole nor Ryder will look at me.

My hand goes to my hair. My naturally wavy hair Ryder told me to straighten for tonight. My hand trembles as I brush my fingers over the mask that covers who I really am.

Ryder wasn't seen with me tonight.

He was seen with Sloane.

I turn to face him. "Ryder?" His name leaves my lips in a solemn whisper, and Ryder closes his eyes in disappointment.

"Sloane deserves better than you!" Lennox shouts from behind me. "She deserves better than any of us."

The volume of Lennox's voice catches my attention, and I spin in time to see him lunging toward Ryder, ready to strike again.

Spinning on my heels, I step into his path and shove his arm up and around, using centrifugal force to my advantage. He trips to the side before I twist my body and shove him hard, past Ryder and into the wall.

"ENOUGH!" I scream at him as I lean all of my weight into pinning him against the wall. "I CAN'T. I JUST FUCKING CAN'T WITH THIS SHIT RIGHT NOW!"

Lennox stills, and worry sets in. He can push himself off the wall any time he wants and come at me. I caught him off guard and used that to my advantage, but if he gets back up, he has strength on his side. Instead, his muscles relax as he opens his palms and nods against the wall. I release him, stepping back to face Cole and Ryder, who are staring at me with dumbfounded looks on their faces when the situation hits me.

Stepping away from Lennox, I square myself on Ryder, hoping to distract him from what he just watched me do.

"You planned this?" I wave my hand around the room, my face heating up with anger under my mask. "You never wanted to bring *me* here." I punch at my sternum, my fingers poking hard into my ribs. "You used me."

My accusation sets Ryder on a different path, and he straightens one of the cuffs on his shirt sleeve before staring me down.

"Trust me, you'll know when I use you. Am I understood?" He challenges me right back, and I don't have the common sense to back down.

"Yes." I snarl, exposing my teeth to him before saying through a clenched jaw, "Master."

I get the reaction I was looking for.

"Don't push me. You've managed to break every single rule I gave you tonight. I've seen your sheet, Amara. I know you like it rough. You love being restrained, gagged, and fucked hard while you're told what a good girl you are. I also know what you don't like. Don't make me punish you in front of Cole, because I can think of five things I want to do right off the top of my head." I turn my attention to Cole, who watches me in silence. There is no humor on his face, and my shoulders slouch in defeat as I return to Ryder's harsh scrutiny. "Now drop your gaze to the floor and follow me out of here. You'll speak to no one." Ryder's face is already puffy and red where Lennox hit him.

Lennox doesn't wait for us to leave. Straightening his jacket, he pushes past Cole, almost knocking him to the ground on his way out, and leaves us to ourselves.

Ryder watches him leave, then looks at me. I decide to back down, taking a step toward the door when Cole blocks my path.

"That was an impressive move there, Sunshine." Cole karate chops the air like he's some sort of ninja.

"Was it?" I shrug but make sure to hold his stare.

He chuckles before stepping aside, winking at me while muttering to himself, "Keep your secrets then. I love a challenge."

I pull my shoulders back and lift my chin to exit as defiantly as I can.

I have no doubt they'll figure it out sooner or later, but neither of them has helped me, so why should I make anything easy for them?

Frustration gnaws at me as I step out of the room then wait for Ryder to lead me out of the club.

It's taking too long for me to find Grayson's killer, and I don't know how much longer I can stay with Ryder under his roof before I lose what little I have left of myself.

Like a drop in air pressure before a storm, a sense of apprehension sits heavy in the air around me.

Something's coming.

RYDER

"Now tell me the real reason you dropped in to see me." Seated behind my desk, I'm the poster child for calm and collected. Under the desk and hidden from sight, my foot taps in agitation as I wait for my father to get to the point.

"Can't a father just stop by his son's work and say hi?" He feigns offense, and I tilt my head, challenging him to continue the charade. He chuckles. "Fair enough. This retirement is harder than I thought. I miss"—he gestures to the room around us—"this."

I smile. I'm sure it doesn't reach my eyes. While I believe he misses being involved, there are a number of other places he could go that would be higher on his list.

He's here for a reason, and we haven't gotten to it yet.

Nash sits casually in a seat, waiting for his next orders. We were going over some family business when my receptionist buzzed to say my father was waiting. I catch his attention and tilt my head to the door, excusing him. He'll be around for most of the day. We'll catch up later.

My father leans back to address him on his way out. "We missed you at Eros this weekend."

While Nash isn't an elite member, I have brought him along as a guest for some of the exclusive events in the past.

Nash stops and smiles respectfully. "I had some business to attend to." Nodding to us, he turns to leave and closes the door behind him.

My father points over his shoulder. "He's a good kid."

Another terse smile from me.

Calling him a kid is calling me a kid, as we are the same age, and my father knows this. It's his way of saying he is still more experienced than I am. It's his way of showing me my place.

It's a place I don't accept.

My father is old school. Ways of doing business have evolved, and he is a dinosaur among the wolves now.

"It was—nice—seeing you and Sloane at the masquerade ball. So things are going well there? Are we going to get a date for the wedding soon?"

I'm not sure what to do with the information my father just shared with me.

Out of all of us, Lennox is the closest with our father. Being the firstborn, there was just some kind of connection they had that my other brothers and I couldn't penetrate, and I was positive Lennox would have told him it wasn't Sloane with me at the club last weekend.

Either he hasn't gotten around to it, or he has decided to hold on to my lie for himself.

"I think Sloane is planning a party at the house to announce the dates soon. Is this why you dropped in? Did Mom put you up to this?"

He relaxes and chuckles at my question before nodding.

I gave him a lie he can cling to, and he's happy.

It still isn't the reason he's here.

"Speaking of weddings, that girl, from dinner, has she left yet?"

Bingo.

This is why he's here. To find out information about Amara.

He knows her name. He bought her for me.

I shrug and play it down.

"She's tying up some loose ends. She works closer with Nash on the business," I lie.

Nash doesn't know why I have Amara here, but he'll cover for me if my father starts asking him questions.

I check my watch, catching my father's attention.

"Am I keeping you from something?"

"Not at all. Dagen is dropping by shortly."

My father is already standing. He got the update he wanted about Amara, and he's more than happy to move along. I rise with him and walk him to the door.

The tension in the room immediately dissipates as I close the door behind him, and my thoughts turn to Amara.

If my father had known it was her at the club, he would have demanded she be returned to Portland, and I don't know what I would have done.

I wish I knew Lennox's reasons for not telling our father, but his silence saved us both. At the same time, his presence back at the club set us back.

I wanted nothing more than to get Amara out of the club unnoticed and back to the house so I could spend more time with her, but Lennox showed up and everything went to shit.

Amara sat quietly in the passenger seat on the drive home, and I allowed it. Too much had been revealed on all sides, and the excruciating look of anguish on her face when Lennox told her everyone thought she was Sloane rattled me.

After she finally cracked, she began to let her guard down.

She opened her front door, and I was about to walk through, but now it's closed shut. Lennox barged in, and I let her down.

Amara announced the following day she would be looking for a place of her own and spent Sunday making calls to book viewings.

I've had Nash tracking her to make sure nothing goes through, but I'm on borrowed time now. Something needs to fall into place. The last two days at work have been dull. Amara has been in and out of the office. Yesterday she had a long lunch and a business meeting I can't find any information on, and I haven't been able to run into her in the office. She's been working late into the evening, calling my security team for a ride home, going out of her way to show me she doesn't need me.

The urge to throw something settles into my bones. I always get the answers I want. I've never been denied information. Until now.

There's always someone who knows something or has proof; I just need to look in the right place. Grayson's killer is still out there. The reason he died is still unknown. Hopefully, the lead Cole has will be the key to proving my innocence and finding out what happened to him.

I need to pull Amara back onto our path. I've given her a few days. That's enough time and space, and I'm ready to talk everything out.

My phone buzzes and I respond, telling my assistant to let Dagen in before shaking these thoughts out of my head.

"Hey. I ran into Dad at the elevator." Dagen's observation sounds more like a question.

"He dropped by to check on business." I roll my eyes, and Dagen nods in understanding before taking the seat my father just left.

"What happened to you on Saturday? Both of you left

rather quickly, and Cole took off shortly after. You left me with those guys at the table. Fuck, do they know how to party. I didn't stumble home until the next afternoon. Thanks for throwing me under the bus." I chuckle, and he leans forward. "Seriously, you can't tell them I'm pining for some chick then abandon me like that. They made it their mission to find me pussy." He shakes his head.

"Well, you are pining."

"I am not. Fuck off with that."

I back off. Dagen is easy to read, and I know when to tone it down. The truth is, he *is* hung up on the one who got away, and he doesn't want to face it.

Anyway, who am I to give advice? I was too stupid to hold on to the only woman I've ever loved, and now I worry I'm going to lose her all over again.

We get a lot of things right, but the Saint boys sure know how to mess up their love lives.

"Fine. Did you find out anything?"

The reason we went to the club was to get close to the Lucciano organization and solidify our support with Elia's next in line. By the sounds of it, Dagen did us a solid by staying with them after Cole left.

"Lots. They wanted to let us know they appreciate the Saints' backing. Their organization is already split. There is no love lost between Elia and the other group, so there is no point in Ratchet and his deserters sticking around. Now Creed and his team are cleaning house. They've been weeding out the traitors and the ones who stayed behind as eyes and ears for Ratchet. The search for the heir has picked up, but now both sides are looking. Ratchet and his group think if they can find the heir first, then the rest of the organization will have to follow them over to the dark side. All hell is threatening to break loose over there." Dagen shakes his head, and I'm happy we aren't in the thick of things.

We will have to make our allegiance public, which will draw some backlash, but I'm happy with the side we are on.

My phone vibrates on the desk, but I leave it where it is. There are no meetings I want to take more than this one right now.

"So what do we have to go on for the heir?" If we can help find their connection and ensure Creed's side remains, then the other faction will die off—figuratively or literally. I really don't care at this point.

"They had a lead on the hospital, but it was a dead end. Any documents or information is gone. They didn't say how, but they narrowed down the year. It clears Cole and me." He stares at me. We both know it doesn't exclude me—or Grayson. "They're currently trying to locate five women, and they are confident it is one of them."

"Why's it taking so long?"

"You know the life. Most of them didn't use their real names. Makes them harder to track, but not impossible."

I raise my eyebrows at him. "Not impossible? Are you saying—"

"I told them I'd look into it, see what I could find. I have some feelers out. It's good for all of us if we don't go behind their backs."

"Agreed."

Dagen shifts in his seat as he changes the topic. "How is Amara? She had her mask on, but her body language was off when you two left on Saturday. Then Cole left and Lennox stormed out shortly after."

Dagen startles as his phone buzzes, and he pulls it out of his pocket to look at the screen as I answer.

"I have Amara under control." I don't feel like getting into the details right now.

"You sure about that?" Dagen looks up. His expression has turned serious, and he points to my phone. "Cole is trying to get ahold of you. He says to turn on the local news now."

I pull the remote out of my desk drawer and aim it at the screen to the side of the room. I click through channels that don't catch my attention until I get to the one I want.

I know it right away because it's Amara's face I see on the screen. She's wearing the same outfit she wore yesterday.

Long business lunch my ass.

Dagen and I gawk at the screen while we listen to the obviously prerecorded segment, and it turns out my little flower hasn't been silent. She's been busy.

The host listens with great interest as Amara talks about her brother's unsolved murder. It's the story we worked tirelessly to suppress from the media two and a half years ago. An image of Grayson pops up on the screen; the same damn photo that sits in a frame in Amara's office stares back at me.

Amara goes on to share as much as she knows about his death, and she asks that anyone with any information contact the number on the screen. It isn't lost on me that she doesn't ask them to contact the cops. She knows well enough by now not to trust anyone else. I've taught her that with my actions.

Irritation burns through me as I read the numbers on the screen. It's her personal phone number.

Lifting the receiver, I punch in the extension I know by heart. It rings, then connects, but it isn't the person I want.

"I want Ms. Scott in my office right now," I demand, and there is a commotion on the other end of the line. I think Amara's assistant might have dropped the phone.

"Uh, um, I—I'm sorry, Mr. Saint. Amara left for the day right before lunch. She, um, said she wouldn't be b-back."

Fucking great.

I slam the phone down.

"What is she thinking?" Dagen's question reminds me I'm not alone in my office.

"She isn't," I growl, ready to snap.

There are only so many places Amara has left to hide from me, and when I find her, we are going to settle everything between us once and for all.

25

AMARA

I've spent the last couple of hours in an odd void.

My suitcase is open on the bed, and I've packed and unpacked it three times.

The cold case segment just finished airing. I only know by the time—I couldn't bring myself to watch it.

My arms tingle with anxiety. On the nightstand across the room, my phone has been lighting up with notifications for the last ten minutes.

I walk over, but I don't pick it up for fear of everything becoming real and crashing down all around me.

The most recent notification displays up at me.

Ryder: YOU BETTER BE HOME WHEN I GET THERE.

I imagine there is a long line of messages just like this one preceding it, but I don't bother to look.

After leaving the club on Saturday, all I felt was helpless. When I had the idea to contact the media and revive Grayson's story, I felt my strength return, and I clung to it. I didn't question my choice until the minute it aired, and I've felt sick with nervous energy ever since.

I just wanted to be seen and heard.

And loved.

But Ryder is going to be disappointed in me, and he'll probably send me away again. This time for good, and I can't take another rejection from him. So I start packing my things again when a soft knock on the door catches my attention.

I pause, frozen with worry in the middle of my room. The door slowly opens on a slow creak, and Sloane peeks her head in.

"Hey. I heard you in here and thought I'd check on you. You're home early." Her gaze stops on the open suitcase on my bed before snapping back to me. "Everything okay?"

I look down at the items in my hands and back up to her, shaking my head in a trance.

"Oh no. Here." She reaches for my things, and I let go of them before she drops them on the dresser and leads me to the bed, pushing the suitcase to the side so we can sit down on the edge. "What happened?"

How do I tell her *everything* happened?

"I went on TV to talk about Grayson's cold case. I thought maybe I could...do that. For him." I thought I had cried out all of my tears, but the little sting around my eyes tells me there may be more coming.

"Oh, Amara." Sloane's concern rattles me. She looks afraid for me. "I don't know how to say this." She takes a minute while she glances around the room. "You don't know how volatile everything is. Depending on what you said, you could be in a lot of danger right now. I'm worried for you. Does Ryder know what you did?"

I shrug.

By the tone of his last text, he does.

I can't live with the guilt that has been eating away at me any longer.

"I need to tell you something. Ryder took me to Eros on Saturday, and I feel bad for—" I pause to sniffle back my emotions when Sloane fills the silence.

"You have nothing to feel bad for. I know you did. I—um, picked out your dress." She glances sheepishly down to her hands before meeting my gaze again.

"I don't understand." I lean back from her. "You knew Ryder took me there to pretend to be you?"

"What? No, I mean—I knew Ryder took you there. I didn't know you were pretending to be me."

"I wasn't. Ryder wanted to give the impression I was you."

She huffs out an irritated breath. "Those fucking brothers," she mutters, shaking her head. For the first time since I arrived in this house, I feel a kindred connection to Sloane. "What happened?"

"Lennox happened," I answer, and Sloane flinches at his name. "He thought I was you, and he took a swing at Ryder."

"That explains Ryder's black eye," Sloane muses out loud, and I nod.

"He looked devastated when he thought I was you. Then he was really pissed, and he told Ryder he didn't deserve you." I'm already in deep trouble, so I take the chance and push for more. "Is there something going on between you and Lennox?"

Sloane looks hesitant to answer. After a moment of awkward silence, she responds.

"A long time ago, there was." I must look confused because she settles her hand on my own quickly and continues, "This was before Grayson and I were together. I think you know, before we went out, Ryder, Grayson, and I were best friends. We did everything together. One night we went to a club

Ryder's dad owned. Lennox was the manager. From the moment I met him, I was attracted to Lennox. There was something about him. I loved the way he looked at me, but he was my best friend's oldest brother, and he was ten years older than us." She glances away before she speaks again. "Lennox and I—have history. I don't want to go into it, but shortly after, Grayson pulled me aside and told me he had feelings for me." She meets my gaze again. "At the time, the age difference between Lennox and I seemed larger than it does now, and they both knew about each other. Anyway, I had a decision to make."

"And you chose Grayson," I offer, to help her out.

She shakes her head. "No. I chose Lennox. It was the hardest decision I ever had to make. I loved them both, with all of my heart." Her eyes shine as they fill with emotion.

"But if you chose Lennox, why were you with Grayson?"

I immediately regret my question.

Sloane looks like she's ready to cry.

"Lennox didn't choose me. I had written him a note to tell him how I felt, and I received it back the next day, unopened, with a letter of his own telling me not to choose him and to let him go."

"But you ended up with my brother?" My heart aches listening to Sloane's story. We have more in common than I thought. We were both rejected by a Saint.

"I was honest with Grayson. I told him I had chosen Lennox, and I showed him the note he wrote back to me. He was there for me. He comforted me, and he still loved me, and we built what we had off of that, and I will forever love your brother."

I watch her tears fall, but my own face feels wet, and I realize I'm crying too.

"My point is, I made my choice, and Lennox made his. We

are now living with the consequences of those decisions. That might be why you attracted some of his anger on Saturday."

"But you were okay with me going with Ryder?" I speak slowly. This is the part that is confusing to me.

"There are some things you don't understand, and I don't feel it's my place to tell you since this is between you and Ryder. I really can't give you any more. I'm sorry." She shakes her head, and I decide to confide in her.

"I think I made a mistake going to the media. It didn't feel like it at the time. But now I think Ryder's going to be really mad. I just feel like Grayson is gone and no one cares, and I'm all alone trying to fight for justice for him, and no one is helping, and life is just going on without me."

I meant to say "him," and my Freudian slip gives me pause. I've been angry that Ryder is engaged, that his life is going on without me when I can't go on without him.

Sloane squeezes my hand. "There's a lot going on that you don't know about. Ryder will get over it. He just—"

Her pep talk is cut off by the door to my room swinging open, and Ryder steps in, looking like he's one straw away from breaking.

I jump up from the bed, and Sloane follows me up as Ryder stalks toward us. Sloane steps in front of me as he nears.

"Just calm down for a minute, Ryder. I've got this under—"

"Leave us." Ryder's eyes are on me, but it's clear he's talking to Sloane, and she opens her mouth to try again, but he talks over her. "NOW."

Sloane glances back at me with a smile that hides her pity. "It'll be okay," she whispers to me before telling Ryder she is going to take Henry out for a while. She steps away and walks out of the room, closing the door behind her.

I wish I had her confidence. I don't see what she sees.

I see the burn of betrayal in Ryder's stern expression.

Ryder's focus remains on me, and I glance to the bed at my suitcase.

I guess it's too late to make that hasty exit.

Ryder follows my line of sight before returning to hold me captive in his stare.

"I warned you, Amara. I told you, if you defied me again, I would show you what you are afraid of."

His threat isn't waiting for a response, but I open my mouth to try anyway, and the breath is knocked out of me when Ryder closes the distance between us, wraps his fingers in the hair at the base of my neck, and pulls me forward into a deep, claiming kiss.

My feet stumble over themselves as I struggle to remain upright, and my head spins at the anger and passion behind our connection.

His tongue pushes into my mouth, taking control of my senses, and I grab onto his shirt, my fingers digging into the sides of his muscular torso.

The fine line between lust and rage swirls into the taste of him on my tongue, and I groan as he pulls away. He studies me as I gasp for air and try not to fall over.

The kiss is confusing because Ryder still looks furious.

"I told you I would expose you. I would show you who you really are. I see you, Amara. I want you to remember: you brought this on yourself."

"What are you going to do?" My tone is weak.

I'm now truly worried. I'm not afraid for my safety. I know Ryder would never harm me, but I'm quickly learning that physical pain isn't the worst thing Ryder can inflict on me.

He tightens his grip in my hair, and I wince as he pulls me into his face. The motion makes me arch my back, and my nipples harden against my better judgment.

Was this the reaction I wanted from him? Did I want him to show me this domineering side of him that I've missed?

Maybe.

"You were a brave little girl going on TV and telling the world you were still looking for Grayson's murderer. Those were your exact words, Blossom. You put yourself in front of everyone in this fucking town; you drew the target on your back yourself. Now I'm challenging you to be that brave with me."

I panic. "I—"

My head swivels from side to side as Ryder rattles me in his hold, and my scalp stings.

"I'm not done talking." I settle and wait. "Good. Girl." He tugs at my hair with each word. "Now, you can be brave and place yourself in my control—and trust me, I will take complete control—or you can leave now and never return."

The thought of his ultimatum hurts more than the hold he has in my hair, and I entertain my tears. I've come so far, and I put myself out there to find justice for Grayson, but I'm lying to myself if I leave it at that.

I won't survive Ryder sending me away again.

The memory of the last time it happened replays in my head, and I'm not strong enough to push the thought out. I stood in front of him with Grayson, my mother, and his father in the room when they announced I was going away. I begged Ryder to keep me, as though I were some kind of pathetic pet, and he told me to leave.

There's nothing here for you, Amara. His vacant words are still fresh in my mind as though he said them yesterday.

There's nowhere left for me to go. Everything I want is standing right here in front of me.

Leaning in, his lips brush against mine. He licks then sucks my lower lip between his teeth before biting down. The pain is enough to send a warning shock through my body before he releases my lip.

"Do your worst." My heart speaks for the rest of me, and I hear the defiance in my words before I realize I've said them out loud.

His eyes burn into me as he observes me with a wolfish sneer, holding me in place by a fistful of hair before he bares his teeth at me in a primal sneer.

"I intend to."

26

RYDER

Do your worst.

She has no idea how deeply she's condemned herself with those words.

But she did give me what I've needed all along. The one thing she knows will set me free.

Her consent.

Sucking her lip in between my own once again, I taste her sweet words on my tongue.

I settle into the freedom of myself and nibble before releasing her mouth back to her.

There will be plenty of time to take everything I want. For now, I'll settle for the feeling of regained control.

I had lost it for a moment.

When I saw Amara on the screen, placing herself in danger, I lost everything.

She has no idea of the severity of her new situation. She doesn't understand the players involved, and she stepped way out of line.

The fear of losing her again shattered me, and this can't

continue. I won't go any longer without her, and the choice was hers.

Submit or leave.

In reality, there was no choice to be made. The ultimatum was me forcing her to face and accept what I already know:

Amara Scott has always been and will always be mine.

If she can't accept her reality, then I'll end up losing her either way, and I'd rather set her free then live through her death like I did with her brother.

All of my plans will fall apart if I lose control of the narrative. Years of searching for Grayson's killer and trying to clear my name while placing blame where it is due will go down the drain if my lies unravel.

"Do you know what I see?" I reach up to her face with my free hand, running my fingers over her soft skin. She doesn't respond, so I continue, "I see a scared little girl."

I'm not fucking around anymore, and she knows it.

"I'm not afraid of you." Her timid tone betrays her words, and I chuckle maliciously.

"No. You're not afraid of me." I sniff the air around her. She smells delicious, and I drop my hand to her breast, cupping her and tightening my grip until she gasps. I lean in, capturing her breath and speaking low into her space. "You're afraid of something much darker."

"W-what's that?" Her pupils dilate as she asks her question.

Her body capitulates to my hold. She rests her head in my grip and follows my lead wherever I place her.

I want this moment burned into my soul.

I want this right here to last forever.

I savor the tension, dragging my lower lip up over her own before licking her face, letting my depravity loose before sucking my tongue into my mouth, tasting the saltiness of her skin.

Has she been crying?

"You're afraid of yourself."

She doesn't respond.

She tilts her chin at me in the only show of defiance she knows won't earn her a punishment.

Releasing her breast, I drop my hand under her shirt and move deftly to her bra strap at the back, unclipping it with one hand, and her upper body relaxes at the release. I keep my hand on her skin under her bra and return to the front, this time pinching her nipple until she sucks in air with a sharp hiss.

She melts for me just like she used to, whimpering softly as I increase the pressure of my hold.

"Say it, Blossom. Tell me who you belong to. Or better yet, tell yourself."

I watch her grapple with handing over her power. I imagine she's weighing whether or not she'll maintain control like she did in the club in Portland. They must have eaten her up and loved every minute of it. I'm sure they got off. They got what they wanted, but it was all a lie.

She played them and took what she needed. She needed to feel used, then, when the moment came to have her completely, she pulled back, and they were none the wiser because they got what they wanted.

I'm not that simple.

My needs aren't as basic.

"I belong to—you, Ryder."

"Do you now?" I mock. "Show me. Shove your hand down your panties and play with what's mine."

She listens to me, shifting her hips to get her palm into her pants. She looks at me with wide eyes as she starts. She's still staring up at me with my fingers tangled in her hair, and I laugh in her face.

"I said show me. Don't pretend to show me. I want to see

your mouth go slack and your eyes widen while you make the cunt I own spasm around your fingers."

She swallows hard.

I won't back down, and she knows it.

If she wasn't planning on giving me everything, she should have chosen to leave.

Biting her lower lip, her hand moves differently now, slowly picking up pace, and she shifts her hips.

I notice the change in her face instantly. Her eyes glaze out of focus and her body is heavier in my grasp. I release her nipple to wrap my hand around her and hold her up.

"That's it. Be my dirty little whore, Blossom. You crave all of this control over yourself, so fucking take it. Own it and force that body of mine to come."

Amara's eyebrows pinch tight, euphoria etched into the lines on her face as her hand feverishly grinds into her clit between us.

She holds nothing back. Her free hand slides around my stomach, and she fists the shirt at my side in the same way I'm fisting her hair. I'm not sure she even realizes she's done it as her body moves on its own, her hips grinding, chasing release.

"Now tell me who you belong to," I growl at her as her breaths turn to short pants.

"You."

"Say it again."

"I belong to you."

"Fucking say it again." I tighten my grip in her hair.

"I belong t-to"—Amara's body rocks and seizes before she draws out her last word with a wail—"YOU!"

I make sure her eyes are open and she's looking right at me when she says it, realization dawning in her post-orgasm haze.

"Yes, you do, Blossom. You fucking belong to me. And I'm far from done with you. On your knees."

Her hands are at the button on my pants before she hits the floor, and I'm already hard. Hell, I was hard the moment she challenged me to do my worst.

Reaching forward, I catch her by surprise when I grab either side of her blouse and rip it open, sending buttons around the room before pushing it off, and the bra I unfastened slides off her shoulders and down with her top.

Wide eyes look up at me, and I shove my fingers into her mouth and over her tongue, making her gag, but she doesn't pull away. She settles her legs under her body and braces her hands on my legs, preparing to take me.

Removing my fingers, I wipe her spit around her face and over her forehead, pushing her hair out of my way. I want to have a clear line of sight to her beautiful eyes while she sucks me off, and she surprises me as she leans into me, her mouth wide, her tongue out.

I wish I could have done this to her when she had that thick layer of eyeshadow on on Saturday night.

"Fuck," I mutter as I shift forward, and she licks up a dribble of precum. Instead of closing her mouth, she leans back, showing it to me on her tongue, and I lose my shit.

Grabbing her face on either side, I guide her around my cock and push in slowly, groaning every inch of the way.

A momentary flash of jealousy surges through me. Amara was good, but she was never this good. I've never had this good.

Pulling myself all the way out, I stare, mesmerized by the length of my cock as she releases me with a string of cum running from my tip to her tongue before it dips low across her tits and she dives back, sucking her perfect lips around my width.

Taking control from her, I hold her head still and pump myself into her face, her body seizing when she holds still and gags. The sound is music to my ears.

I pull her off me a second time, and there is more of me to wipe across her face and mix in with the tears escaping from the corners of her eyes.

The intensity isn't enough.

Pulling the head of my cock out of her mouth, she releases me with a pop, her wide eyes staring up at me, waiting for my lead.

I guide her into a standing position and reach around her to the suitcase she left open.

"You're not fucking going anywhere," I growl as I push the suitcase off the bed, and it clatters to the floor, spilling its contents all over.

I'll burn that thing to keep her here if I have to.

Pulling at her pants, I release the buttons, shoving everything down together, and I'm not gentle when I pull her feet out of each leg.

I'm hungry.

Lifting one of her legs and resting it over my shoulder, I grip her ass tight, pulling her into me. My mouth devours her whole as I growl into her pussy, smearing her juices all over my face.

I've missed her scent.

I've craved her taste.

She adjusts the foot she left on the ground so she doesn't tip over, and I continue to take, pushing my tongue deep inside of her until she bucks and grinds against my stubble. Her fingers comb through my hair with harsh tugs every time I hit a sensitive spot on her clit.

Lowering her leg from my shoulder, I stand quickly to witness the heady look of pure rapture still dancing across her features. I pull her mouth to mine, sucking her tongue and licking her lips to share her taste with her, and she takes everything I give her.

Spinning her to face the bed, I shrug my pants all the way off and pull my shirt over my head, freeing myself completely to take her like the base animal I crave to be.

I bend her forward, and she braces her arms on the bed, arching her back and offering herself to me, but her pose isn't good enough. I want her completely spread and unable to control my onslaught.

I tap her leg, urging her to lift it onto the bed and do the same with the other until she is kneeling. Then I position her knees forward and out so her ass juts back toward me, her feet dangling off the edge of the bed. Then I settle her head onto the mattress before reaching in between her legs and running my fingers up the length of her pussy, and she moans into the covers.

"I don't want to use a condom." It's the closest I'll get to asking her permission.

"I said what I said. Do your worst," she growls against the sheets.

I don't give her a chance to brace for me. Gliding into her warm channel like I took her throat, I push all the way in, and she deflates against the bed with one long groan.

I pull out and slam in again, and she spasms around my shaft as she spreads her legs wider, her hands fisting the bed sheet around her.

Having her back like this is surreal. I feel like I'm dreaming, and I reach around to rub through her wet folds just to hear her moan for me again.

I never corrupted Amara; I was drawn to this insatiable need in her. I felt matched with her darkness.

Do your worst.

Fuck me. She's damned me with those words.

I'm all hers, and if this is what is going to end me, I'm fine with going out in her arms and buried deep inside her.

Gripping her hip with one hand, I drill into her as I slap her firm cheek with my other hand, reddening her ass. Her head arches back as she groans and grunts with each smack. Her hips writhe as her body rides along with me, out of control in a stampede of sensation and aphrodisia.

"I told you you would know when I used you, Blossom."

Amara's head sluggishly dips to the side. "Fuck, yes—use me." She's slurring her words; my little flower is back with me.

My cock still buried deep, I lift her hips and push her forward, stomach-down on the bed. I climb over her and comb my fingers into her hair, lifting her head up for better access to her ear.

"Tell me I hurt you."

"What?" Her pussy clenches around my cock as I continue fucking her.

"Tell me I hurt you." I never repeat myself, yet here we are. "Tell me I had that power. Tell me I still have it. Tell me you couldn't let me go."

Tears roll down her face freely, and her body twitches and grinds against each thrust. "I couldn't let you go."

Her body tenses around me, and I know she's close to coming and sending us both into the release we need.

"You are mine." I pound her into the bed with such force that her nightstand moves, and the little broken glass pieces of her butterfly catch my attention as they rattle around.

The view of Amara capitulating underneath me and the sound of the shattered glass clattering against itself is mesmerizing, and I let myself loose.

"That's you, Blossom. You're my little broken butterfly, and I'm going to put you back together the way I want you."

She turns her head, entranced by the sight of the glass shards rocking on her nightstand, and I wrap my arm around her throat.

Propping myself above her, I lift her hip with one hand and plunge myself into her over and over while reaching underneath her to rub her sensitive clit. She breaks free, the sound of my name wrapped in her wail as she shudders against the bed, and I follow her over.

The first sounds I hear as I pull myself back from the euphoria of my orgasm are Amara's soft sobs, and I shift off her and turn her onto her side, facing me. Laying my head on her pillow, I guide her onto my outstretched arm, and I brace for the moment she shuts down.

But it doesn't come.

She doesn't tell me she needs to go. She makes no excuse to leave my care.

I know she's deprived herself of the care she should have had from so many other men, and the fact that she's staying with me makes my heart ache.

She is hesitant, but she's trying.

While I'm happy she never truly let me go, I'm filled with so much sadness for her. I let her down. I wasn't strong enough to protect her then.

I hope I am now.

"Talk to me. Tell me what your tears are for." I kiss the top of her head, and she sniffles before answering.

I can't begin to heal what I've fractured if she closes down on me now.

"I love you, Ryder. I always have, but I won't hurt anyone. Not even to be happy."

I gave Amara an ultimatum. Submit or leave, and she chose to stay.

The ultimatum is now mine.

I need to surrender myself and place my complete trust in her or free her.

This can't be one-sided.

It's all or nothing, and I will never settle for anything less than everything where Amara is concerned.

Consequences be damned.

It's time to tell her Sloane is not my fiancée and Henry is not my son.

AMARA

I told Ryder I loved him a few minutes ago, and we've been sitting in silence ever since.

With every passing second, more doubt creeps in, and I'm at the point where I'm no longer crying against his chest.

I'm frozen in fear.

"Um."

Ryder's body tenses, and he jumps like I've just slapped him out of a trance.

"Oh, shit. I'm so sorry. I've waited to hear you say those words for so long, I guess I thought I might never hear them again. This feels like—I can't describe it. I feel like the richest man in the world. Like I'm invincible, and I froze. I had this crazy thought that if I moved, it wouldn't be real."

"Well, don't go jumping off any buildings." I try to lighten the mood for my own mental health, and he shifts beside me, pulling me up to eye level with him.

Some of my makeup is smeared across his face. His lips are a faded shade of the lipstick I had on earlier, and I realize I must look even worse.

"I love you, Amara. I always have."

His words are genuine. His tone, tragic.

The anguish in his heart as he speaks steals my breath.

"There's something I need to tell you."

A chill blows across my flesh, and my skin prickles with goosebumps. I lift the covers on my side of the bed and slide under, and Ryder follows me. His hot skin touches my own, and I prepare myself for whatever he wants to share with me.

"Henry is not my son."

Nope. Not prepared for that.

My words lodge in my throat along with my breath, and his hands tighten around my arms while he waits for me to say something.

"I don't understand."

Ryder needs to give me more to go on, as I have too many questions fighting to be the first out of my mouth.

"Henry is Sloane's son, but he is not mine. Sloane and I have never—" Ryder looks down between us.

"You're engaged, and you've never..." My forehead rises with the look of shock I'm sure is on my face.

"Well, we've kissed a couple of times in front of family, for show, and it was the most awkward thing—for both of us. I mean, she's like my sister." Ryder contorts his face as though he just ate something sour. "Amara, Sloane and I aren't really engaged. It's a lie, and there is a reason for it. There are only four of us who know the truth. Well, five now." He stares into my soul with that piece of information.

I sit up straight, tucking my legs under me and squaring myself on him.

"I have so many questions." At least, I think I do. My mind jumps from one to the other like my brain just ate too much sugar.

"I know you do, but I think you're overlooking something really important that you need to know."

My gaze flits around the room. Nervous energy surges through me, and I look at Ryder, urging him to tell me.

"Henry is Sloane's son. Sloane's and—Grayson's. Henry is your nephew, Amara."

Time stops, and his memory comes crashing into me.

My eyes sting as my heart swells with more love than I know what to do with.

"I—I'm an auntie. Grayson's still here?" Without warning, I bawl. My lips tremble and my hands shake on Ryder's body. I follow my tears as they rain down onto my fingers, and I slide my palms back, revealing something I must have missed earlier.

"What's this?" My fingers trace the dark ink on Ryder's chest.

"I couldn't let you go either, Amara." Years of sorrow burden his words.

A dark tribal tattoo of a flower stares back at me.

He carried me around with him all this time.

I was always his.

And now I have a piece of Grayson too.

I trace my finger down the thorny stem of his tattoo. "Tell me about the night he died. Sloane told me you were together."

He shifts his weight, pulling himself up to sit against the headboard. He adjusts the pillow behind him before covering my hand with his own and setting it back on his tattoo.

"We were. But not like that. Neither of us had any idea that Grayson was looking into anything. Sloane came over because she was worried. She'd just found out she was pregnant, and she wasn't sure if she and Grayson were ready to be parents. She just wanted to talk it out before she told him, and she wanted my advice. Grayson was killed that night. He never knew he had a son."

A flash of familiarity hits me. When Henry and I giggled about eating our vegetables at dinner, there was something overwhelmingly comforting about the moment we shared. I realize now, he sounds like Grayson when he laughs.

"Oh my God! Henry is mine. He's me. He's Grayson. Oh my God, Ryder. Where is he?" I make the move to bound off the bed to find my clothes, but two strong arms pull me back to my place.

"I'm sorry, Amara. You can't. You can't tell Henry—or anyone—what you know. This is the part where you get to know our secrets, but with them comes the responsibility and the burden of keeping them safe. You can't treat anyone or anything any different. Literal lives are on the line, and I made a promise to Grayson that I would protect Sloane if he ever couldn't."

"What haven't you said?"

"Grayson's killer is still out there. If they thought Sloane was still looking for them, or if she hadn't moved on, or if Henry was Grayson's son, either of them could be next. We don't know why Grayson was murdered, and, until we do, we don't know who is safe. Henry is just a little boy. This information will confuse him, and he may say something he shouldn't. We can't risk it."

"So you and Sloane pretended to be engaged and announced that Henry was yours. You did that for Grayson?"

He nods, confirming he's the man I used to think he was.

"So you're telling me you didn't stop looking for—" I choke on the rest of my sentence.

"We never stopped looking for Grayson's killer, Blossom. It's Sloane, Cole, Dagen, and me, but we've only found dead ends, and we can only do so much under the table."

"And I messed everything up." I fill in the blank Ryder is too kind to.

"Yes and no. When I saw you on television, my world blew up. We've all been too afraid to put ourselves out there. We don't know where the next bullet might come from. Cole messaged me on my ride back here. He has an idea; he wants to track you. He thinks if anyone makes contact with you, we'll be able to cut them off. You need to let us handle this, Amara. There is only one way to get the information we need, and it isn't asking nicely. I will kill anyone I have to for Grayson, and to clear my name."

"So you are a suspect. Why can't Sloane tell the authorities she was with you that night?"

"I told her not to. They don't have enough on me even without her testimony, and creating our cover story was more important. It keeps them safe. Besides, her parents would just contradict her. She snuck out that night to talk to me. They would tell the cops she was at home in bed, and it would look even more suspicious."

As Ryder opens up, the adrenaline of the last few hours leaves me feeling tired, and I curl my body around him, resting my head on his chest, listening to his heartbeat.

"Do you have any idea who might have killed Grayson?"

My head lifts with Ryder's chest as he takes a deep breath.

"When we find out why he was killed, I think we'll find out who it was. We have a theory. You saw the video Grayson left me. He was checking something out, but that's all we know. My family and the company we keep have many secrets. Secrets, I'm sure, people would kill to keep buried. Those guys you saw us with at the club have their own shit going on. They are our allies, but, while we consider them loyal business partners, we can't put all of our trust in one place because that is when we get blindsided. The head of their organization is dying, and they are scrambling to find his lost heir. There is a lot you don't know. I will tell you, but you need to give me time. I'm not lying to you. I'm protecting you, but at the same time,

I'm protecting Sloane and Henry as well." He tenses for a moment, and I lift my attention to him. He's processing something in his head. "I also have a theory that it might be Lennox."

"What? You think your brother killed my brother?" I had an inkling it might be one of the Saint brothers. The murder happened on their property, and any security footage of the area was wiped or missing. I was doubtful though. I thought it was more likely an associate.

"I haven't cleared him yet. Sloane doesn't think it's him, but we haven't ruled him out, so we can't bring him into our plans.

"So why didn't you take Grayson's video to the police?"

"Your mother only sent me that box of Grayson's things recently. She was cleaning, and she thought I would want to have some of his stuff."

I crane my neck up to look at him, and I must be wearing my feelings on my face.

"What?" Ryder asks.

"She never asked me if I wanted his stuff."

He stares at me for a long minute, clenching his jaw before he simply says, "I'm sure she just didn't think about it."

He could be right. My mother never talked about Grayson's death with me, and every time I tried to bring it up, she would rush me onto another topic. It must have been painful for her to lose her only son.

"So what do we do now?"

"Cole and Dagen are chasing down a lead, but we're running out of time and ideas. Our parents want us to commit to a wedding date"—he chuckles acerbically—"and every day that passes takes the information we need further away from us."

We lie in comfortable silence as I process all of the information Ryder shared with me.

For the first time in years, I don't feel the surge of anxiety that comes with feeling out of control. My palm is open and lying on Ryder's chest instead of clenched in a tight fist.

Everything is still spiraling all around me, just like it normally is and even more so, but I don't feel the need to manage anything about the space I am in.

"I want to help you."

Ryder jumps at my words before hugging me tight and settling once again, and I wonder if he was drifting off.

He clears his throat. "How so?"

"Well. I think I already have. You said Cole is going to try to follow me, and I already sent out my number asking for tips. Maybe I can do a little more. You know, take a look at the crime scene, ask the news station to run the episode again. Maybe if it's me poking around, someone will get nervous. I'm sure I look like an easy target all by myself."

He lifts me to look at him and raises an eyebrow. I have only seconds to pitch my idea before he shuts me down, so I hurry to continue.

"I'm serious. I can do this. For Grayson and my nephew. I can do this, Ryder."

"I won't let you dangle yourself like bait. You don't know what these people are capable of. You don't know what I'm capable of. You don't even know who is on your side here."

"I know you're on my side. That's all I need." My smile is weak. I'm still getting used to the idea that we both want the same thing.

"I lost you once, Amara. I won't lose you again." The finality and regret in his words make me doubt myself, but I know what Ryder sounds like when the odds are against him.

If they don't get a lead soon, everything will go away. He has to know this is our best shot.

"I know you won't. That's why this will work." I sit up beside him, pulling my legs into me, and face him.

He stares at me for a long minute before speaking cautiously. "I'll talk to Cole and Dagen and let you know what we come up with. Until I know we can guarantee your safety, you stay put and defer to me. I'm warning you now: you will wait for my lead on this. Do you understand me?"

"Yes." I answer with complete confidence, but I cross my fingers under the sheets.

It's a bad habit I picked up as a child. No one knows about it, not even Ryder.

I will listen to him to the best of my ability, but if something goes wrong, this is a promise I won't be able to keep.

28

RYDER

Waking up with Amara's naked body wrapped around my own felt like a dream. I used to have dreams like this, and they would put me in a bad mood for the rest of the day when I realized they weren't real.

But there she was this morning, sleeping with her head on my chest and looking like an angel. Strands of her hair moved gently with each breath she took as she made the occasional murmur.

I watched her facial expression change with whatever was happening in her head as she slept. Her eyebrows scrunched together in an intimidating expression. At least, it looked like she was trying to be threatening. I thought she looked adorable.

I fucked Amara two more times before we fell asleep tangled in my own bedsheets, and that is why I haven't been able to lose this stupid grin I showed up to work with.

An important business meeting cancelled on me this morning, and a deal I've been working on stalled in negotiations, and I'm still on top of the world.

Nothing is going to sour my mood today.

As if just thinking that thought has jinxed me, my phone buzzes.

It takes me a moment to follow the conversation on the other end of the line because my assistant is speaking in a hushed tone.

"Mr. Saint, I have Alicia Scott here to see you. She doesn't have an appointment, but she says she's like family."

Motherfu—

Well, at least my dopey smile is gone.

"Send her in, Constance." I glance at the clock on the wall. "Take an early lunch."

"Thank you, Mr. Saint."

Less than a minute later, my assistant opens the door, showing Amara's mother into my office before bowing her head and excusing herself.

"Leave the door open, Constance. Thank you." I maintain a polite tone, but only until she is gone. My tolerance may be slipping, but it isn't my assistant's fault. Keeping the door open is my way of telling Alicia she isn't staying long.

"What are you doing here, Alicia?" I overlook the formalities and stand. I don't want her to take a seat and get comfortable.

If my brusque attitude fazes her, she doesn't show it. Instead, she looks around the room and smiles brightly. "I thought I'd stop in and surprise Amara with a mother-daughter lunch to catch up."

She's checking in with me.

She wants me to know she is keeping up her end of the bargain. But her end of the bargain isn't *pretending* to be a mother to Amara. It is *actually* being her fucking mother.

I know Alicia hasn't had the easiest life. She came from the same background my own mother grew up in. Who we become is only partly a result of our upbringing though. Alicia and my mother grew up not knowing what it was like to have extra money at the end of a paycheck. It's why both of them ended up working in Elia Lucciano's clubs before they met the men who took them out of that existence.

Their paths went in different directions when they met those men. My father was a close associate to the Lucciano family. He made his own money, and he made a lot of it. Alicia's husband didn't have the business sense to grow an empire. They were both shortsighted. Instead, they stuck with odd jobs, blackmail, and selling their own daughter into our family.

Alicia knows what she knows. She operates within her upbringing, and that is why she doesn't fully understand that I am not buying Amara. I just want her to care, to truly wonder about her daughter, and I had hoped this would be the start of that.

But it isn't.

She's reporting to me like an employee hoping to get a bonus for doing their job.

"Amara's office is down the hall." I glance over her shoulder at the door.

She fidgets with her purse. "Oh, yes. I know. I thought—since I'm here—I'd stop in and say hello."

"Alicia, we are not friends." I stare her down, and her smile falters a fraction.

Pity sours my spirit. Alicia looks lost. She's no doubt done okay for herself. Despite their lack of business sense, Amara's family had some money to their name when her father died, and it's my business to know she landed on her feet. I wonder if Amara knows her mother is the kept mistress of a fast-food magnate.

Alicia looks like she's missing out. She has servants, she can fly anywhere and buy anything she wants, but her fire is missing. I had hoped she would have found her heart in reconnecting with Amara, but I just don't think she gets it.

"You have some nerve speaking to me like this." She breaks eye contact when I cock my head to the side at her audacity.

Her voice grates in my ears. Now my patience is slipping.

Old habits die hard, and Alicia thinks because I've given her money that this puts her above me on the ladder of life. She thinks she has something on me now, and, true to form, she's trying to exploit it.

I slide my hands into my pocket and straighten my spine. Deserving or not, she is Amara's mother, and I give her a chance to walk away.

"Do I?" My heart quickens as saliva pools in my mouth.

Amara's mother is nothing more than a mouse in my world, and, like a cat, I do love to play with my food before I rip it apart and swallow it whole.

A smarter person would back down.

Alicia crosses her arms, and I'm not sure if she's becoming defensive or if she's forging herself against me. For her sake, it should be the latter.

"Yes. You do. Maybe I should go to your father and tell him what you've done behind his back."

I'm half a second away from strangling her in my office when I hear the voice that settles my demons.

"What has he done?" Amara steps into the room from behind the open door, and I wonder how long she was standing on the other side, listening.

Alicia's empty threats wash away as Amara steps close to us. Her breasts push against her blouse just enough to pull her buttons tight.

"Oh, hello, honey. I was just stopping in to surprise you with lunch, but I know it's probably short notice."

It takes everything I have not to roll my eyes and huff out

loud at Alicia's pathetic attempt to get out of a lunch she had no intention of going through with in the first place. She must have shown up hoping to check in with me, then catch Amara when she was on her way out in the hopes that she already had plans.

Amara is unfazed. "What has Ryder been doing behind his father's back?" She tilts her head, curiosity written on her face.

Alicia glances at me and shrugs.

"Well—um, it's just that—"

I'm sure Alicia didn't think this through.

She thought she would tell Amara about me, and I would lose her, but now that I watch her try to find the words, I think she's realized there is nothing she can say that won't implicate her as well.

I stare at her indifferently. She's the one who brought the shovel. I'll let her dig her own grave for a while. Then I'll push her in it.

Alicia looks at me, silently pleading for me to cover up our little lies.

She's putting her faith in the wrong person.

"Alicia, I honor my business dealings." She almost looks relieved. She shouldn't. "However, a broken deal is fair game, and you broke our understanding when you threatened me." After last night, I never want to keep another thing from Amara, but I was unsure of how to approach this. I had an arrangement with Alicia I was bound to—until now.

I turn to Amara. "Your parents sold you to my father when you turned sixteen."

"WHAT?"

Alicia takes a steady step out from in between us to distance herself from her daughter's shock, and I let the truth fly.

"You know our parents arranged our marriage." Amara nods. "What you don't know is that your mother and father sold you to our family, and my father accepted with the caveat that nothing happen while you were underage. That arrangement ended when your father passed away and Alicia broke the deal and moved you out of Seattle. What your mother is referring to are the recent funds I sent her when I was acquiring your company."

Amara blinks hard at me. She looks like she's going to fall over. "You bought me—again?"

"No." This is the first time I hear emotion in my words. "Alicia called asking questions and suggesting a new deal. I made it clear to your mother I was not buying you. I was buying her apathy." I stop short of telling her I also tried to buy her a caring mother.

I wait for Amara to say something. Despite my last name, I'm no angel. What I want from her is the purest thing I know, but I'm riddled with sin in all of this. It's time to give Amara the power to do what she needs to do. This is the moment to trust her unconditionally.

I'm the only one who thinks this though.

Alicia catches her attention from off to the side. "Amara. I'm so sorry you found out like this." Her tone holds no remorse.

What she's trying to do is release herself and place the blame on my shoulders.

Amara's mouth drops open. "Are you for real? You're sorry I found out? Are you not sorry—oh I don't know—that you sold me? TWICE?" Amara throws her hands up in frustration.

I wait in silence. If Amara asks me any question right now, I'll answer it with complete honesty. She has been stripped of control for too long, and, while I want to take it from her now and then, I think she is at her best when she has the power to decide when to relinquish it.

"Don't be mad at me." Alicia tilts her head in my direction, hoping to pull me into her line of fire. Amara takes a moment to examine me.

I stay still.

I give her every opportunity to judge me and tear me apart. I'm no saint, and Amara deserves her day of reckoning with me. If she's hurt and wants to do it here and now. I'll allow it. I don't share the level of fear her mother is projecting.

I own my actions.

Amara returns to her mother. "Who do you think I'm going to be mad at? The one who wanted me enough to buy me, or the one who sold me?"

Amara's question hits me in the gut.

I would buy her a million times.

Alicia stumbles back a step. Amara's accurate summary landed on its intended target. Alicia's lower lip trembles, and I hope this is the wake-up call her mother needs in order to work on repairing their relationship, but only for Amara's sake.

If she can't fix the damage she caused, then Alicia can rot away somewhere. I'll make sure of it.

Amara doesn't wait for anyone else to direct the conversation. Squaring herself on her mother, she raises her hand and points her forefinger at Alicia.

"Here's what you are going to do: you're going to leave with the money you have, and you are not going to come back here." Amara steps in front of me, as if to protect me, and a surge of pride creeps up my spine. "You will not say anything to his father, or I will tell Mr. Saint myself how you tried to blackmail his family." Alicia pales at her threat. My father is not a man to cross. "I'll reach out after I've had some time to process this. If you wish to mend the rift you've created between us, then we'll talk about all of this then. Do you understand me, Mom?"

Amara falters on her last word.

Alicia nods, and Amara steps back in silence. She doesn't

say goodbye. Pointing to the door, she excuses her mother. Alicia fidgets with her purse and drops her gaze to the floor. Her lies are finally out where they can be seen and judged, and she's too beaten to look up at me.

Amara waits until Alicia leaves the room before quietly walking to the door, and I don't say anything to stop her. She's asked Alicia for time, and I'm sure she needs that from me as well.

Instead of exiting, she pushes the door closed, shutting us in. The empty click of the lock catches me by surprise.

My heartbeat picks up once again, this time for a different reason, as she closes the distance between us.

I test the waters between us. "Blossom."

She levels me with her stare.

"How long have you known?"

Amara stares me down, waiting for me to respond, but she isn't mad. She just wants answers.

"I found out just before you turned eighteen. Dagen was actually the one who told me when he discovered something he shouldn't have."

She stands still while she processes what I've told her. I've known all along.

"And you sent me away." Amara is close to working something out in her head, and I help her out.

"You are mine, Amara. You always have been. If our parents wanted to pretend you'd been bought and sold, so be it. But the fact that you had a price put on you—it made you—"

"A possession." Amara whispers to herself, and I nod.

It's the one thing Amara never wanted to be.

"When your mother broke the deal and moved you away, it took you off the board. You were no longer a pawn. I thought it was the best way to keep you safe until I could protect you myself."

Amara's eyes lower to the ground between us. "You should have told me. I know why you didn't, but you should have."

I nod once. I won't argue that point. I've made mistakes. I've done a lot of things to Amara.

"I won't apologize." I'd do everything all over again and without remorse if I knew I would have her back like I do now.

"I know. But you will make it up to me. Then we'll talk about it—later."

I lower my head to make eye contact. "Will I now?" I deliver my question as a challenge.

Unlike her mother, Amara doesn't shy away from my gaze. She pinches her lips together and nods, batting her lashes at me.

I know what she's getting at. I sucker punched her with this secret, and she wants her pound of flesh in retribution.

It's like guy code. If I blindsided one of my brothers and wanted to make things right, they'd get a free punch.

She's asking for her free punch.

But she's not one of my brothers. Our dynamic works in a certain way, and I know by looking at the glint in her eye she is going to show me what it feels like to spin out of control, and I'm not going to like the lesson.

All humor leaves my face.

"Done." I resign myself without asking what my punishment will be, but I add my terms. "Whatever happens does not leave this room." She nods her agreement and I continue, my voice dropping dangerously low, "I say this with absolute certainty, Blossom: you will never have this opportunity again."

She closes the distance between us and places her warm palm on my chest before drawing her finger down over my abdomen and stopping at my belt.

"I know."

"Very well." It feels unnatural to hold my hands at my sides when I want to comb my fingers through her hair. I lower my head to the side, barely brushing my cheek against hers, and I whisper into her ear, "Do your worst."

I pull away from her, and Amara shudders.

She looks back up at me and sucks her lower lip between her teeth. "I intend to."

My phone rings, and she leans around me, lifting the receiver then dropping it back down before punching some buttons. I assume she's forwarding my calls.

Anticipation burns through me. Possibilities of what she is going to do both excite and terrify me.

I feel these emotions when I am on the other side of this scenario, but they are not the same. They come from a different place. When I have Amara's control, I am excited by the known, not the unknown. I know what I'm going to do to her, and I can't wait to uncover her reactions.

At the same time, there is a level of worry that I'll miss something she needs. Holding her trust in my care can be overwhelming at times.

This is different, but the same.

"You'll sit in your chair. I want your pants around your ankles."

It takes me a few seconds to understand what she's saying.

"I'm not sure how this is a punishment," I murmur as I circle my desk.

She stays quiet as she follows me around, watching as I reach for my belt.

My cock springs to life the moment he clears my zipper, and she places her hand on my chest, gently urging me to sit down.

Placing her palms on my knees, she spreads them and

nuzzles her body in between, and I jump when she wraps her fingers around my erection.

"Unbutton your shirt but leave it on." She lowers her head, licking at my tip, and I groan. My fingers find the first button as the soft warmth of her mouth spreads down my shaft.

Her head bobs as her spit coats my length, and I push open my shirt, anxious to feel her touch.

I really don't see how this is a punishment.

Standing, she reaches under her skirt, pulling her panties down and kicking them away with the toe of the black heels she still has on.

Fuck, she's amazing.

I'm lost in excitement, and I almost miss her next words.

"You won't touch me. You'll remain still"—she leans over, brushing her lips against the shell of my ear while I inhale her intoxicating smell—"and you won't come."

Wait—what?

"Amara." I hate that panic is the only thing I hear in my sad excuse for a threat.

"Hands under your thighs," she orders.

It's hard to concentrate when her glazed eyes and hazy look are such a distraction. I know this look. She is ready, and she's telling me this is the only way I'm getting any right now.

This is her one shot.

This is her worst.

Fuck me.

Holding her stare is the only thing I'm allowed to do as I place my hands at my sides and grip the seat.

Amara pulls her skirt up, showing me her trimmed pussy, and I groan without shame as she moves to the chair and climbs on top of me.

My head shouts at me to grab her and pull her down around every inch of my raging hard-on. I grit my teeth as she lowers herself at her own pace, moaning as she tilts her hips for better access.

My head drops back against the chair, and I watch her find a rhythm, her hips rocking and grinding as she raises and lowers herself, slowly picking up her pace.

We fall into a manageable flow, and I tell myself I'll just jerk off after she leaves when her fingers go to the buttons that are stretched tight across her chest.

I'm mesmerized by the supple skin on her stomach, and my eyes climb to her chest.

A growl forces its way out of my throat when she shoves her bra up and her tits fall out—just out of my reach.

Fuck, I want to motorboat her right now, but I'm pretty sure it's against her rules.

She continues to ride me, my cock wrapped tightly in her cunt, and I rein myself in, urging the building sensations to subside for a little longer.

A surge of desperation hits me when she moans loudly, picking up her pace and pinching her own nipples right in front of my face.

I look from my chest to hers, silently willing her to lean forward and make skin-on-skin contact, but she doesn't.

Instead, she grips the headrest of my chair and looks into my soul as she fucks herself on me.

I'm holding myself back with everything I have. Her face goes slack, her lips part, and I force the image of her sucking my cock far out of my head as the muscles in my thighs and back tighten to keep myself from coming with her.

My teeth clench as she starts to moan. The little sounds she makes hit my ears like a fucking symphony.

I know I have a grimace on my face. I can't physically hide how difficult it is to watch her take her pleasure but not be able to take my own.

I'm about to start reciting my ABCs when her body tenses and convulses around me, a loud whimper escaping her lips.

As the aftershocks hit her, her pussy spasms around my cock, and I'm about ready to lose my mind when she settles enough and lifts her body off of mine. My cock timbers to the side in all of its erected glory.

He's still ready for his happy ending.

Poor guy.

I watch as she gathers her panties from the floor, pulling them up her legs and smoothing down her skirt.

I stay still as she meets my stare, her face warm and flushed. She's glowing, and I'm glowering.

She adjusts her bra and buttons up her top without a word.

Combing her fingers through her hair, she looks like nothing happened.

I, however, am a mess.

My heart is still pounding. I'm in such a foreign headspace, I don't know what to do.

She smiles then. "One more thing. No coming until it's with me, later tonight." She winks at me. She fucking winks. "I bet you wish you had that information earlier."

Son of a—

I watch her leave and shut the door behind her, then I check the clock on the wall. The time spurs me to get dressed and compose myself, but it's no use.

When Constance checks in with me once she returns from lunch, I tell her to cancel all of my meetings for the rest of the day.

There's only one thing occupying my mind now: all of the dirty things I'm going to do to Amara when I get my hands on her next.

29

AMARA

It's amazing what a good nooner can do for the rest of your day.

My productivity shot through the roof, and my cleared head meant I could fill it with all of the details I needed to handle my deadlines and meetings.

Except for my meeting with Ryder. That one was cancelled, and I don't think he came out of his office for the rest of the day.

He texted me to tell me he had some business with Cole after work, so they were going to grab dinner together. Then he made a point of listing all of the things he had planned for me tonight. His frustration was evident in the number of spelling mistakes he kept making.

I've been at home and off work for an hour, and I'm still chuckling about it.

I check the time on my phone. Sloane is due home any minute. She picked up Henry from his daycare, and they went out for a treat. I asked her if we could spend some time together and watch a movie, just the three of us.

We had a long talk over breakfast about everything Ryder shared with me last night, and I've already promised I can keep their secret. I've become practiced at controlling my emotions, and I've ensured her Henry won't suspect a thing.

The cardboard box lying on the floor at my feet holds many fond memories for me. It is filled with old movies Ryder and his brothers watched as children. Mrs. Saint often brought out the box so I could watch them when I was over.

The front door opens just as I find the one I was looking for.

"I'm in here," I call over my shoulder, flipping the disc over in my hand to read the back of the cover. I'm pretty sure this one doesn't have anything Henry shouldn't be watching.

The door opens behind me, and I talk over my shoulder as I finish reading the cover. "I found a movie Ryder used to watch with his brothers as a kid. I think Henry—"

"I'm not here to watch a movie."

I startle at the voice's dark authority and snap my gaze to the entrance.

The room falls into complete silence, and the hairs at the back of my neck stand on end.

Lennox glares at me from the door. It's the same look he levelled on me when he thought I was Sloane at the club.

I stand, and my hands reflexively smooth the front of my clothes. "Of course not. I'm sorry. Um—Ryder isn't here."

My mind scrambles to replay what I just said out loud. After telling Sloane I had everything under control this morning, did I just let something important slip? No. I didn't say anything about Ryder. I only mentioned the movies.

I release a steady breath and keep an impassive expression on my face.

"I'm not here for Ryder." The despondent way Lennox says

Ryder's name fills me with despair. It makes me think their history is a tragic one.

"Why are you here?"

It's a stupid question, really. Ryder told me the brothers all have access to the place if they need it, but something about the way he is sizing me up tells me the question is valid.

A chill snakes its way down my spine as he takes a few steps into the room without answering me. Where Ryder stalks me like a wolf, Lennox moves like a panther. His broad shoulders are all muscle, yet he moves with a quiet agility that would mean certain death for any prey who underestimated him and got too close. And here I stand, trapped in a room and gawking at him like a damn deer lost in the headlights.

"Stop looking into your brother's death."

My hackles raise, and I speak without thinking. "You mean his murder."

He chuckles darkly at the semantics and takes another step toward me.

From what I gathered from Ryder and Sloane, Lennox rarely makes an appearance in this house. Yet, by the way he consumes the space around him, I would think he owned the place. He leaves my accusation hanging in the room, and his savage confidence is unsettling.

The uncomfortable silence provokes me to speak. To fill the silent space around us with a distraction.

"I won't stop." My body deflates in resignation.

Lennox nods inwardly, biting the inside of his cheek between his teeth. He doesn't look surprised by my response.

"Back off or they'll never find your body." For a fraction of a second, Lennox's expression morphs into something I can't place.

I take a step back as my mind races with what to say next.

If Lennox had intentions of hurting me, he wouldn't do it here. There's staff and security all over the place.

Or would he?

After our altercation at the club, I'm certain he knows I'm hiding a little secret. Someone his size doesn't just get maneuvered out of the way and nailed to a wall without understanding the power behind why.

If he tries anything here, I'm confident I can at least fight long enough for Ryder's security team to run in and stop him.

No. I'll stay still and hold this card in my hand until I need to play it. I'll show them all just how strong I am.

Our standoff is broken when Henry rushes around Lennox and into the room. Sloane's voice follows.

"Sorry we're late. Henry just had to stop at the pet—" Sloane stops mid-step as her gaze meets mine.

She tenses, and I realize my face must be showing my fear, because she shifts her attention to Lennox.

"What's going on?" She crosses her arms and straightens her spine as she levels a this-better-be-good stare at him.

The corner of Lennox's lip twitches. "We were just discussing her television appearance."

So he did see the show. It looks like I'm doing a stellar job of putting myself out there.

Sloane shakes her head and types something into her phone. Then she squares herself on Lennox and props her hands on her hips.

"You need to go." Sloane's tone is firm, but she tilts her head a fraction, as if trying to reason with him in silence.

Henry tugs at the movie in my hand, and I let it go as I focus on the show playing out in front of me.

"And what if I don't want to leave? Do *you* want me to go, Sloane?" Lennox lowers his voice.

The heat in the room just shot up to an intense level, and I'm not sure we're all talking about the same thing anymore.

"Uncle, watch with us." Henry commands his attention, and Lennox softens into a completely different person as he kneels down, takes the movie from Henry's hands, and looks at it.

His smile doesn't reflect in his eyes as he hands it back to Henry.

"You know, this was your dad's favorite movie when he was your age. Ryder would always pick it when it was his turn to choose the movie." Lennox speaks with the sadness of long-lost happier days, and his memory surprises me.

That earns him a grin from Henry. "Really?"

A commotion at the door draws all of our eyes, and Nash enters with two guys behind him.

"Lennox." He turns to Sloane and me. "Ladies." He smiles at Henry. "Little man." Nash turns his body back to Lennox, looking a little hesitant. "I've got orders from Ryder. We need to escort you from the premises for the night." Nash delivers his marching orders with nonchalance, as though he's talking about the weather. He breaks his stare with Lennox and glances at Henry for a moment.

"I'll remind you, this is my house too." Lennox is firm with the three men around him, but his tone isn't as harsh as it was with me just a minute ago, and I already sense a fading tension between the men in the room.

"Yes. Absolutely. It is. But this is something you'll need to take up with Ryder. Maybe we can leave these three to do their own thing." Nash smiles at Henry, and Lennox takes a long, solemn look at the boy.

Worry creeps along my skin. It's a stupid thought, but I'm terrified Lennox will be able to tell by looking at me that Henry has a secret. Maybe it was better when I didn't know this truth.

I understand now why Ryder kept it from me.

"Sorry, kiddo. Another time." Lennox addresses Henry, who shrugs before finding the best seat on the couch, oblivious to the strain all around him.

Lennox curtly lifts his chin at Nash, and the three men leave the room. Lennox turns to follow but stops when he reaches the door. Turning toward the room once more, he looks past me, as though I'm not even here, and settles his eyes on Sloane. Gone are his harsh features. Instead, a forlorn feeling washes over me.

His voice is low as he speaks. "This isn't over."

Then he's gone, and I'm left wondering if he was talking to me or Sloane. I steal a glance at her, and the ashen look on her face tells me she's wondering the same thing.

Sloane stays still, staring trancelike at the door Lennox left through. Knowing a bit of their history makes this understandable, but I sense there are a lot of unresolved issues between these two.

Sloane was entirely selfless when she pushed Ryder and me back together, and I hope I can be that kind of a friend to her when she needs me.

"You okay?" I whisper, hoping Henry doesn't hear us.

She smiles, then looks at me. Her happy expression is only for show; her eyes hold so much sadness. I don't know Sloane well enough to tell what she's feeling, but, if I had to guess, I would say she was lonely.

Her eyes focus on Henry, and she holds up her hand, asking for a minute as she circles the couch, takes the movie from him, and puts it in the player.

The opening scene begins, and Henry doesn't wait for either of us to join him. He takes his place in the middle of the couch, and Sloane returns to me, lowering her voice.

"I'm good. Seeing him was—unexpected. How about you?

Did he say anything to you?" Sloane looks both hopeful and worried.

"He told me I'd end up dead if I kept looking for Grayson's killer."

Her eyes widen and she nods in thought while the movie plays on.

"Hey," Nash calls under his breath from the door, and we pause to look at him. "Everything good?"

Sloane nods. "Fine. Thank you, Nash. Can you ask Marta to bring us the bottle of red I have open on the counter and two glasses?" She smiles, and Nash leaves us.

As soon as he's out of range, Sloane turns her attention back to me.

"What exactly did Nox say?"

Nox. This is the first time I've heard anyone call Lennox by anything other than his full name. I don't think she realizes she said it either.

"Um"—I glare at the ceiling, trying to remember—"first he said to stop looking into Grayson's death, then he said, 'Back off or they'll never find your body.'" I quote the second part word-for-word. Then I tell her this was when Henry ran into the room.

Her forehead creases as she considers my recollection.

"So he didn't threaten directly," she mutters to herself before asking, "Did you feel threatened, Amara?"

I do a double take at her question, and she shrugs her shoulders in a knowing expression before explaining herself.

"You know Ryder. The Saint boys are all the same. If they mean to threaten you, they don't dance around. Lennox said you'd end up dead. He didn't say *he* would kill you. I know Lennox is intimidating, and you don't know him like—" She pauses at whatever thought has just entered her mind. Taking a deep breath, she shakes her head and tries again. "Switch it around. If it was Ryder who acted like that and said those things, how would you take it?"

Her question brings everything to a halt.

I don't know Lennox, and I have no history with him. Sloane is right; Lennox has always been cold and private from my perspective.

I put Ryder into the scenario. If it was Ryder walking in and saying those things, matched with his actions and the look on his face—

"I would have thought he was warning me."

30

RYDER

"So tell me again why you wanted to come out with me tonight. I mean, I'm not complaining, but don't you have a little spitfire at home waiting for you?" Cole chuckles into his beer, and I glance around the dive, hoping to place a familiar face so I don't have to answer his question.

No such luck.

"You said your guy has some information on Grayson. I want in on it." It's a half truth.

Cole eyes me up then shrugs, accepting my answer.

The truth is, I want to see Amara desperately right now, and this is why I should stay away a little longer. I'm still wound up, and I don't have enough control over myself yet.

Depending on what happens here, Cole may need to bust some bones, and I could use the release.

This is what listening to my little flower is doing to me. I honored her request and didn't jack off in the nearest bathroom after she used me as her fuck toy at lunch.

I've been an ornery asshole all day.

I need to punch something.

Movement over Cole's shoulder catches my eye as a scrawny guy approaches us. I lift my chin, indicating the intrusion, as the guy skittishly looks around the bar to see if anyone is looking.

"Lucky." Cole turns and stands, slapping the guy on the back as though they know each other. I don't remember if I got his real name at any point, so "Lucky" it is.

Lucky flinches at the connection, and Cole doesn't step away. Instead, he towers over the sniveling mess and clamps his hand in the lapels of his jacket, pulling him onto the barstool Cole just sat on. Cole takes the stool beside him so we both flank his sides.

Only Cole's smile is friendly, and I stare at our guest, expressionless.

I'm already starting to feel better.

"Heyyyy, Mr. Saint. Um, thanks for meeting me here. Uh, I almost have all of that money I owe you."

Cole mentioned the guy has actually been making his payments, which is oddly impressive because usually such extensions are only so people can settle their affairs.

Cole nods, his smile tight on his face. "Paying your debt has nothing to do with why you're still here with us, Lucky. You have something to tell us, or are you defaulting?"

Lucky looks between us, and the light from behind the bar sparkles on the sweat glistening his forehead.

"N-no. I'm not defaulting. This is—uh—the bar where I saw those guys talking, the ones I told you about, and I've been trying to find them for you."

"I want a name." Cole takes another sip of his drink, and Lucky breaks a partially smug smile.

"I can do you one better." Lucky tilts his head back and toward the corner of the bar.

Cole and Lucky stay turned toward our conversation. I'm

the only one who can naturally look over their shoulders without turning around.

Two men are playing a round of pool in the corner. I don't recognize either one.

"Which one?"

Lucky startles at the low sound of my voice but settles quickly. "The taller one, wearing the jean jacket."

I take a second look. The men in the corner are deep in their game, and our guy isn't looking around. He isn't expecting anything. I look at Cole and nod.

"You know what happens if you play me." Cole stares at the poor bastard sitting between us. It wasn't a question, but Lucky nods anyway. Cole clarifies, "On your daughter's life."

I hold my expression firm to back Cole up, but I know he wouldn't harm an innocent kid. Lucky doesn't know that though, and he pales but holds firm. "I know what's at stake, Mr. Saint. I'm turning my life around for her. I'm telling you, it's him."

Cole sits in silence as the seconds pass before pinching his lips together and nodding to himself. Then he ducks his head toward the guy cowering between us.

"Well, Lucky. You have three payments left, then you don't want to see my face again. Understand?"

Lucky doesn't skip a beat. Standing, he lowers his sight to the floor. "Yes, sir."

As Lucky promptly exits the bar, Cole turns to watch him leave and steals a glance at the two in the corner. Without skipping a beat, he takes another drink and slides onto the stool Lucky just left.

"Recognize him?" I ask, squaring myself to the bar in front of us and taking a twenty out of my wallet to cover our drinks.

"Yep." Cole stares at his empty bottle before setting it down. The waiter comes over and lifts the bottle to ask if he wants another. Cole shakes his head. When we are alone again, he continues, "He's a Saint lackey. Mostly a body, muscle, backup. He has worked at Saint's Wharf from time to time. He could have had access to the security tapes. It'd be a stretch for him to get them, but probably not impossible." He takes a pause, weighing the truth in his next words. "Depending on who he was working with—or for."

"What's his name?"

"Steevers. I prefer his new nickname though."

"Which is?"

"Unlucky." Cole flexes his knuckles into a fist.

An increase in noise from across the next-to-vacant bar catches my attention, and I nod as the two guys make their way outside through the back doors. Steevers pulls a cigarette out of his jacket pocket as they exit.

Cole stands and makes eye contact with the bartender, shaking his head. The silent order is understood.

We are not to be disturbed.

Unlucky's sheer stupidity isn't lost on me. First he crosses the Saint family, then he brags about it, and now here he is, enjoying a drink and a game of pool in a Saint-owned establishment. This guy must really think he's untouchable.

The cold winter air fills my lungs as we step into the alley, and both men turn to face us. Steevers's eyes go wide for a fraction of a second, his cigarette hanging from his lip.

"You got a light?" Cole asks as he approaches.

Their tentative smiles are strained, but the one with Unlucky reaches into his pocket and pulls out a lighter as I level him with one swift punch to the face. Steevers reaches for his gun, and Cole grabs the front of his jacket, taking him down with a blow that lands, and I hear the crack of bone from where I'm standing.

"YOU BROKE MY NOSE!" Steevers hollers into his

hands, cupping his face, and blood pours down onto his shirt. Cole removes the gun and slides it into his belt at his back.

The guy at my feet struggles to stand, and I tower over him. "You know who I am. Stay down. I don't know your name. You want to change that?"

I'm betting he knows of me; the guy looks up at me and Cole from the ground before raising his hands in surrender. He stays on the ground, leaving his friend to fend for himself.

"Word around here is you have something I want." Cole grabs Steevers by the jacket again and easily lifts him to his feet even though they both weigh about the same.

Cole doesn't clarify further, and Steevers pales. He knows exactly what Cole is asking for.

"Hey, man. I don't know what you're—"

"Skip the bullshit. I want the video from Saint's Wharf."

Cole doesn't give him a chance to lie. He lands his boot on the side of Steevers's knee and follows through until another sound of bones cracking fills the dark alleyway.

Steevers howls in pain, and Cole lets him drop to the ground to roll around for a moment. The guy at my feet looks like he's going to vomit or pass out. Good. I'm sure the stories he'll tell will go a long way in supporting our reputation around here.

"If you don't know what I'm talking about, then you're of no use to me, and Seattle will wake up to the news of two bodies found in this alley." Cole pulls Steevers's gun back out and checks to make sure it's loaded.

Steevers gets the message.

"Whoa. Wait. Okay. Um, I might have something. But I want out. I want your promise that I give you this and I don't get killed."

Cole ignores his bargain. "How did you get the security video?"

"I—shit—I can't tell you that. I'm dead for sure." Cole lifts the gun to Steevers, testing his loyalty, and he doesn't back down. "Look, I was supposed to destroy it. That's all I'm going to say."

Whoever is responsible for Grayson's death also has a reputation here if Steevers won't name them to save his own life.

I have a moment of panic for Grayson and Amara. If Cole kills this piece of shit now, then we might never solve this. I clear my throat, catching Cole's attention. He puts the gun back in his belt.

"Here's what I'm going to—promise. You get me the security video, and you have three days to"—he kneels down, digging his fingers into Steevers's broken leg until he screams— "get this checked out and disappear. After that, our truce is up, and word goes out."

Steevers takes a second too long to respond, and Cole grips his knee. The guy twists his head back in a silent scream. Cole is giving him a head start, and he must know this is the best offer he'll get.

"G-got it. I'll send my woman with it. I'll contact you when I have it."

Cole stands, looking down on him with a disgusted sneer. I share his disdain. He's using his girl as a shield to guarantee we won't kill him as soon as we get what we want. The asshole doesn't know for sure we won't kill her.

"You try to leave, and I'll let it slip that you never destroyed the video you were supposed to. You have twenty-four hours."

Steevers nods furiously at Cole's threat. If he's scared enough of whoever he was working for, he won't want them to know he didn't follow orders.

Cole turns his attention to the guy lying at my feet. "Your friend had too much to drink and fell. Get him some help."

He scrambles over as we step back. As they scurry out of the alley, Steevers yelps and groans, dragging his limp leg and banging into garbage cans.

"Do you think he'll follow through?" I watch as they disappear around the corner.

"He has no choice. If he has it, we'll get it." Cole takes a step toward the back door of the bar when my phone vibrates in my pocket.

Sloane: Lennox is at the house with Amara.

"Shit," I hiss at the message, and Cole stops walking. "Lennox showed up at the house. He's with Amara."

I pull up Nash's number and hold the phone to my ear as Cole stays still beside me.

The phone line clicks, and I don't hesitate. "Nash, Lennox is in the house."

"Yes. He dropped by about five minutes ago. He—"

"Get him out of there now, Nash. Off the grounds. I'm on my way."

I disconnect the call. I know Nash will do as I request, but he'll be confused. We've kept our plans hidden away from anyone who isn't family.

I pass Cole in the alley. I'm reaching for the door when he murmurs, "Your hellion can take care of herself."

I round on him. "This is Lennox we're talking about."

He shrugs and opens his mouth to say something then closes it again. I know my brother well enough to tell when he is keeping something from me.

"What aren't you saying, Cole?"

He raises his hands, silently urging me not to be mad. "I might have learned something about your girl." A sharp pain pinches behind my eye; no doubt I'm having an aneurysm.

Cole chuckles at my glare and continues, "I went back and checked on her life in Portland. Something didn't sit right with how she handled Lennox at Eros. It turns out, Amara doesn't go to yoga class for an hour and a half each week on Wednesdays."

"Cole." I warn him to speed this up.

"Okay—fine. You're no fun," Cole mutters, and my patience snaps.

"Just you wait, Cole. One day, you're going to meet someone who drives you batshit bonkers, and you're going to need something from me and I'm going to be all like"—I throw my hands in his face in air quotes—"'whatever guy, you're no fun,' and you're going to want to knock my teeth out."

"Never gonna happen, little brother." He chuckles. I don't laugh with him, and he decides to get back to his story.

"For the past two years, Amara has been taking self-defense and mixed martial arts classes in a room at the back of the yoga studio."

I stare incredulously at the stupid grin on Cole's face. "When were you going to tell me this?"

Now my brother tosses his head back and laughs before wiping a tear from the corner of his eye. When his steam runs out, he sighs deeply.

"Honestly, I was kind of waiting for her to have enough of your shit and drop-kick you like a sack of potatoes. I would have paid money to see that." The goofy grin on his face is testing my patience.

I pull the door open so hard it groans on its rusted hinges, and Cole catches me before I tear through the bar.

"Ryder. Just wait. Really. Your girl can take care of herself. I didn't tell you because it's clear to me she isn't going to hurt you. Knowing you, you probably gave her a lot of reasons, but she hasn't kicked your ass yet, has she?" My silence is Cole's answer, and he continues, "You said it yourself: Amara holds onto power in different ways. She's trained every week to strengthen herself. I think it's amazing that she did that. You know Amara better than any of us. Why do you think she hasn't said anything?"

He nods over my shoulder at the bartender, who returns the gesture, and Cole starts walking toward the front door. He isn't waiting for my answer. This is my food for thought.

I had just taken a punch to the head, and the room was a little out of focus, but I recall Amara stepping easily into Lennox, and then he was up against the wall. She looked worried, but still diffused the situation, then brushed off her movements as a lucky break.

My mind was on other things that night. I should have noticed what Cole saw.

We're already stepping into the parking lot when the cold chill finally hits me and pulls me from my thoughts.

"You want me to follow you to the house?" Cole turns to face me when he gets to his bike, and I check my phone.

Nash already texted. Lennox left a few minutes ago without incident.

"No, but thanks for—all of this." I leave the details hanging between us, but Cole knows I also mean setting me straight about Amara. He nods, digging his keys out of his pocket.

He fires up his motorcycle and waves before riding out, and I get into my own car with thoughts of my flower still invading my head.

Cole is right: Amara could have taken a shot at me many times. Instead she obeyed, surrendered, and submitted.

She didn't tell me because it's a piece of her she wanted to hold on to until she was sure she was safe to share it, not because she was planning to use it against me.

I just haven't earned that piece of her yet, but I will.

Nash is already waiting for me outside the front gate as I park and get out of the car.

"What was he doing here?" I circle my car and walk to their building, nodding at the guys to pull up the security feed. I enter in my code to access the tapes.

My brothers and I are the only ones with access to our video footage, and Nash waits behind me as I finish logging in.

Once the system unlocks, I step aside and allow Nash to type in the time, and I watch the screen as Lennox pulls into the yard.

"He said he was here to talk to Amara Scott, and she was home, so I let him in." I don't respond. Instead, I tap through the cameras to follow Lennox as he made his way through the house. Nash fills the silence. "I'm not sure what happened here, but Lennox is right; this is his house too, and I technically work for all of you."

I glare at him then, because we both know he is angling to be my right hand.

He tries to redeem himself.

"Listen, Ryder, I can't protect your house if I don't know where the threat is coming from."

He's not wrong, but I'm not ready to bring anyone else in. I promised Sloane we would keep Henry safe, and I won't endanger him.

Instead, I go with what we all know. "Amara's life is in danger since she went on TV."

Nash nods in agreement. "We all saw it."

"Everyone has," I mumble dryly to myself in frustration before addressing Nash again. "Until further notice, you are to brief me on her movements and clear any visitors with me."

Nash waits a few seconds, and I know he's hoping for more. He's not getting it right now. I lock up the video feed.

"I'm going to talk to Sloane and Amara. Keep everyone out for tonight. Have the cook bring any food or coffee out here. No one else gets in until the morning. Understood?" Nash nods, and I loosen my tight smile and leave the security building.

As I near the house, my body warms with all of the events of the evening, but there is one thing—one little thing—that heats me above all else, and that is the thought of what I'm going to do to Amara once I get her alone.

The house is quiet when I step through the front doors, and I follow the light coming from the family room. The last five minutes of a movie I used to watch when I was a kid are playing on the screen, but that isn't what I'm drawn to.

Circling the table, I take in the sight before me. A half-drunk bottle of red and two drained glasses sit on the table, along with some empty candy wrappers and a demolished bowl of popcorn.

Sloane smiles up at me, and I place my finger on my lips to keep her quiet. She turns her attention from me to the duo passed out beside her.

Henry's head rests gently on Amara's shoulder as his little hands hold one of her arms as though it's a teddy bear. Amara's head is back against the couch but tilting in toward her nephew in a loving gesture.

"They giggled together through the whole movie." Sloane's laugh is soft, and I take another minute to enjoy my flower.

Judging by what Cole said, Amara could probably take any one of us in a hand-to-hand fight, yet here she is, sleeping soundly and trusting us to watch over her.

"Get him to bed. We'll talk in the morning." There's no point in asking her what was said when I saw everything on the security cameras.

Sloane stands, lifting Henry up into her arms, and his limbs dangle at his sides as she leaves the two of us alone.

Wickedly, my eyes lower to Amara's body. Try as she might, her flannel pajama bottoms and robe are the furthest thing from a turnoff.

Lethal or not, my little angel left me wanting today, and that can't go unpunished. The muscles in my cheeks tighten into a sinful grin.

This day has been too long.

I am suddenly starving, and my sleeping beauty knows she has a price to pay.

It's time to collect.

31

AMARA

I'm hit with déjà vu when I open my eyes and look at the movie playing on the television.

I'm sure I already saw this part.

The male body stretched out beside me startles me to fully awake, and I meet Ryder's gaze. He's taking me in. My stomach tightens in anxious excitement.

Ryder knows what this does to me. I always loved when he would stalk me and take me over. There's nothing like feeling hunted—at least, when Ryder is my predator.

Somehow, I ended up sleeping on his hard chest, and his arm is wrapped around me while his fingers comb through my hair.

He casually sips a glass of red wine with his free hand, and I glance around to find the rest of my company.

"I sent them to bed. We're alone."

Ryder makes it sound like a threat, and more shivers tickle across my body.

"Where do they sleep?" This seems like a question I should

have asked sooner. "I saw them going into a room near mine once."

"They have my parents' old room when they want it, but lately they've been staying in the pool house." Worry settles over me. I hope I'm not kicking them out of the house. Ryder continues talking. "Relax. They enjoy it out there. The deer come right up to the door in the morning. Henry loves feeding them, and security is out there all night. It's like a vacation home for them."

He shifts, and I lift my weight off him so he can stand.

He takes the last sip of his red wine, then sets the glass down and extends his hand to me.

The events from earlier hit me. "Ryder, Lennox—"

"I saw everything on the cameras, and I'd rather not talk about him unless there is something I don't already know."

Something has shifted between us. I expected Ryder to come rushing in here, guns drawn and ready to fight for my honor, but this version of Ryder seems more calm and collected.

"No. That's it." I take his hand. He pulls me up, then leads me from the room. I follow with a yawn, still trying to wake myself up.

A soft jerk on my hand tells me we aren't going upstairs to bed, and I pad quietly behind Ryder as he pulls me down the hall and into the library.

The smell of old paper, leather, and a fire long since extinguished hits me. My face flushes at the sight of the large leather chair.

"I replaced a lot of furniture in this house, but I will never give up this chair," Ryder muses to himself before turning his attention to me. "Do you know why I love this old piece of furniture so much, Blossom?"

I nod and force myself to meet his intense stare.

"Why?" His expression turns dark.

His thumb rubs along my wrist as he waits, and I get the feeling he's monitoring my pulse.

"Because you found me here and made me read that part of the book out loud." He smiles affectionately before stepping into me. Wrapping his fingers around the back of my head, he pulls me forward, placing a chaste kiss on my forehead.

The tension between us increases as he drops his hand to the belt tied loosely around my waist and gently pulls. My robe opens, exposing my little white tank top underneath, and the tickle of my nipples hardening under his scrutiny makes me shiver.

"While that is a favorite memory of mine, it isn't why I kept it." Ryder's eyes rake over me slowly, and he licks his lower lip before pinching my nipple through the fabric. A thought nags at the back of my head.

"Are you sure you can't think of another—more obscene—reason I may have wanted to hold on to it?"

He didn't see that. I was alone.

"Wh-why did you keep it?" I try for a genuinely curious tone.

Ryder's finger plays with the elastic band of my pajama bottoms before his hand cups my mound over the fabric and squeezes gently, rubbing my labia together. I groan for him while his eyes move from side to side as he watches my expression crack.

Reaching his free hand out, he pulls a book off the shelf and hands it to me. A dizzying wave hits me, and my cheeks warm at the sight of the familiar cover.

My dirty little secret stares up at me.

The cover is as worn as I remember it. A woman and man locked in a heated embrace stare up at me, just like they did that night, beckoning to me to read their erotic story like the little voyeur I was.

He lowers his head, his lips brushing along my ear as he whispers, "I saw you. That night when you thought we all went outside to go swimming. I stayed behind. I stood right over there"—he nods to a section of the room I wouldn't have been able to see from the chair—"and I watched you hold this book in one hand while you read to yourself. You were covered by a blanket, and your leg was draped over the arm of the chair. What was your other hand doing, Blossom?"

"You—how did you—" All of this time, he never said a thing.

It's clear what I was doing by the book I was reading, and Ryder knows it, but he isn't backing down. For him, the fun is in getting me to admit to the things that make me feel shame.

"I was touching myself."

I remember the night this happened. I was sure I was alone and had dared to rest my head against the back of the chair and—

Oh God, I remember moaning.

It was spontaneous and soft, and it startled me out of my haze. I couldn't help myself. The elicit words on the page mixed with the thrill of being so close to Ryder and masturbating in his parents' house while I imagined him doing everything in that book to me.

"Do you know how hard it was to watch and not touch you?"

Small pieces from that night come back to me. I was almost seventeen and so curious. Ryder never made his intentions clear until after I had turned eighteen, but he made sure no one else took an interest in me before then. At the time, I had thought he was helping Grayson look out for me like the overbearing brother he was, but he was keeping me for himself.

His grin is mesmerizing, and curiosity pushes the question

out of my mouth before my brain catches up. "Why are you smiling like that?"

"Because now I get to touch you." He delivers his answer while he slides my robe down my arms and drops it at our feet.

Sliding one finger in the elastic of my pajama bottoms, he runs his hand along my waist before grabbing my flannel pants by each side and sliding them down. He coaxes me to step out of them.

I grab the bottom of my tank top and lift, but I'm halted when Ryder meets my gaze and shakes his head.

"That stays on for now. Sit down."

My bare ass rubs against the soft leather with a creak as I lower myself into the oversized chair. Ryder drops with me, kneeling on one knee.

His chuckle comes out on his breath as he looks at me, and I lower my eyes to the book clutched on my lap as I sit hunched forward into him. It isn't until he guides me to lean back that I realize how tightly wound I am.

I relax the muscles in my shoulders and rest my body against the back of the chair, just like I did that night.

"Read it out loud."

Memories of the time he told me to read for him send an anxious thrill through my body, and my skin prickles into goosebumps at the nostalgia. "Where should I—"

"I believe it's still marked." He levels me with a hint of mischief in his eyes.

I got the better of him today, and I left him wanting. Now it's time to settle that score.

I return his smile.

I'd be lying if I said I haven't been thinking about this moment all day long. I knew exactly what I was getting myself into setting him up like I did.

I slide my forefinger along the pages, and it slips between

the earmarked corner and the page before it. As I open the book, he opens my legs. His fingers caress my thighs, moving ever so slowly toward my pussy.

Skimming the page, I find the paragraph I'm looking for.

His smile breaks when I lick my lips to get ready to speak, and his gaze zeroes in on my mouth, his expression falling in a moment of pure depravity.

Then I read.

Before I finish the first sentence, Ryder dips his fingers between my outer labia and slides lazily through my folds as he listens to me. He casually licks his lips while his voracious eyes draw me into his spell.

"I told you to read, Blossom." The corner of his mouth twitches into a grin.

"Oh—yes—right." I clear my throat and turn my attention to the page in front of me as his wicked chuckle teases me.

My next sentence is met with him lifting and guiding my legs, hanging them over each arm of the chair and leaving me entirely exposed to him, his face mere inches from my core.

I swallow my nerves and force my gaze to remain on the page as I keep reading the story. He spreads my lips wide before dropping his head to lick along the area I already know is wet with need.

I fumble along, slurring my words when he sucks my clit into his mouth, and his tongue continues to work every sensitive spot he comes across.

Before I realize I've closed them, my eyes shoot open with a jolt at the stinging sensation between my legs. Lifting my head off the back of the chair, I meet Ryder's admonishing gaze.

His open palm lies flat on my pussy, covering the area he just slapped.

"I didn't tell you to stop." His taunt makes me shiver.

Shit.

I can't remember where I left off, so I pick a random paragraph and continue reading. As though our stories are the same, the female is spread out on the bed before her lover, and he explores her body as Ryder explores my own.

My own need builds, and I wriggle my hips as I read, determined not to stop this time. Ryder's hands move under my hips, cupping my ass cheeks and holding me in place while he teases me into a mess.

"Just—um—wait—I'm going to come." My hips involuntarily buck, begging him to send me over the edge.

Ryder stops what he's doing. "Is that you speaking, or the book?"

A growl screams through my head. "It's me. Please don't stop."

Ryder tsks me as he smirks. Then he drops his mouth to my clit and wastes no time building me up and sending me toward the edge.

I writhe in his hands as my final crest approaches, and he stops.

He stops.

My eyes shoot open and meet his once again.

"You'll read that book, and you won't stop, or I will edge you all night. Am I understood?"

I nod furiously, desperate to please him so we can both get what we want. I start reading again. I'm sure I've already read this part, but I don't care. The knot twisting tight in my stomach needs to be released.

As I glare at the words on the page, Ryder continues to touch me, gliding his fingers easily into my wet pussy while his lips latch around my clit and he sucks me into a frenzy. He edges and eases me back two more times before addressing me.

"Come when you want, but don't stop reading until you do. Then I'm going to fuck you into this chair just like I wanted to that night." He rises onto his knees, then stands. Unzipping his pants and pulling out his already stiff cock, he returns to his place on the floor in front of me.

"Fuck yes." My own words surprise me.

They are words I haven't used for a long time.

They come from the part of me I've repressed.

I read from the book, but the words hold no meaning for me. My mind switches to autopilot, and I simply move from one to the next as my body surrenders to Ryder, and he takes control.

When his finger slides from my opening to trail my arousal down further to my ass, I lose my spot. I quickly jump to the first paragraph I see on the page and keep reading.

I think I'm getting louder as I read. Ryder works the tight muscle at my back entrance, locking his mouth around my sensitive nub as he pushes just enough to make me see stars. I yell a random word from the page as I buck wildly against his face when my orgasm hits me.

"Thank fuck." Ryder jumps up, tearing the book out of my hands and smashing his mouth into my own before grabbing my little top and tearing it down the front. I gasp for air as he pulls my hips to the edge of the chair, pushing my legs out and into the arms as he leans over and slides into me without warning. His length fills me whole.

Ryder wastes no time building up to a harsh pace, and my body reacts, winding itself tight again.

My back slides into the chair with each thrust as sweat coats my body, and my fingers dig into the worn leather as a second orgasm rushes into me.

As I tip over the edge into oblivion once again, it is Ryder's growl I hear as he joins me, grunting and groaning expletives. He lowers his weight on top of me as his hands move to the sides of my face, and he leans in for a devouring kiss that sucks the breath out of me.

"You're my absolute, Amara. I should have never let you go, and I want you back. At the time, I was trying to protect you. Grayson thought sending you away would give you a life away from who we are and what we do, and I agreed with him. We were wrong. I was wrong, and I won't make that mistake again. I'm not telling you to accept your place—I'm asking you. Please, Blossom. Give me the chance to love you and show you every day from now on how much you mean to me. I will never let you go again."

My face is wet before I realize I'm crying, and Ryder cups my head, waiting for my answer.

I nod as a sob escapes me. Ryder leans in, kissing me just like I wished he would have on the day I was sent away.

My defenses are down, and I have no desire to run away. I want to feel every emotion with Ryder, and I wrap my arms around him, clutching the back of his shirt as he pulls me forward into a commanding embrace.

I don't know what this means, and I'm not sure Ryder does either. Nothing has changed outside of this room. Sloane and Henry may still be at risk, and Grayson's killer is still out there.

As my heart rate returns to normal, Ryder shifts off of me and reaches for my robe. Before he allows me to take it, he dips his head to my breast and sucks my nipple into his mouth, earning a moan from me.

His grin tells me we aren't done with each other tonight, but I think our time in the library has come to a close.

He stands and offers me his hand to help me up, and I wrap my torn top around my body before finding my pajama bottoms.

I turn to him while I put them on. He already has his pants up, and he's looking at his phone with concern on his face.

"What is it?" I ask.

His gaze meets mine. "It's my father. He wants to have a family meeting—here—tomorrow night. He wants all four of us there. Me and my brothers."

I thought Ryder always got along with his dad, but the worried look on his face tells a different story.

He adds, "Something's wrong."

RYDER

The last time my father called a family meeting, it was to announce his retirement and discuss the handling of the family businesses.

That was two years ago, and before that, we never had one.

My father didn't just request our presence. His message was worded in a way that told me we were all to show up. End of discussion.

I kept Amara home with me during the day, and I sent a message to my secretary to let everyone know we were out of the office on business.

Until I know what is going on, everyone is to remain on lockdown. Sloane and Henry made a day of it out in the pool house, and I brought in one extra guard just to sit out there with them.

Cole has been messaging me all day, and neither one of us has any leads on what this is about. The timing is bad. Our guy is supposed to get us the missing warehouse security footage by the end of today, and no one has heard from him yet.

I sent Amara up to my room when Nash notified me of our

first guest's arrival with instructions not to come down until everyone leaves. I don't need a run-in with Lennox, and my father isn't a fan of hers after she tried to accuse us of killing Grayson somewhere between the main course and dessert.

"Hey. Any idea what this is about?" Dagen is the first through the door.

I shake my head, and he steps into the house when I catch someone entering behind him. Dagen turns to greet Cole with a nod. Before he turns back, headlights light up the front entrance, and Dagen looks past our brother to see who it is.

"It's Lennox. I need a drink." Dagen keeps his jacket on, and I point toward Dad's old office.

It's a general space now, but back when it was my father's, all meetings were held there because it is a little more soundproof than the rest of the house.

"I'll see them in." Cole nods toward the office. None of us want a repeat of what happened at Eros.

I'm not ready to ask Lennox about his showing up and threatening Amara. I worry it'll come to blows if I do. The last thing I want my father to see is his sons fighting each other in his old home.

The less my father hovers in our business, the better.

I nod and turn before Lennox gets to the door, but when I near the office I hear two distinct voices. My father must have pulled in behind him.

"How's business?" I ask Dagen as he pours a drink from our cabinet. He reaches for a second glass and fills it before handing it to me.

"It's slow, so it's given me time to look into some side projects. There's no new information there though." Raising his brows, he adds the last part before anyone joins us, and he shoots me a glare that tells me he's talking about the identity of the Lucciano heir.

The door opens before I respond, and my father joins us, followed by Cole, then Lennox, who meets my glare without a greeting. I take my drink and find a chair while everyone serves themselves.

My father is the first to speak. "You boys are quiet. Everything okay here?"

We all murmur that we're fine, and Dagen speaks above us. "Just wondering why we're all here."

He shifts his focus to Lennox, who grumbles, "Don't look at me. I don't know anything."

My father huffs at our bickering before taking his seat behind the desk.

That's our dad. Always at the head of the table, always the one sitting behind the desk. Even in his retirement, he has his hands in everything. He's sitting there just like he used to, except he doesn't run the family business anymore.

We do.

"I understand there was a situation on Saturday at Eros." My father's eyes shift between Lennox and me.

I open my mouth to come to Amara's defense, and Lennox cuts me off. "Just a disagreement between me, Ryder, and Sloane. It won't happen again."

At the wrong name, I look over and meet Lennox's hard stare. The stern look in his eyes tells me to shut up.

I return my attention to my father and nod in silence, agreeing with my brother's lie.

He's keeping Amara a secret from our father. I catch Cole looking inquisitively at Lennox as well.

"Very well. Boys, I'll remind you that you cannot demand everyone else follow your house rules when you don't follow them yourselves." Our father looks at each one of us as he speaks, then takes a sip of his drink.

Grumbles and curt coughs fill the room as we all agree with

him in our own way. We learned a long time ago not to defend our actions with poor excuses, and he moves on to asking each of us how business is and if there is anything we want to add.

The conversation moves at a boring pace; he manages to make fifteen minutes of light chatter feel like a few hours. My impatience builds because I know we haven't gotten to the reason we are really here.

Finally, it's my turn to talk about the company and what we've been doing, and I sense the change in my father as I speak.

Whatever his reason for being here, it has to do with me. He grows more tense with my every word. He's looking for his segue into the conversation, and I'm pretty sure I know what it is.

Amara.

He's waiting for me to bring her up. I've avoided talking about her this whole time, and his clenched jaw is telling me he's pissed about it.

"And how is the takeover going?" our father finally asks.

I shrug and shake my head.

"I've told you. My acquisition of the company was my own venture. I used my own funds. This is a family meeting." I attempt to separate her from this.

My father hits his boiling point.

"Okay then. Let's talk about family affairs. Does anyone here want to tell me why a certain woman was all over the news this week talking about your friend being murdered at a Saint-owned warehouse?" My father's knuckles go white around the glass in his hand, and the room falls silent.

No one says a thing. It's a slippery slope talking to our father. While you would think your first instinct would be to speak up and try to give your side of the story before he really gets angry, you would be incorrect.

Saying the wrong thing is worse than saying nothing at all in times like these, and Cole and Dagen are staying silent because they don't want to be responsible for digging Amara's grave.

They also don't want to give any indication that they know anything, so neither of them will look in my direction. My father stares me down—so does Lennox.

My father breaks the silence. "I recall you telling me you had everything under control, boy."

I wince inwardly. I hate it when my father calls me "boy." I always have.

"That was unexpected, but it is being dealt with." I take a sip of my drink to settle my nerves and buy me time to think of an answer that will pacify the situation.

"How are you *dealing* with this?" he asks as everyone turns their attention to me.

"I have our team in touch with the television station and any other news outlets that may decide to pick up the story. I have been told it's been suppressed and removed from their online site and no new information will be posted." By "our team" I mean our lawyers and the companies we hire to gloss over facts and pay people off.

My father lets us sit in uncomfortable silence for a few minutes while he considers my information. I almost startle out of my seat when he speaks again.

"And the girl?" my father asks.

Lennox shifts, pulling his phone out of his jacket pocket to check the screen before sliding it back in and returning to our conversation.

I start lying through my teeth.

"Her time here is almost over. She has been dealt with and silenced, and she'll be returning to Portland next week to continue with the company from there until I see fit to remove her from her employment. I made it abundantly clear what will happen if she attempts anything like that again." I don't use Amara's name in front of him. It's best if he keeps calling her "the girl." It's when he gives someone a name that I start to worry.

As for sending Amara away, that will never happen again. I've bought us one week—then I have to come up with a reason for Amara to stay or hide her away somewhere. As I wait for my father's ruling, I mentally list all of our options.

"Very well." My father doesn't sound convinced, but the night is dragging on, and I'm sure he's ready to leave now that he's said his piece.

Cole and Dagen shuffle in their seats, and my father lifts his phone off the table. He taps the screen a few times, mutters about the late hour, and sets the phone back on the desk.

I'm halfway to standing before he breaks the awkward silence.

"Boys, while I have you here, I want to update you on your mother."

"Everything okay?" Cole's concerned tone matches how I feel.

"Hmm? Oh, yes. She's doing well. She had a bit of a setback last week when her memory loss got the better of her, but her doctor had assured me that might happen because he had to adjust her medication. He's monitoring her now. She hasn't had any problems since. I wanted to let you know. I also wanted to tell you to visit her more often. She talks about all of you boys, and I know she misses you." My father is not a caring man toward anyone who isn't my mother, so watching him painfully ask this of us makes me feel like an asshole for not seeing her more.

"I'll call her tomorrow. We'll have her over more. I know Henry loves seeing his grandmother."

Of all the lies I've told tonight, this one was the hardest.

While I love Henry as if he were my own, I've hated telling my mother she has a grandson when she doesn't.

"If that's everything, I need to get home and see your mother." Everyone looks relieved the meeting is done. Then my father turns to me. "I want to know when Amara Scott is out of your life for good."

He doesn't wait for my answer.

It wasn't a question.

And there's her name.

Lennox speaks first. "I'll walk you out, Dad." He glares another round of daggers at me before he leaves the room behind my father, and I'm left with Cole and Dagen.

I wait until the front door closes before I leave the office and return to the main area. Then I make sure both of them are gone.

"You're sending Amara back to Portland in a week?" Dagen looks between Cole and me in confusion.

"Fuck no. I'm just trying to buy her some time."

Cole adds his two cents. "That's not a lot of time, brother."

From the front hall, I call Amara's name up the stairs. I want her to be a part of our plans from here on out, and we'll all need to sit down and share what we know.

"Amara's not here." Sloane startles all of us when she steps out of the dining room.

I turn to face her. "What do you mean? She's in her room; I sent her there myself."

"I was on my way inside, to get some snacks for Henry, and I heard her talking to Nash in the driveway. They didn't see me. I couldn't make it all out, but Nash said he would take Amara where she needed to go. He said he'd message you to let you know."

I pull my phone out of my pocket and check. There are two messages, and neither is from Nash.

Amara: I got a call about Grayson's killer. It can't wait. I've got backup.
Amara: 147 Holston Rd. Suite 12 clear
your name

The messages came just over five minutes apart from each other.

"Son of a bitch. Who's at the pool house with Henry?" My skin feels clammy as I ask Sloane the question.

"It's Yuri. Why? Is Henry—" Sloane looks ready to bolt, and I grab her.

"Henry is fine, Sloane. He's safe. I need you to get him and come into the house for tonight. Dagen, get Yuri in here now."

Dagen takes one look at the expression on my face and doesn't stick around for an explanation. Sloane runs out of the house with Dagen right behind her.

"Ryder?" Cole is trying to play catch-up, but I don't have time.

I turn and run toward the basement, and Cole follows close behind me. I open the gun safe at record speed and grab the first gun I see. I check the clip and the safety before securing it in my belt, and Cole does the same as I talk out loud, saying everything that comes to mind.

"I told him. I told Nash to inform me if Amara left. Sloane heard him say he'd text me, but he didn't." I grab a third gun to give to Dagen, then I close up the safe. "Fuck, dammit! Amara said she got a call about Grayson's killer. How fast can you pull up the call log? I want to hear the recording. Cole, I think Nash—"

Cole's expression sobers as everything registers. "On it."

He turns and runs back down the hall, taking the stairs two at a time. He's already out the front door when I get back to the main floor, and Yuri joins us with Sloane and Henry in tow.

Yuri is one of my most trusted guys on our security team. I hired him myself, so he has no allegiance to anyone else in my family. Yuri is the father of a friend of mine, and he is ex-military. He has no desire to work his way up the ranks. He was just looking for something he could do until he retired.

He straightens when I address him with my orders.

"I'm putting you in charge. No one—NO ONE—but the three of us are allowed past those front gates until we return. Call in the next team on duty; they're starting early. Lock this place down. All conversation happens face-to-face. Nothing over the airwaves, no radio." Yuri nods, and I turn to Sloane, pausing briefly at the look on Henry's face. "You sleep in here tonight, and you stay together at all times."

Sloane clutches him close to her chest and nods, trying to hold back her tears.

"Amara?" Sloane whispers, and my breath catches in my throat.

I shake my head, asking her not to go there.

"Dagen, you're with me." I don't wait for anyone. I turn and run out the front door, getting up to full speed as I head for our security building at the front gates.

If Amara left with Nash and he didn't do as I asked, then he isn't on my payroll. Thoughts of what I'll do to him if I turn out to be right push me to top speed down the driveway.

The sound of an engine behind me tells me Dagen has his car. I see Cole through the windows, hovered over the computer. He waves me in.

"I just heard from my guy. He says his woman took the security footage and contacted Amara directly. She didn't trust him not to set her up. That must be who contacted her. Nash has Amara in one of our vehicles."

"The meet is at one forty-seven Holston Road," I tell Cole, and he's already shaking his head.

"GPS on their vehicle says they aren't going anywhere near there. It looks like they are heading out to our dumping grounds. I think they're going to kill her."

"We go now."

When Amara's life is on the line, clearing my own name isn't important. I don't have time to listen to the recording. If Amara isn't being taken in that direction, I'm not going there anyway.

Cole grabs our handheld GPS tracker and follows me out to where Dagen sits in his car, waiting for us.

I round the car to the passenger seat, and Cole opens the door to the back seat. "You got a body in here?" he asks, and I glance back at the large duffel bag on the seat.

"It's my rock-climbing gear. Just move it over." Dagen starts the car.

I told Amara I would never let her go again.

I thought I had everything under control, and now the one thing I want more than anything has been ripped away from me right under my nose.

33

AMARA

The butterflies in my stomach have been fluttering like crazy all day. Ryder has been preoccupied ever since he received that text from his father last night.

His words contradicted his actions when he told me I had nothing to worry about, yet he wouldn't let me go into work or leave his sight all day.

I watched through the window of the room I first stayed in as each of the brothers then their father arrived, and I spent the first fifteen minutes pacing back and forth around the room. I should have asked if I could join Sloane and Henry tonight, but I can't go out there now.

I don't get calls from anyone other than Ryder, and he's currently busy. So when the ringer on my phone pierces the silence, I startle and run across the room to answer it.

I don't want to give anyone a reason to come upstairs and deal with me tonight.

"Hello?" In my haste to stop it from ringing, I didn't look at the caller ID.

It's a woman's voice. "You the lady on TV asking for proof of a murder?"

"Yes. That's me. I—"

"I have something I'm supposed to hand over, and I don't want any trouble." Her voice is low and rushed. I don't know her, but she sounds terrified.

"Okay." With my phone pressed to my ear, I take two steps toward the door before stopping in my tracks.

I can't interrupt Ryder and his family. His brother and father won't take kindly to me barging in there, and Ryder already thinks Lennox is involved somehow.

"I have a memory stick, and I'll give it to you, but you have to come now and come alone."

I don't want to ask her if she knows what's on it for fear she'll hang up on me, but I know Ryder will never allow me to leave alone. "I'm not sure I—"

"I'm texting you the address. I'll be there for forty-five minutes, then I'm gone, and I won't call again. Come alone, or I'm out. I don't want any trouble over this. I'm just turning it in."

I pad silently down the hall, careful not to make a sound. I don't want to alert anyone in the office of my presence. I can see a sliver from the top of the stairs. The door is closed, so they must all be in there by now.

"Send me the address. I'm coming," I whisper into the phone.

"Forty-five minutes." And the line goes dead.

I turn the ringer off and wait for a half a minute. Then the text comes through, and I open the map app. It's about twenty-five minutes away from here by car.

I can't let this go. I promised Ryder I would wait for his lead on this, but by the time their meeting is over she'll be gone, along with whatever video evidence she has. Ryder won't be able to clear his name, we won't find Grayson's killer, and Sloane and Henry won't be safe.

Henry—my nephew. Grayson's son.

If Ryder were in my position, he would do the same thing.

Regret hits me hard as I take cautious steps down the stairs clutching the keys to one of the cars Ryder let me borrow last week. I'm breaking my promise to Ryder, but there isn't anything I wouldn't do for my family.

Everyone I trust is in that room, along with everyone I don't.

The floors in the front hall are sturdy, so I don't need to creep along them to get out of the house undetected. I hope if Ryder hears the door he'll think it's one of his guys. I walk at a steady pace, my heart thudding into my chest as I reach for the heavy front door.

As soon as it closes behind me, I suck in a deep breath of the freezing night air. I should have worn my heavier coat, but I didn't have time to go through the front closet, and I didn't want anyone coming out to check while I was in there.

Zipping up the thin jacket, I run down the stairs toward the car that's parked where I left it.

"Ms. Scott? What are you doing out here?" As I'm circling the trunk of the vehicle, the deep voice catches me by surprise, and I trip, slamming myself into the side as I startle.

"Oh. Shit. Nash. Um, I'm—going out." I look from Nash to the front door, and he follows my line of sight.

"I'm not sure I can allow that. Maybe we should go back inside and talk to Mr. Saint." He extends his arm to lead me back toward the house, but I'm not willing to give up any ground.

"Wait. You can't. I have to go. It's—I'm leaving."

I push off the car and open the driver's door. Before it opens all of the way, a strong hand slams it shut.

"I'm sorry, Ms. Scott. I need to send you back inside." He pulls his jacket back, showing me the gun he's carrying.

I'm losing time.

"Look, Nash. I need to go. I don't have time to explain, and I can't go in there and get Ryder. I—dammit! If I don't go now, I won't be able to clear Ryder's name in my brother's death. I can't say any more. I—" My words stop as I go for a different approach, and I cry.

Nash's expression changes, and I feel like I'm gaining some ground, so I keep talking. "I can't take Ryder out of his meeting, and I only have forty minutes left to get there." When Nash leans his head to the side to consider what I'm saying, I panic. "You can drive me then. You just can't come in. Please. I have to leave now."

Nash looks over his shoulder toward the front gate.

"Fine. But I'm bringing one of the security guys. We won't stay in the car, but you won't see us." As Nash offers his terms, I shake my head, and he stops me cold. "We come with you, or you don't go at all."

I don't have time to argue, and I pull out my phone and text Ryder so he knows where I am. I'll send the address from the car.

"Fine. But we go now."

Nash pulls out his phone and taps the screen.

"Who are you messaging?"

"My security partner and Mr. Saint. We have a car at the front gate." Nash turns to walk down the driveway, and I follow behind. The cold air bites at my cheeks, but I don't care.

This might be it. This might be everything we need.

As the gate opens, a man steps out of the security building and nods at Nash. I follow them to their vehicle in silence, glancing at my phone to see if Ryder has the message yet. He doesn't, and I'm not surprised. I don't think any of them will be checking their phones until the meeting is over.

Assuming Nash will sit in the passenger seat, I slide into the back seat behind the driver. Worry gnaws at my stomach when Nash joins me in the back, leaving the front seat empty.

Neither of the men say anything as the other man starts up the vehicle and pulls onto the street.

Nausea bubbles in my stomach as the car makes two more turns and no one says a thing.

My confidence drains out of me as futility sets in.

Neither of them asked me the address.

I've made a mistake.

The time to get out of this has long passed, and there isn't anything I can do now. The doors locked when the car started moving.

Streetlights wash over us in waves as we drive down the street, and I slide my hand into my pocket, wrapping my fingers around my phone and trying to decide what move to make.

I wish I got to tell Henry I loved him. I'm happy I got to say it to Ryder.

The cold night around me blurs as tears fill my eyes.

Nash sighs beside me.

"Give me your phone." He speaks matter-of-factly, as though I should have known all along he couldn't be trusted.

I slide the phone out of my pocket, and the screen opens to my message to Ryder telling him I had backup. I don't have time to type out an SOS.

A split second before I hand it over, my eyes land on the microphone icon, and I turn off all rational thought and go for it. Tapping the little button, I turn myself away from Nash and speak as clearly as I can into my phone.

"One four seven Holston Road. Suite twelve." Nash notices too late and dives at me to try to get the phone out of my hand

and stop me from hitting send. I finish my message: "Clear your name."

I hit send.

"Son of a bitch." Nash rips the phone from my fingers and stares at the screen.

Removing his own phone, he sends another text, and my heart breaks.

Nash is working for someone, and that person now has the address where my informant is waiting.

The screen on his phone lights up a minute later, but I can't see who it's from or his response.

"Sit tight and we won't hurt you." Nash reaches into his jacket, removing his gun and holding it on his lap. At least it isn't pointed at me, but I get the warning. I sit in silence as we continue to drive farther away from Ryder and the life I wanted with him.

If they aren't going to hurt me, then there's a chance I'm being taken to Grayson's killer. If I fight Nash now, he'll just shoot me right here.

The driver—I never got his name—slows at a yellow light, and the car slides on a patch of ice before we stop just inside the intersection.

After a few seconds, I reach to my side and try the door handle. It's locked, and there is no way to open it from back here.

Nash shifts in his seat and grips his gun as he stares at me, and I return my hands to my lap.

The streets are deserted. The extreme cold weather warning and the storm that is about to roll in has everyone staying at home. Even in this heated car my toes feel painfully cold, and I wiggle them in my boots, willing blood to reach them as the light turns green and the car rolls through and we continue to wherever we're going.

I recognized the streets and neighborhoods for the first ten minutes, but now none of the landmarks or street names look familiar. Not only that, but the buildings are starting to thin out, and it looks like we're heading out of the city. The cold in my toes spreads through my body at what that might mean for me.

The occasional set of headlights come then go, and I continue to look around for anything I can use to my advantage.

The men stay silent.

The sign overhead tells me we are heading east, and the car turns off the main highway and onto a side street.

I keep looking at the quiet all around me. Half a minute later, there's a set of headlights behind us.

The road in front of us stretches into darkness, though I see some lights up ahead illuminating a bridge. A little voice in my head decides to get out now.

As if reading my mind, the radio in their car crackles on, and I hear Cole's voice, shocking us all. "Amara, fight. They're gonna kill—"

"Shit." The driver slams the radio off, and Nash mutters profanities as he turns to look out the back window.

The car is still behind us, and our driver picks up speed. I glare at Nash, sizing him up.

"What? Are you going to yoga me to death, Ice Princess?" He sneers as he shakes his head. He's confident he has the upper hand.

I don't hesitate.

I click my seat belt off at the same time I swing. My fist connects with Nash's face, and his head snaps back.

I climb across the back seat, pinning the hand that's holding the gun to his lap, and yell, "I'M—A FUCKING—QUEEN!" I land three solid punches with each word as tears roll out of my eyes.

Our car swerves then straightens out as the driver swears, yelling back at Nash, "Get her under control!"

With the way the car is moving, I'm not going to get any more strong punches in, so I go for Nash's eyes, gripping my fingers around the sides of his head and burrowing my thumbs into his sockets until I feel a soft pop on one side and he screams, bucking wildly to get me off his lap.

I fall toward the back of the driver's seat, and the car swerves again, but it doesn't stop.

I look over Nash's large frame. The headlights are still behind us, and I know in my heart Ryder is coming for me.

When Nash's hands go up to his face, I realize he isn't holding his gun. A second after that, his body freezes.

He realizes it too.

My time is up. If he gets his gun back, I'm dying in this car tonight. We both fight and push at each other when my foot touches something. I reach for it as Nash dives down with me, trying to punch me as he goes.

His fist grazes my cheek but doesn't connect because of the rocking of the car.

My hand touches the cold metal, but the heat from Nash's hand on mine tells me this is it. I can't relinquish any ground.

As we both struggle to right ourselves, a flash of light appears between us, and a painful blast fills my ears.

RYDER

"Can't you go any faster?" I tap on the dash and glance around. "I don't see them."

The streets are empty.

Dagen just makes it through an intersection before the light turns red. "The roads are slippery. We're no good to Amara if we're stuck in a ditch."

I know he's right, and it's a good thing he's driving.

Cole shows me the handheld from the back seat. "We're still a bit away, but we're driving faster than they are, and they just stopped at a light. Remember, they think we're still in a meeting."

They. Two members of my own team.

It wasn't hard to rewind the security camera back five minutes. It was hard to watch as Amara followed them into one of our cars and they drove her away.

I don't have time to think about how she defied my instructions and put herself in this situation. There's only one thought in my mind, and it's getting her back. Everything else will wait until she is safe.

Cole speaks again. "I saw the security schedule when I was out there pulling up Amara's phone recording. Did you know Nash and Grant have been working the same shifts for a few weeks now?"

I don't answer him. I'm sure the look on my face says it all.

Our security guys are supposed to rotate between shifts and team members for this exact reason, and I would have known this was happening if I didn't delegate the scheduling to —Nash, my fucking right-hand man.

I was right to keep my secrets between Sloane and my two brothers.

These two must have been watching and waiting for the go-ahead to take her.

But who gave them the order?

"Sloane said she saw Nash pull out his phone. If Nash didn't text you, who did he text?" Dagen keeps his eyes on the road as he asks his question.

That's the million-dollar question.

The memory of Lennox checking his phone while we were in our meeting hits me in the chest.

"There." Cole lifts his arm between Dagen and me, pointing out the front windshield at a set of taillights in the distance as the car turns off the highway. Glancing back at his GPS, he confirms his hunch. "Yep. That's them."

Dagen clears his throat. "Guys. They're getting too far out of the city. If they notice we're onto them, they might just kill her and be done with it. But if I turn off the headlights, I'll have to slow down."

We sit in silence for a few seconds before Cole reaches his hand out to me. "Give me the radio."

I reach for the radio. Even though Dagen isn't close to our family business, we are all still connected through the same security protocols.

I lift the receiver from the dash and hand it back. "What are you going to do?"

Cole looks hesitant before he shakes his head.

I'm not going to like this.

"I'll bet they left their receiver on so they could hear the moment we found out about Amara. I'm going to send her a message."

My heart sinks into my stomach. As soon as Cole says anything over our open line, they'll know, and something will happen.

But what choice do we have?

I'm prolonging the inevitable, and we need to give her a chance.

I can't leave her in the dark like this.

Closing my eyes, I nod, and Cole takes a deep breath before holding a button on the side of the radio.

"Amara, fight. They're going to kill you."

The three of us sit deathly still as Dagen picks up speed. There's no point in hanging back now.

Nothing changes for a few seconds as the car in front of us continues on.

Dagen breaks the silence. "Maybe they didn't have the ra—"

Suddenly, the other car makes a sharp swerve to the side, and the three of us react with our own profanities. The dark shadows of two bodies in the back look as though they are fighting, but it's too dark to tell what is happening.

"I think your spitfire got the message," Cole murmurs.

"Uh, guys?" Dagen's eyes are still on the road, and I see the cause of his worry as their car continues to swerve on the icy road toward the bridge up ahead.

The car fishtails for a moment, but whoever is driving recovers, and I release the breath I was holding when a flash and loud pop from the back seat of the car in front of us stops my heart.

If anyone says anything, I don't hear it.

I don't hear anything.

The car straightens out and starts crossing over the bridge, and hope drains out of me.

If Amara was alive, she'd—

I don't get a chance to finish my thought as I watch the car swerve hard to the right. It fishtails once more, and this time it doesn't recover as it busts through the old railing and goes over the side of the rickety bridge.

"She's alive." My face feels wet as I say the words, and Dagen nears the bridge and slows down.

I turn my attention to him. "What are you doing? Get out there!" I can still save her.

"I can't drive onto the bridge." He points to the broken railing the car just busted through. "That's a lot of damage, and it's old. The weight of this car could take us all down."

We need to get to her.

I get my seat belt off, turn in the seat until I'm on my knees, and reach for the duffel bag in the back.

"You said this was your rock-climbing gear?" I don't wait for Dagen's response.

Unzipping it, I find what I need right away and spin back in my seat to open the door.

On the side of the road, I wrap the rope around my midsection a few times, then knot it like I used to when we would go sailing.

"What are you doing? This is crazy." Cole looks scared. In my life, I've never seen this look on his face.

"I have nothing if I don't have her." The weight of my conviction sinks into my soul. If Amara dies, I may as well follow her, because there will be nothing left for me.

As soon as the last knot is tight, I grab the remaining rope and start running onto the bridge. Thankfully, Cole is right behind me. Dagen is farther back.

The wind whips around, and frigid air shocks my lungs. I brace myself as I get closer to the spot where the car broke through the barrier and they went over. I toss the end of the rope back to Cole, who picks it up.

The car comes into view only five feet down and a couple feet out from us. A few large, dead tree trunks have wedged into the riverbed below, and freezing water rushes violently around the car as it remains where it landed, hooked up on a large tree trunk. It's pierced through the passenger window and out the driver's side, which is the only thing keeping the car from being pulled down the rapids.

The first face I see is Grant's. He fumbles with his seat belt before turning to face me, and the dead tree groans under the weight of the car.

He knows he's fucked.

I want to put a bullet between his eyes and leave him out here for what he's done, but I know Grant will tell me everything I need to know once I get my hands on him.

As his eyes meet mine, he opens his mouth, but movement in the back seat catches my attention.

Thin fingers push against the window, and Amara's face presses to the glass as she shouts, "I CAN'T GET OUT!" She bangs at the back window, and I realize she's trying the door.

Then I notice the rising water beside Grant in the car, and he continues to fight with his seat belt.

Grant is blocking Amara's only exit.

Without weighing my options, I pull my gun out of my belt, raise it to Grant's head, and shoot.

"Amara, this is your only way out." I drop the gun on the

bridge beside me so I can reach for her, and the trunk cracks but holds.

Grant's dead weight jerks a couple of times before Amara is able to move him out of the way enough to climb over him. She's covered in blood as her hands and arms scramble to lift her weight toward the window.

Pulling her shoulders through, she reaches her hand up. She's clutching a phone between her ghost-white fingers.

"T-take it. It's Nash's." My world tilts on its axis. She should be fighting for her life, but she's fighting for ours. She's still trying to help Grayson and clear my name.

"Let it go. I need your hand," I yell over the rushing water, and my fingers ache as the cold sets in. I can't believe she's still pushing through in that freezing water.

The point becomes mute when the branch snaps and bends, jarring the car and moving her a couple of feet farther away from me, and she drops the phone in the water.

"NO!" she screams and meets my eyes. Hers are full of tears and regret. "I love you, Ryder. When you tell Henry, tell him I loved him so much. Okay? Tell him. Okay?" Her sobs cut my heart open.

She doesn't believe she's getting out of this.

She was going to use her last breaths to save us.

The severity of our situation grips my heart and sends me into a panic.

"Listen to me, Blossom. Give me your hand. I know you're scared, but you climb out of that fucking car and come back to me. NOW!"

She doesn't hesitate. Pulling herself through the window, she steps over Grant, lifts herself out of the car, and reaches up toward me.

The last piece of the trunk breaks away. The river sucks the car under as she keeps moving up and toward me, but it isn't enough.

I'm going to lose her.

I don't look back.

I don't double-check my knots.

I don't check to see if Cole is ready for me.

As the freezing water consumes the car and attempts to swallow Amara up and take her away from me, I dive in.

AMARA

Every inch of my body aches as the cold sets into my bones, and I struggle with my limbs to get them to move how I want them to.

Hopes of getting the evidence we need from the woman who called me are long gone, but I have the next best thing. If Ryder can clear his name, maybe he can protect Henry.

Wrenching the driver's body as best as I can, I climb up his corpse and push out through the window, holding out Nash's phone and yelling at Ryder to take it.

He's shouting at me, but I'm not focused on his words. The water comes barreling down the river and slams into the vehicle.

This car is going under. I feel it giving up.

The wreckage takes a dip as the debris around me strains to hold us in place, and the phone slips out of my hand. I scramble to get it back, but it's gone and below the surface before I have the chance to see where it went.

"NO!" I've lost my last chance.

When I look back to Ryder, I know in my heart this is the

last time I'll see him. I can't leave anything unsaid, but I don't have time, so I say what's most important first.

"I love you, Ryder. When you tell Henry, tell him I loved him so much. Okay? Tell him. Okay?"

The car surrounds me like a tomb, and with each movement, it breaks away a little more. Acceptance is all I have left, but I'm not ready to go.

Ryder leans over, rage etched into his features.

"Listen to me, Blossom. Give me your hand. I know you're scared, but you climb out of that fucking car and come back to me. NOW!"

He's fighting for me.

That last word is all I need. I will fight for Ryder and my family until I take my last breath. I begin moving my limbs, bracing my arms and legs against anything that will get me out of the car and closer to Ryder.

As my waist clears the window, the last of the support from the car beneath me gives way and breaks free.

I don't stop.

I keep moving up as the car moves away, and Ryder takes one step back.

My hips are through the window. A new feeling of strength pushes me forward and up, and I stretch myself toward the bridge. My knees clear the window, and I stand tall as the current rages around me.

The car is going under.

This is it.

Water swells then fills the car as it slips below the surface.

I brace my foot against the door, then I jump up as hard as I can and reach out.

Just before the river takes me under, Ryder comes toward me, headfirst and arms out, and I stay stiff. With my arm extended, I suck as much air as I can into my lungs.

I thought I was cold, that my body could feel no more, but the frigid temperature as my head goes under shocks me, and I momentarily seize up when my arm is tugged forcefully away from my body.

The river surrounding me fights to whisk me away, and I kick my legs as hard as I can against the rapids.

I open my mouth for air, sure that my next breath will take me to my watery grave, but my lungs expand, and I gag.

I'm above water, and I open my eyes.

The first person I see is Dagen on the bridge, then Cole, who is pulling on a rope and yelling. Ryder is in the water with me. He's shouting something, but everything is garbled.

Exhaustion hits me in a wave, but I push through it, blocking out everything around me. I focus everything I have on kicking my legs against the current.

I am a fighter, and fighters fight, so I keep going, unsure if I am actually doing anything, as my body has gone numb.

When the lights above the bridge dim, I look up to see we've made it back to the pier underneath. Ryder climbs onto a ladder at the edge and pulls me closer and up with him.

"Shit. I broke your wrist." He tucks my hand into my chest and wraps his body around mine.

I want to tell him it's okay because I don't feel anything, but my words won't work, so I look up at him and smile. At least, I think I'm smiling. I can't feel my lips.

Cole joins us, bracing Ryder against the post under the bridge to keep us on the ledge.

"Fuck, you guys know how to have a good time."

Ryder turns his attention toward Cole, and they talk to each other as the sound of rushing water comes back to me.

My body must be snapping out of its shock, because my teeth chatter together and I begin to shiver when Ryder looks at me again.

"Cole is going to carry you up the ladder on the other side. I'm too weak from the rapids. I can't get both of us onto the bridge right now, and we can't stay down here. You'll freeze to death if we don't get you into the car. He's going to put you over his shoulder. If we help you, can you stand for a second?" As Ryder speaks, Cole looks at me over Ryder's shoulder with a cautious smile.

Can I stand? I have no idea what I can do. I try to stretch my legs, then I nod.

Cole helps Ryder onto the narrow platform, and they each hold an arm of mine before Cole steps in and tilts me forward over his shoulder, and I close my eyes.

I keep my eyes shut, but I listen to what they are saying in case they need me to do anything.

Once we're on the bridge, Cole sets me on my feet and spins me to face him, pulling open my jacket.

"WATCH HER WRIST!" Ryder yells from behind me. Then he takes over, removing my jacket and shirt before tugging at the button on my pants.

"What are you—"

Ryder's tone is final. "Dagen is gonna get you into the car. You need to get out of these and warm up."

My body continues to shudder as a blanket is wrapped around me as soon as my shirt is off, and Dagen lifts me into his arms and runs off the bridge. Ryder and Cole are talking with each other as they follow us off.

"We have a team on the way out. They'll be here any minute. Should we call an ambulance?" Cole is asking the questions from over Dagen's shoulder.

Dagen is the one to reply as he opens a door to the back seat, and it's the first warmth I've felt since we went into the water. "Get her in the car. Ryder, strip and get in with her. They'll have more blankets in a minute. There they are."

I follow his line of sight to the approaching cars in the distance.

"Wait." I stop Dagen from getting me into the back seat and demand their attention. "You have to go to the address."

I lost Nash's phone, but maybe the woman is still there. Maybe she gave me more time.

Dagen turns me, ushering me into the warmth as he answers, "As soon as they get to us, I'm going to the address with one of our guys. Cole will get you home safe."

I get in and move myself to the far side of the vehicle. A moment later, Ryder joins me in his underwear. He slides across the back seat, and I lift the blanket, inviting him under with me.

"Now, don't get any funny ideas, Blossom." He smiles, wrapping my blanket tight around me and waiting for his own.

A burst of laughter hits me, then another giggle. All of my emotions crash into me at once, and I cry as I laugh.

"You okay, Sunshine?" Cole asks nervously from the front passenger seat as he closes his door and blows warm air into his fisted hands.

The question makes me laugh harder, and I can't control myself.

Am I okay? I am a lot of things, and "okay" is not one of them.

Then the first day I saw Ryder again after all of that time comes back to me, and my thoughts settle on one part of our conversation.

My giggle sounds hysterical. Ryder cradles my head, concern etched into his features.

"I told him," I say, my teeth chattering and my body shaking.

"You told who, baby?" All three sets of worried eyes are on me now.

"I told N-Nash. I t-told him someone would put a b-bullet in his head," I mutter, and their worry morphs into surprise as I finish my thought. "I just didn't think it would be m-me."

I can't stop my sobs from coming.

"Oh, Blossom. I'm so sorry. You were so brave. I love you." Ryder pulls me closer in an embrace, kissing the top of my head as my body heaves, wracked with anguish.

Cole's face softens as Dagen's door opens, and a couple more blankets are handed back to us, along with a backpack of supplies.

Dagen steps out, and a few different voices start talking outside the car.

Cole tells Ryder to stay put, and he doesn't argue when Cole leaves to join the group.

Instead, Ryder wraps my feet in warm socks before opening more packages.

"Stay under the blanket. This will warm up your hands and feet." He keeps his focus on taking care of me. Once I have socks and gloves filled with warmers on, he does his own and pulls a blanket around himself before he rejoins me, rubbing his hands over my body and kissing my forehead until the doors open again and his brothers rejoin us. This time, Cole is in the driver's seat, and Dagen shares the update from the passenger side.

"Okay. Cole is driving you both home. We have a medical team meeting us there. We all agree: what happened here cannot be shared with anyone yet." Dagen looks at me. "I'm heading to the address you gave us. We'll be about five minutes late, but maybe we'll get lucky." He hesitates and glances between Ryder and me. "Is this a good time to say welcome to the family?" Ryder groans, and Cole smacks Dagen on the arm. "Yeah, I didn't think so."

Dagen leaves, and a member of their security team takes his

place as Cole starts up the car. He talks to Ryder over his shoulder. "Keep her awake."

Exhaustion takes over as he says the words, and my eyelids instantly feel heavy.

"Hey. You heard him. Eyes on me." Ryder smiles, and I open my eyes and smile back.

The car rocks gently from side to side, and the motion makes me want to sleep for just a little while. I move my fingers in my gloves; the numbness is gone. They hurt, but I'm happy I can feel them. I pull my gloves off, and a sharp pain makes me gasp.

I feel my broken wrist now.

My adrenaline must be wearing off, because every inch of me hurts.

"What is it?" Ryder lifts his weight off of me and pulls the blanket back. I brace my wrist with my good hand, and he relaxes a fraction.

A wave of nausea hits me. "I don't feel so good." My body feels weak and clammy.

Ryder sits up and pulls the blanket completely open, his eyes raking over me, and I think he says something under his breath as he shifts, drawing the attention of the guy in the front seat, who startles when he looks back. He takes off his seat belt and turns to face us.

"Um, Cole, we have a problem." Ryder sounds panicked all over again.

I slide my good hand to cover my midsection where he is staring, and when I pull my hand away, my fingers are coated in a fresh layer of blood.

"You're bleeding?" I worry.

"No, baby. You are."

I am?

The car is a flurry of activity as Ryder pushes my hand out

of the way when I try to locate what's wrong. Reaching into the pack beside me, he pulls out some fabric and pushes it into my stomach, but I don't feel that either.

"Cole, get to the hospital. She's bleeding out into the seat under her. How did I miss this? STAY WITH ME. DON'T CLOSE YOUR EYES." Ryder sounds angry. He sounds like he should be yelling, but his voice is miles away. Maybe I have water in my ears.

"It's okay," I comfort Ryder.

I don't really feel anything. I want to say it can't be that bad, and I reach my hand up to touch his cheek when I stop and hover my fingers in front of my face.

"That's a lot of blood," I murmur.

I'm going to fall asleep for a little while.

I tell myself it'll just be for a few minutes.

I don't want to go, but I think this time I have to.

"AMARA!"

36

RYDER

From the second Amara passed out as Cole raced to the hospital until the moment the emergency room staff finally got me to let them take over as they rushed her down the hall and toward surgery, I slipped into autopilot.

My body was not my own.

My actions were not my own.

Everything I am and will ever be, I gave to Amara in those hellish minutes. They kept ticking by, and I surrendered myself to her as she lay lifeless.

My world crumbled to dust when Amara lost consciousness in my arms.

I saw my pain written all over Cole's forlorn expression as he pushed me into a private room to wait and began doling out orders to everyone around us. I heard their voices, but no words registered as our people came with updates and left with new assignments.

Then, the moment of truth came. The flurry around me ceased when the surgeon entered, and Cole cleared the room before shutting the door and standing in front of it with his arms crossed over his chest.

I was thankful he didn't leave me to hear the outcome on my own.

Clearing his throat, the doctor pointed to a set of chairs near us, and I hesitated before he finally spoke. "Mr. Saint, she made it through surgery. We are all optimistic, but I need to discuss a few things with you. May we sit down?"

I nodded and introduced Cole as my brother before asking him to join us. I wouldn't have caught everything the surgeon told me on my own.

The glances they exchanged told me Cole and our team had already been talking to the doctor, and I wondered how much he knew about our private situation.

It turned out, a good-sized piece of broken glass was lodged in Amara's abdomen. I'm sure it must have happened when she was fighting to get through the smashed driver's side window, and I still hate myself for not catching it sooner.

He told us her condition was listed as serious. Then I was led to another private room, and there she was. Sleeping peacefully under the covers, unconscious to the world. I listened to the doctor tell us how he expected her condition would be upgraded to fair, but right now they needed to keep her here, in observation, and the next eight hours were critical.

I am now four hours in, and she hasn't woken up yet. Cole has reminded me over and over again it is because she fought hard to survive, and she lost a lot of blood. Dagen has been in and out over the last couple of hours, but neither of them has given me any updates.

Every time I ask a question, they answer by telling me it can wait while they exchange glances with each other.

Amara's hand lies limp in my own; her breathing is soft.

"Okay." I release a deep breath, startling Cole out of the

chair in the corner where he closed his eyes for a rest. "Tell me where we are. I mean it."

Dagen turns away from the window as Cole pulls himself out of the little chair and stretches to his full height. Another look passes between them before Dagen lifts his chin to Cole, telling him to speak for them both, and he does.

"We have information, but that doesn't mean we have all of the facts. So you can't go running off with what we tell you." Cole levels me with a serious glare. "Got it? You'll stay put, and we'll figure this out the right way?"

Outside of Amara and Sloane, my brothers know me better than anyone. I am ready to tear out of here and go after the first name they drop. The only thing keeping me from leaving is lying helplessly in a hospital bed at the moment.

"This is bad. Isn't it?" I ask.

Another hesitant look travels between them.

"Fine. I stay put." I lift my hands in surrender. I'll do whatever I need to to protect Amara.

Dagen speaks first. "I went to the address Amara gave us. I went in the back way, and—she was already dead." He looks at Cole, then back to me. "Someone else was there." Dagen shakes out his arms at his sides and glances around, as if to avoid whatever he needs to tell me next. "Fuck, Ryder. He's our brother. He didn't do this. I know he didn't."

My heart sinks. As much as I accused him behind his back, I'm not sure I ever believed Lennox would have been involved.

"Tell me what you saw, Dag."

"I didn't see enough. When I arrived, a woman was lying on the floor dead. I don't know how she died, but there was blood—and *he* was standing over the body. I couldn't see a gun or a knife with him. The guy I went with must have made a noise, because something startled Lennox and he bolted. I didn't go any closer—I didn't want to leave my prints or evidence behind. Besides, I don't think her killer would leave anything to find. The building is under renovation, and the security cameras are being upgraded, so there isn't any footage. Cole has someone looking for cameras in the surrounding buildings. Maybe we can determine when Lennox got there and if there was anyone else."

Cole steps forward. "About that. I hired an outside team for this. Someone with no connections to our family. As soon as I hear anything, I'll be on it, but I think it's best if I head back to Portland and take care of some business as soon as I can. If I stick around here too long, it will raise suspicion. Dagen will stick around until I get back. Until then, no moves without me. I'm serious, Ryder. We need more to go on."

"What more do you need?" My voice is getting dangerously close to yelling, and I point at Dagen. "He saw him with his own eyes. I really don't want to believe this either, but they're not safe if he's out there." I point to Amara's sleeping body, and the insinuation that I am including Henry and Sloane in this is silent.

Cole takes a step closer so he can lower his own voice. "Let's just wait to see if anything pans out. I mean—this is Lennox we're talking about. I know we all aren't as close as we used to be, but he's still our brother." He lets his own silent message linger between us.

There isn't anything I wouldn't do for my brothers, and in my time of need I would hope they would have my back first and ask questions later. But it's been a long time since I felt that close to our oldest brother.

"Fine. But he doesn't come anywhere near us. I'll give him some rope, but if he fucks up, I'll be the one on the other end, hanging him with it." I pause for effect while I gather my thoughts and stifle my anger, then I return my attention to Cole. "How are Sloane and Henry?"

Cole takes a deep breath of his own and stretches his neck to the side to release some of the tension building in the room. It's a habit he's had since he was a kid. "They're fine. Safe at home. Sloane keeps texting me to ask about Amara. You might want to give her a call as soon as you know something. She's a lot like your girl there, and I worry she's going to march her ass down here if we don't fill her in soon."

The hint of a grin tugs at my cheeks, and it hits me: I feel like I haven't smiled in a long time. Those two are a lot alike.

I nod.

I turn my attention to Amara and take a step to her side, brushing a section of hair off her forehead. "When are we moving her?"

I assume Cole set some plans in motion while I was mentally checked out for the hour when Amara was fighting for her life on the operating table.

"As soon as she is listed in fair condition. The doc would prefer we wait until she's back to good, but we need to get her out of here and back to our medical team at home so we can hide our tracks. That's probably why they're hesitant to move her out of serious. I'll talk to him in a bit. Don't worry; he's been dealt with." That's Cole's way of saying he's been paid off or threatened and he's on board with keeping his mouth shut and helping us.

Dagen clears his throat before speaking. "That leaves Nash and Grant. What do we do about them?"

With the immediate threat now behind us and Amara safe and recovering, I'm back in control of my surroundings.

"We do nothing." My answer is final, and both of my brothers meet my gaze. I clarify, "The car will be found downriver in— what?—a couple of days once the storm passes. Police will come to question us. Make sure we have some of our own on the case. As far as we know, they left work together last night, and that is the last we saw of them. Cole, change their schedules to reflect new end of shift times." I check my watch. The sun should be coming up soon. I fall into what I do best: finding calm within the chaos and controlling the outcome. "Have Yuri back up then erase all of our video footage from the point where everyone arrived last night. If they ask, our security system went offline when the storm started rolling in. If Dad asks, we tell him the same story."

"And Lennox?" Dagen asks.

"He won't ask." I shake my head.

If Lennox is behind this, then he knows full well we are onto him. If in the wild chance he is not, then he won't think anything of Grant and Nash going missing. He isn't close to them.

Cole nods, then reaches for his jacket. "I'm going to hit the road. I'll be back in Portland by breakfast. I'm putting Dagen in charge of our team here. There are two guys outside the door. They're with us."

Cole joins me at the side of Amara's bed, and we both look down on her sleeping form.

"I knew—you know," Cole mutters beside me.

"You knew what?" I shift my gaze to Cole.

He speaks while I follow his line of sight back to my flower. "I knew you loved her—I mean, back then, I knew you wanted Amara. I could tell by the way you looked at her, like she was this secret treasure, when you thought no one was looking at you. You'd get this dopey look." Cole chuckles as he reaches for Amara's hand and covers it with his own. "This one is fierce. She's going to be just fine, Ryder. Hold on to that."

I turn to respond when my body jerks into Cole's, and his arms wrap around me, pulling me into a suffocating hug.

I don't remember the last time any of my brothers hugged me.

I attempt to release the embrace, and he only pulls me in closer. Then I realize Cole is struggling hard to control his own emotions, and he sniffles. "Fuck, Ryder. When you went in the water—I thought—I thought that was it, you know, and—shit. Don't ever fucking do that again."

From over Cole's shoulder, I catch Dagen's gaze as he shrugs and nods. I hadn't considered how close we all came to losing something.

We break apart when a nurse enters, pulling a notepad out of her pocket and clicking on her pen. She circles the bed, checking monitors and making notes before reaching for the blanket at Amara's side. She lifts it to check her midsection before meeting our stare, and Cole steps toward her, flashing her a smile and asking if she can get the doctor for a status update.

He knows I'm anxious to get her home and under my own care and protection.

The nurse falls for his boyish charm and smiles flirtatiously back at him before telling him she'll do her best. I groan inwardly, rolling my eyes. In all honesty, I don't care what Cole does as long as he brings my girl home for me.

"Can I sit with her on my own for a bit?" I ask Dagen, since Cole is already on his way out, and he nods, following Cole to the door.

"Sure thing. I'll be right outside. I'll send one of the guys for breakfast."

I'm pulling my chair to her side before the door is shut, and I waste no time cradling her hand in both of mine and placing her cool fingers to my lips as I close my eyes.

I think of all the things I want to say to her and how I wish we could go back to just twenty-four hours ago, when I woke up with Amara's naked body wrapped around my own.

A tug from between my hands catches me by surprise, and I open my eyes to the best sight I've ever seen.

Amara's beautiful eyes are open, and she's looking right at me.

My world crashes into me all at once, and I surrender myself to her in a way I never thought I was capable of.

I cry.

37

AMARA

The sound of a piano playing a mellow song breaks through my consciousness as I open my eyes to confusion.

The last time I woke up, I found Ryder, crying, at my side in the hospital. Everything after is a blur, and this isn't the same room I was in.

This time, Ryder is smiling. He looks happier than I've ever seen him.

"Where are we?" My voice is scratchy, and I clear my throat, prompting Ryder to reach over and pour me a cup of water before standing and placing the straw between my lips.

Water has never tasted so good.

"We're home." Ryder returns to his seat, sliding it closer and taking my hand in his.

Home.

I glance around the room, and its familiarity registers as I see the swirly pink pattern on one of the walls. I didn't recognize it before because the furniture has been removed, along with the toys and books.

"I know you don't like this room, but—"

Dagen joins us, cutting Ryder off. "It's the best place for her. It has a bathroom, and she's next to your room." He circles to the other side of the bed and looks at me. "The only way I could convince Ryder to leave your side and get some rest was if you were right next door."

I smile at Ryder and squeeze his hand back.

"Thank you. It's fine."

And it really is.

There are pieces of myself I left behind when I went over the bridge.

My memories of that night are fragmented and blurred. I remember small pieces, like why my wrist is wrapped in a cast.

I remember Ryder came for me. He came after me when he had the chance to go to the address and clear his name, and he fought for me. He jumped in the freezing water, risking his own life for me. When some pieces pop into my head, I have to push them out. I'm not ready to fully acknowledge the danger I was in and the fear I felt.

When I look around the room, I no longer feel alone. Instead, the room offers me hope, a second chance, another shot at life and love. This room holds a rejuvenating strength now.

"You're playing music?" I look around and see a stereo sitting on a shelf in the corner.

"It was so quiet in here, and those stupid machines beeped, and—I just couldn't sit here and listen to nothing." Ryder's expression is filled with pain, and I smile in understanding when Dagen gets up and turns off the piano concerto.

"So is everything good now?" I look hopefully at Ryder.

The last thing I fully remember is sitting in the back seat of Cole's vehicle. Dagen was going to find the woman who called me.

"God no!" Ryder chuckles sardonically. "It's all gone to shit." His sudden smirk contradicts his words.

"But you're smiling. You look happy."

"You know what? I am happy. I'm really fucking happy. Everything can burn down all around us, and I'll be right here with you for the rest of my life, grinning like an asshole because I have everything I will ever want."

Ryder's shift from dominant arrogance to utter joy is unsettling, and I look over at Dagen, who is shaking his head and rolling his eyes.

"I think you broke him, Amara. I don't know how to get his factory settings back."

My laugh is quickly followed by a wince when a sharp pain rips through my stomach, and Ryder's smile fades, replaced with the controlling seriousness I know.

Ryder places his hand on my shoulder, gently holding me to the bed. "Stay still, Blossom. It's going to hurt for a bit. The doctors had to take a big piece of glass out of you. The nurse will be in shortly with some painkillers."

"How long have I been—out?"

Ryder's eyebrows pinch together. "About three days since the last time you woke up in the hospital. Do you remember that?"

"A bit, but—" I shake my head.

I remember seeing Ryder at his most vulnerable moment, his tears rolling down his face. At the time, it felt like a dream.

"You were sedated while we transported you here, and the doctors felt you needed to rest and let your stomach heal, so they extended it for the first couple of days."

"So what's going on then? The woman?" I ask.

"Dagen found her dead; anything she had with her was gone." Ryder opens his mouth to continue, but he stops. Tilting his head to the side, he reaches up and brushes my hair off my cheek. "This isn't your fault, Amara."

He knows me so well, and his words don't help. I feel responsible for that woman's death. She sent me her location, and now she's dead.

"Who was she?" I ask. I now owe a stranger a life debt, but I don't know how I can help her rest peacefully.

"She was the girlfriend of a guy who used to do jobs for the Saints. We're trying to find him now. He sent her to deliver the evidence in his place. She's listed as Jane Doe at the morgue. I'll let you know if that changes."

Ryder glances at Dagen a little too long.

"What aren't you telling me?"

The room sits in a serious silence.

"Dagen saw Lennox there that night." I try to sit up, but Ryder is faster than I am, and he steadies me against the mattress before I hurt myself. He quickly continues, "Stay put, Amara. I won't tell you again." Something stirs inside of me at his command. "There's more. A security camera from a nearby building caught another woman running away from the area around the exact time it all happened."

Dagen catches my attention. "While we don't know who Jane Doe is, we might be able to ID the other woman. Cole is driving into town as we speak to pick up the information we have on her so he can hunt her down before she becomes the next target. We need her to identify Lennox as the shooter. We need to make sure—it's just that...he's our brother."

"I get it." I stop Dagen from explaining more. There isn't anything I wouldn't do for my family. I would always give them the benefit of the doubt first.

"Authorities found the car with Nash and Grant. They were by the house asking questions yesterday, and it's been handled. They don't need to talk to you because you were home all night in your room while we had a meeting downstairs. Unfortunately, the storm knocked out our security cameras around that time." Ryder's matter-of-fact tone tells me this is the story I'll be going with, and I nod my head in understanding.

"So where do we go from here?"

Ryder leans in a little closer. "Who do you belong to?"

I stare, dumbfounded, while my body heats up at the change in topic. Ryder watches me in stoic silence, and the serious expression on his face tells me he expects an answer. Dagen leans back in his chair and watches our conversation in silence.

"I belong to you." I sheepishly lower my voice to answer as I shift my focus between the two brothers.

"Will you marry me, Blossom?" His sincere question makes me gasp, and another pain in my abdomen reminds me to stay still as Ryder shrugs. "I mean, after I call it off with Sloane."

"What?" A woman's voice from the door startles me, and I jump as Sloane enters the room and rushes to my side. "You're awake and you're getting married? This is—oh my God—I'm gonna cry. Yes, our wedding is totally off, Ryder. This is the second happiest day of my life."

She wedges herself in the space between Dagen and the bed and leans in, kissing my forehead and motioning like she's going to hug me without putting any pressure on any part of my battered body before spinning to speak to the men.

"Wait. Is this why you sent me out to get ice cream? You knew she was waking up, and you wanted to talk to her first." She props her hands on her hips and levels both brothers with a hard stare, and I have to take deep breaths so I don't hurt myself laughing.

Dagen throws his hands up in the air. "Don't look at me. I'm lactose intolerant."

"Well, I got back just in time, and—oh, shit." Sloane's happy expression falls as she turns back to Ryder, then glances at me. "I didn't let you answer, did I?"

Dagen laughs as Sloane steps away. "Now I understand why I had to not be here. I'm awkward. I just love you both so much." She lowers her voice into a whisper as she steps behind Dagen. "I'm so sorry."

Sloane waves her hands at Ryder, silently telling him to pretend like she isn't there and to try again, then she clamps her hands over her mouth to stop herself from saying anything further.

Ryder clears his throat, drawing my attention from Sloane, and when I look back to him, he's on one knee beside my bed. All humor leaves the room when his eyes meet mine, and he clears his throat.

"I should have done it this way before," Ryder mutters to himself as his hands fidget nervously with my own. Then, looking back to me, he smiles.

"Letting you go was the biggest mistake of my life. That day I told you to leave, I lied to you. I lied to everyone in that room, and I lied to myself. I let you go because I thought you deserved better than me because I knew without a doubt and in my soul that I didn't deserve you. I will never deserve you, Amara, but if you give yourself to me, I will never let you go again. Amara Scott, will you marry me?"

"You mean after we get through this mess?" I motion to the makeshift hospital room around us.

I imagine we still have some lies left to tell and a killer to catch.

"No. I want to marry you this afternoon. Cole will be here shortly, and I'll have someone here to marry us in a couple of hours. We will find Grayson's killer, but I don't want to fall asleep tonight without saying goodnight to my wife."

"But—I'm a mess." I lift my cast off the bed and motion to my prone form.

"While your body is a definite perk, today I want your heart. I'll take everything else when you've recovered." Ryder winks, a salacious grin stretching across his face as he licks his lips.

"You've always had my heart, Ryder. Yes. I'll marry you."

38

RYDER

The moment Amara said yes, Sloane jumped into action, and she hasn't stopped running all over the house since. I'm a few minutes away from asking Dagen to slip a roofie into her wine, but her excitement is growing on me.

As if she can hear me thinking about her, Sloane comes running up the stairs, dressed in a sapphire blue cocktail dress and carrying a garment bag over her forearm.

"Okay, I know this is probably weird, but I just want this to be beautiful. Here's the dress I had fitted when we were pretending. We can do without that god-awful veil, and I'm going to take a pair of scissors to the back so it can lie on top of Amara and not hurt her wound." Reaching into her pocket, she pulls out a jewelry box and hands it to me. "The ring I was wearing is in there."

"I can't give her your ring, even if we were never getting married." I try to hand it back, but she holds up her palm, blocking my attempt.

"Ryder, we both know that was never *my* ring. I know who was in your heart when you picked it." Tears fill her eyes as she smiles. "And if you both decide to get a different one together, then it's still yours. Just exchange it."

The doorbell chimes, and Dagen strolls out from the dining room with a drink in his hand.

"Got it."

I turn my focus back to Sloane.

"Fine. How are you doing with everything?"

No one bounces back better than Sloane. Her resilience is admirable, but she does have tears in her eyes.

"Are you kidding me? I'm a maid of honor. This is so awesome. I just wish Grayson could see it."

"Me too." I look at our guest at the front door. Dagen is reviewing some papers, and the officiant looks around the foyer. "If you want her to have that thing on when we commit to each other, then you better get moving because I'm marrying my girl with or without it in about ten minutes."

Sloane doesn't wait another second. Barreling past me, she disappears into Amara's recovery room, and I walk down the stairs toward my brother when I hear a voice coming in from outside the door we haven't closed yet.

"Dagen, your autocorrect is lit. I think you meant to type 'witness,' but it came through as 'wedding.' It still doesn't make sense though." Cole holds up his phone as he joins us, taking a second glance at the man who is about to perform our ceremony.

The look of confusion on his face is priceless as he takes in my tuxedo, and Sloane races down the stairs yelling something about putting together a bouquet of flowers.

"Canon in D Major." I catch Sloane's attention, and she stops to look at me. "It's an important song for Amara. I think she'll want it played today. Just check with her first," I say, recalling her reaction to the song that played the night I saw her standing on her own at her boss's farewell party.

Sloane nods, then resumes her pace, tearing back up the stairs as fast as she can in her heels.

When I turn back to my brothers, Cole is grinning like an idiot.

"You're fucking doing it." He looks like he's going to hug me again.

"Yeah. I'm fucking doing it, and I have an important question I need to ask you."

"You want me to be the best man?" Cole's grin spreads wider when Dagen cuts him off.

"Fuck that shit. I'm the best man. He already asked me."

Cole looks wounded, so I talk fast. "You both are the best men I know, but Cole, this is really important to me." A lump forms in my throat. "Amara has asked that you give her away."

"Shit. Are you serious? After the groom, that's the most important—I'm just—YES. I'm honored—shit, man—"

Cole has always looked out for Amara, and he is the best person to take her father's place in giving her away. Then he tries to lighten the mood, and I second-guess my choice. "Does this mean she has to call me daddy?"

My possessive nature bursts through, and I smack his chest hard. Dagen joins Cole in laughing at my expense, and Sloane calls down from the top of the stairs.

"We're ready any time."

"We'll talk business later. It can wait." I point to the stairs, and Dagen leads the way with our officiant in tow.

When we get into the room, my line of sight goes no further than my bride.

The nurse clears away, taking a tray of medication with her.

Sloane was able to clip Amara's hair up, and a soft nude lipstick covers her lips. She has some scrapes and a black eye from that night, and the dress sits on top of the covers.

Amara is the most beautiful sight I've ever seen, and I pause at the door for a moment to take her in.

Cole rounds the bed and stands beside Amara, placing his hand over her cast, and she grins unabashedly up at him while Sloane smiles on from her other side.

A minute in, the officiant asks who is giving Amara away, and Cole leans over, kissing Amara's forehead before he drops his voice low, but I still hear him. "There is no one better suited for my brother than you, Sunshine."

Then he steps away and I take his place, staring into her tear-filled eyes as she grins at me. The rest of the ceremony takes less than two minutes as the officiant speaks a line and we repeat it while smiling at each other. Then the officiant asks us if we have any vows to exchange.

I nod and clear my throat. Reaching across to Amara's good hand, I pull her fingers to my lips and kiss her like my life depends on her touch, because that is how I've felt every minute of every day since I first knew she was mine.

"I have nothing prepared, but that doesn't mean I don't have a lifetime of words to say. You have my promise: I will tell you all of the ways I love you every single day for the rest of our lives. I will protect you, I will care for you, I will provide for you, and I will never let you go again, because I didn't just let you go that day—I tore out a piece of my soul. I told you that you were like your broken butterfly, but you aren't. I am. You are so strong and amazing, and it is you who has pieced me back together. When I let you go that day, I let my heart go. And, today, I'm taking it back, and I will die before I let go again."

I've stopped talking for close to twenty seconds before I hear a sound in the room. Amara breaks the silence when she sniffles. Her eyes are filled with tears, and her nose is red and raw with emotion.

The officiant turns to her, prompting her to respond.

"That's beautiful, and I'm so sad because I don't think I'm going to do as good of a job as you. Mostly because that nice nurse just gave me my painkillers, and I love all of you right now." Everyone chuckles, and she tugs on my hand with her good one, drawing my attention back to her. "But I love you most of all, and I really hope someone got this on video because I want to tell you how much I love you when I can think of some better words. This isn't how I imagined my wedding day would go, and, with the exception of Grayson not being here with us, it is perfect."

Sloane's sobs catch my attention, and I glance up to see her smiling at us as tears roll down her face when the words I've been impatient to hear are spoken.

"And now, by the power vested in me by the state of Washington, it is my honor to declare you married. You may seal this declaration with—"

My lips are on hers before he finishes his announcement, and it is one of the sweetest things I have ever tasted.

When I pull away, Amara's eyes are full and wide, and this is the look I've wanted from her since the moment I stormed back into her life, but there's something else.

"You're tired." I comb her hair back from her face, and she pauses a moment before she nods.

"A bit." Her voice is low, but Sloane overhears.

"Okay. Everyone out. I need to get this dress off Amara before"—she looks at her watch—"ugh, I need to go get Henry from daycare soon. No one says a thing around him, right?"

We all mutter our agreement, and Sloane shoos the guys out of the room. I stand up, kissing Amara one last time. My kiss is gentle, but I long to claim her properly.

"I'm going to talk to Cole and Dagen. Close your eyes. I'll be here when you wake up, Mrs. Saint."

Amara gets a second wind at her new name, and she smiles. "I love you, Mr. Saint." She giggles. "It doesn't sound the same when I say it." Her voice is already sounding weak, and I leave her to Sloane's care.

My brothers have already seen the officiant off, and they are closing the front door when I join them on the main floor. Silently, I tilt my head before turning to lead them into the office.

Cole saunters in, making a straight line for the bar and pouring three drinks before handing us each a glass. "I leave you assholes alone for a few days, and you go and get married." He raises his glass. "I'm really happy for you, bro. I mean—shit —you got your girl."

Dagen raises his glass. "I'll drink to that. Congrats, Ryder."

I join them in taking a big gulp.

I'm married.

No, that's not it.

Amara is mine, entirely.

She always was, but now she is on paper, and I'm the richest man in the world.

"Amara will sleep for a few hours, so we have a little time, then I'm all hers."

I nod to Dagen, and he circles the desk, removing a file and setting it on the top before he shares the contents.

"Our body is still a Jane Doe, but we were able to capture some clear video footage from a nearby business. It shows the dead girl approaching with another woman, then the other woman running away around the time of the shooting, and we have a still photo of the car she was driving." Dagen pauses and chuckles to himself.

"What's so funny?" Cole steps closer to the desk. He's smiling at us.

"Well, it's just that this should be the easiest person in the world for you to find." Dagen wipes a tear of laughter from his face, and I smile along with him because I've seen what's inside the file. "I mean, she drives a car with big flowers painted all over it."

Instead of joining us in a laugh, Cole's face falls. "What?"

He looks like he's seen a ghost, and our chuckles cease.

"She drives a—" Dagen stops talking when Cole urgently steps forward, placing his glass on the desk and reaching across for the folder, tearing it open.

He pauses for a few tense seconds.

"SON OF A BITCH!" He flips furiously through the pages before he looks up to us, and I'm too shocked to say anything.

"What's wrong?" Dagen sets his glass down, and we glance at each other before looking back to Cole.

Cole tosses the file onto the desk. A few papers slide out of it as he spins around and takes two steps away, burrowing his fingers into his hair in frustration before he turns back to face us.

"What's wrong is"—Cole lifts the photo he took from the file—"I fucking know her!"

ACKNOWLEDGMENTS

If this is the first book of mine you've read, I want to thank you for taking a chance on me. If you've been with me for awhile, I want to tackle/hug you to say thanks for sticking around. It means the world to me that you're still here.

I want to thank everyone who helped me bring this book to life:

Cover design: Kirsty Still (Pretty Little Design Co.)
Editor: Caroline Knecht
Photographer: Wander Aguiar
Cover Model: Kyle Kriesel

And though they are listed last here, they are never last in my heart, I want to thank my family for their encouragement, interest and support.

Until next time...

ABOUT LUNA

Luna Kayne is a multi-genre romance author located in Canada. She writes dark, explicit, romantic suspense with a hint of humor and angst. Her men are dominant and often stubborn, and her women are usually underestimated. As for tropes and sub-genres, nothing is off the table.

In 2021, she won an IPPY (Independent Publisher Book Awards) award with her novel, *Step Darkly* which earned a bronze medal.

Luna Kayne is the pen name of author *Sheri Landry* who writes non-romance action thrillers and has won awards for her writing under both names.

You can learn more at LunaKayne.com.

facebook.com/LunaKayne

twitter.com/LunaKayne

instagram.com/LunaKayne

tiktok.com/@luna.kayne

bookbub.com/profile/luna-kayne